# SHALL WE DANCE?

Warmer than he had been only moments ago, Trace ran a finger around his collar, striving to loosen the thing and ease his breathing. Riveted to the spirited figure of his daughters' governess, he wondered that Aunt Cellie could have approved the purchase of such a revealing gown for Miss Partridge. It was plainly a gown designed to attract unwary males.

Even he, standing impatiently on the sideline of the dance floor, could not drag his eyes away from her. As an observer, Trace was torn. One minute he beheld her in rapt admiration, and in the next he chafed with inexplicable irritation. Perhaps he should have a word with her. After all, Miss Partridge had not asked him for permission to attend.

He ambled about the floor so that when the music stopped, he stood close enough to seize Susannah's elbow.

"Lieutenant Reardon!" she exclaimed. Flecks of burnished gold glistened deep within her large amber eyes.

"Miss Partridge."

"Shall we dance?" she asked, effervescent as newly uncorked champagne.

"Immediately."

# THE LIEUTENANT'S WOMAN

## SANDRA MADDEN

ZEBRA BOOKS
KENSINGTON PUBLISHING CORP.
http://www.kensingtonbooks.com

To Amy Garvey and Hilary Sares, the very talented and patient Kensington editors, who launched my first novels in the contemporary and historical genres.

I greatly appreciate the guidance and encouragement you've given me along this adventurous road of romance writing.

Thank you.

# CHAPTER 1

*October 1865*

"Lieutenant Trace Reardon, submersibles and torpedoes."

Trace Reardon was not the most popular guest at the party. He'd introduced himself a dozen times to other members of the Naval Academy's new faculty, but welcoming smiles faded as soon as he spoke. His southern drawl marked him as a former Confederate officer and branded him an enemy with little else said. He moved among men who had served in the Union Navy, and only a strict code of conduct prevented him from being ostracized completely.

Held in the home of Captain Reese Devonshire and his wife Clara, the formal afternoon gathering served to introduce the civilian and naval instructors to each other and set the tone for the new school year.

During the Civil War, the United States Naval Academy had moved to temporary facilities in Rhode Island. Having recently returned to its original Annapolis location, the academy had just begun its fall classes under the direction of the newly appointed superintendent, Rear Admiral David Dixon Porter. Porter had appeared at the party earlier and had given a rallying speech. To a rapt and captive audience, the superintendent enthusiastically outlined his plans, calling for changes that would surely stir controversy.

Not that Trace feared controversy. What he feared were delicate almond wafers that crumbled in his hand and weak tea just slightly darker than rainwater. Forgoing the less-than-manly refreshments, he bided his time with a cursory study of Captain Devonshire's home.

The parlor and drawing room sparkled with crystal and sterling. Fresh greenhouse flowers, fine oriental carpets, and delicate bone china served as gentle reminders of Clara Devonshire's wealth and breeding. In the far corner a harpist played Brahms.

Even though Trace had been raised in similar surroundings, the staid propriety of social events such as this no longer fit him comfortably.

Running a finger beneath his collar, which suddenly felt torturously tight, he watched and waited. After what he deemed an acceptable amount of time spent in strained socializing, he politely conveyed his appreciation to his hosts. Attempting to appear less eager than he was to leave, Trace made his way toward the main corridor. He could almost taste the bracing, salt-flavored October air.

Within inches of making good his escape, the sound of breaking glass stopped him in his tracks. The shattering glass effectively startled the entire party. A hush fell over the room.

"Oh no!" The plaintive lament came from a female voice.

Trace had almost reached the corridor, the same

corridor where the sound had originated. As he entered the hallway, a tight-lipped Clara Devonshire sailed by him. She resembled an ironclad, steaming toward battle.

Never able to resist a good battle, he followed.

A diminutive creature at the end of the hall stared down at the shards of glass surrounding her on the polished plank floor. Her palms covered her cheeks in a silent expression of horror. Both her eyes and her mouth were open wide as she surveyed the damage in apparent shock.

"Oh no!" the young woman cried again, staring at the broken pieces. And as if she were alone, she added, "What have I done?"

"You have done yourself out of a fine position, that's what you've done," Clara hissed, in a low, biting tone. She obviously did not want to create a scene, nor be overheard by her guests. "Now clean this up and gather your things. You are no longer employed by this household."

"Oh, but—"

Clara cut off the young woman's protest. "You are the clumsiest girl!"

"It was an—"

Obviously unwilling to listen to any explanation, the captain's angry wife marched past the stricken servant and back into what appeared to be the kitchen. She had not looked back, not noticed Trace observing the brief scene.

But the girl noticed him. Misting amber eyes briefly met his. Raising her chin, she blinked back unshed tears. Trace detected a slight tremble of her lips.

At first glance she appeared unremarkable. She wore a plain black gown with a wide white apron wrapped around her middle. A white cap trimmed with a band of lace sat jauntily atop a cluster of buttermilk curls. Strands of her pale yellow hair fell to frame her face, dislodged wisps brushed against the nape of her neck. At second glance, despite the young woman being disheveled, Trace thought her a pretty little thing.

For an instant his heart constricted in sympathy. He knew how it felt to be repudiated. "Allow me to help you."

He moved toward the mess. Before she could object, he'd squatted on his heels and picked up several sharp pieces of crystal.

"Oh no." She fell to her knees opposite him, immediately engulfing him in the faint, sweet scent of lilacs. "Thank you, but if Mrs. Devonshire finds one of her guests helping me she will . . . she will boil me in oil or something similarly horrid."

"The lady of the house has already dismissed you," Trace pointed out. "What else can she do?"

"I don't know." Her uncertain tone implied the rest of the unsaid sentence: but something dire.

"Besides, you shouldn't be working for someone who would boil you in oil."

The young woman's lips turned up in a soft, barely stifled smile. Her full, sensuous lips were a natural peachy shade, moist and holding promise of tasting just as delicious as they looked.

Not that Trace was interested. He blamed the sudden streak of warmth he felt on the overcrowded parlor that he'd just left.

"The Devonshires had the only position available when I arrived in Annapolis," the unemployed maid told him.

Hunkered down over the crystal opposite each other, they were eye to eye. A rare innocence glistened from the depths of her gold-dust eyes. He knew instinctively that this was a woman without wiles.

Although he rarely made rapid decisions, Trace made one now. "I happen to know of a position as governess that I believe would suit you admirably."

"Oh, sir, I don't know." She shook her head, dislodging yet another buttermilk curl.

"Do you like children?"

"Yes, I love children."

Trace stood. "Then that's all there is to it."

"I don't think so." The golden-eyed woman took the hand he offered and rose to her feet.

"I'm Lieutenant Trace Reardon." He gave a stilted bow.

She lowered her head. "Susannah Partridge."

"You look to be of a responsible age."

"I am four and twenty."

Miss Partridge was much older than he'd taken her for, but these days it was not unusual to meet unmarried women of advanced years. A great number of women had lost their sweethearts in the war. As a result, an equal number of older women competed for husbands with young maidens. Thirty-year-old men, like Trace, preferred the young, naive maidens.

"You are the perfect age, Miss Partridge. I am offering you a temporary position as governess to my four daughters."

"Oh my. Four? You have four daughters?"

"Does so many frighten you?"

"Not at all," she replied staunchly.

"They are young and small. You are bigger than they."

She smiled. "That is comforting to know."

"We've been so busy settling the household, there has been little time to find a suitable governess as yet. My children attend the local school just as all of the officers' children do, so you will not be charged with educating the girls."

"How old are your daughters?"

Trace could almost see her mind spinning.

"Emily is eight, Alice and Amelia are seven, and Grace is five years old," he said.

She frowned.

"They are exceedingly well-behaved children," he assured her in his most persuasive tone.

She kneaded her lip. "Mrs. Devonshire paid me a wage of three dollars and fifty cents a week."

"I shall give you five dollars a week in wages."

Inclining her head, she studied him as if he might show outward signs of being daft. After a moment, she asked, "Who is caring for your children at present?"

"My aunt, who wishes to return to her home in Lowell, Massachusetts, as soon as possible."

And the dear, bossy woman nagged him constantly to find a wife, saying she could not leave until he found one. He, however, did not want a wife. Trace did not plan to father any more children. Four girls were enough females for any man to support in one household. He'd decided to give up on having a son. All he wanted was a mother for his daughters.

Nodding thoughtfully, Susannah Partridge teased the corner of her full bottom lip. Momentarily distracted from the business at hand, Trace fixed his gaze on her plump, seductive, siren lip.

"You hesitate," he remarked, tearing his gaze from her lips to her eyes.

Gently arched brows gathered toward the bridge of her narrow, perfect nose. "You are not concerned about my, my gracelessness?"

"Are you referring to this accident?"

"Yes. I believe I was cursed as a small child."

"Anyone might drop a vase."

"There have been several . . . accidents since I arrived."

Accidents did not alarm him. If anything, it was Susannah's beauty that he found disturbing. Not many governesses of his acquaintance possessed trim, curvaceous figures and soulful eyes rimmed with thick fringes of dark, curling lashes. In a past place and time in his life, Trace would have wanted her for himself. And taken her.

"I have only arrived in Annapolis ten days ago," she said. Snatching a basket filled with rose pot-pourri from the table behind her with one hand, she placed the broken crystal she held in the other on top of the dried petals.

"And I have returned to Annapolis only three weeks past."

Susannah held the basket out for Trace as he discarded the broken pieces that he'd retrieved. "Do you instruct here at the Naval Academy?" she asked.

"Yes." He'd been a student at one time, and had always wanted to return as an instructor. In order to do his best in his new position—and nothing less than his best would do—he needed to solve his personal predicament as swiftly as possible.

"As I see it, you have a dilemma, and I have a problem," she said, apparently mulling over his offer aloud. "I can resolve your dilemma and in doing so solve my problem."

"It would seem so. On the surface."

She still did not appear convinced. Trace withdrew a card from his uniform jacket. "We live in officers' quarters four houses down."

Miss Partridge studied the card. "Yes, I know the house."

For good measure, he bluffed by issuing a stern

warning. "Do not delay in making your decision, for I must fill the position quickly."

"No, I shall make my decision by day's end." She started to turn away and then spun back in a rustle of skirts. "Yes. Yes, I shall be your children's governess. I will come as soon as I gather my things."

"Very well."

"Upon one condition."

Her eyes met his, shining and defiant.

Trace felt a nervous lurch in the bottom of his belly. "What is that?"

"That we agree my employment is to be on a trial basis with either one of us able to serve immediate notice."

"I would not have it any other way."

If he did not find the proper mother and wife before long, Susannah Partridge might prove a tempting dalliance even though she was what he considered to be an "older woman." Trace found the thought of temptation under his roof twenty-four hours a day a trifle unsettling.

As he departed from the Devonshire home, he did so with the hope that he hadn't just made a monumental mistake. Trace could not remember when last he'd acted quite so impulsively.

Hours later, after aimlessly ambling about town wondering if she had any other recourse, Susannah approached Lieutenant Reardon's spacious Georgian house on Blake Row with a fair amount of trepidation. The gray afternoon had deepened into night, but her path was lighted by the gaslights that dotted the academy grounds.

Trace Reardon, as head of his household, obviously could hire whatever help he required. But since he'd said his aunt had been caring for his children, Susannah wondered about his wife, or lack thereof. She should have thought to ask.

She knew so little. She did not even have a clear idea of what a governess did. Questions and doubts assailed Susannah as she paused at the bottom of the steps leading up to the lieutenant's front door. She worried that his aunt might not approve of his hasty choice of a governess. Perhaps his wife, if she existed, would dismiss Susannah out of hand. And were the lieutenant's children so ill-behaved that the lieutenant might have hired the chimney sweep to care for them had the cleaner been available?

When she left her home in Rhode Island to come to Annapolis, Susannah had risked everything. Most of the money she'd managed to put away had been spent on the journey, leaving her practically penniless. Without a position, she would soon be destitute. No matter what awaited her on the other side of the door, she could hardly refuse Lieutenant Reardon's proposition.

He had happened upon her at a desperate moment. Susannah's curt dismissal by Clara Devonshire still stung. Her pride had been sorely wounded. Still, she could not feel more contrite about breaking the crystal vase and certainly meant to pay the captain's impatient wife for it as soon as possible.

Susannah's father used to say that the Lord worked in mysterious ways. Perhaps it was true, but Lieutenant Reardon did not appear to be connected with a higher power in any way. He looked more like the devil. An enticing devil with a charming southern drawl.

But southern wasn't good. If Susannah hadn't found herself in dire straits, she might have turned Reardon down simply on the basis of his obvious Confederate roots. She'd been raised a New England Yankee.

Tall, dark, and formidable, the man soon to be her employer towered over Susannah. She guessed the lieutenant to be at least six feet four inches. His rigid military bearing hinted at formidable strength, power both exciting and dangerous. His dark blue uniform strikingly displayed shoulders as broad as the city of Boston. A man in uniform could always make a woman's heart beat faster.

In one hand Susannah carried a worn carpet-bag containing her sole possessions. In the other she carried her irascible cockatiel, who, although covered, squawked loudly each time she inadvertently swung his cage.

She was about to enter the unknown. She knew nothing about Lieutenant Reardon. For all she knew, she might have been hired to care for children spawned by the devil. If only she had some idea of what waited for her inside the big old house. But she had little choice. Summoning all her courage, she mounted the steps and pounded the brass door knocker.

A uniformed maid responded quickly. "Yes ma'am?"

Oh dear. Belatedly, Susannah realized that dressed in her worn black gown, she looked more like a woman seeking a handout than a governess. She smiled brightly, hoping the young housekeeper would not notice the tattered hem of her dress.

"Bail! Bail!" her bird squawked before Susannah could speak.

A furious flapping of feathers, a few of which escaped from the cage, caused Lieutenant Reardon's housekeeper to step back.

"Oh dear." Susannah shot the girl an apologetic smile. "I'm afraid my bird is a bit agitated. Hush, Bilge. His name is Bilge."

The girl cast her a dark frown. "Are you expected?"

"Yes. I'm Susannah Partridge."

After a swift, sweeping appraisal, the somber brown-eyed housekeeper nodded her head. "Follow me."

Depositing her carpetbag and the birdcage in the foyer, Susannah followed. The prim housemaid stopped at the open door of a small, austere study. The roaring blaze in the fireplace provided the only warmth that Susannah could detect. Lieutenant Reardon worked at a fine, dark cherry desk.

"Miss Partridge is here."

Reardon raised his head from the paper he'd been writing. His ash gray eyes locked on hers.

Her breath caught in her throat. The glint of silver that flashed from the depths of the lieutenant's eyes spoke of a keen perception. Could he detect the nervousness that lay behind her forced smile?

The lieutenant lowered his hooded gaze to her lips. He expected her to speak, obviously.

Susannah choked. And in so doing, she cleared her air passage. She had not taken a full breath since being announced.

"Come in." The lieutenant's curt invitation could have been mistaken for an order.

Taking a sorely needed deep breath, she sailed into the room hoping she would not trip. Clara Devonshire's accusation was true. Susannah was clumsy, and had been all of her life.

The striking southern officer had discarded his jacket. His white linen shirtsleeves were rolled up to his elbows, revealing strongly corded forearms dusted with crisp dark hairs. Unbuttoned at the collar, his shirt fell open at one corner, teasing Susannah's eyes . . . and imagination.

"I wasn't certain that you would come," he said.

"As I am quite fond of children, it would be exceedingly silly of me not to further investigate the opportunity you offered."

"Yes, it would." He looked over her shoulder. "Jane, summon my aunt to the study."

With eyes only for the lieutenant, Susannah had not noticed that the housekeeper had remained. Was it possible that after losing everything else, she was now losing her wits?

"Miss Partridge, please be seated."

Extending his arm, he motioned to one of the two dark-green wing chairs positioned in front of his desk.

"Thank you," she said quietly, adopting an air of strict propriety—a quality that was not actually in her nature. She perched primly on the edge of the chair.

The lieutenant sat down again behind his desk. Resting his right ankle over his left knee, he gave the appearance of being relaxed. But his stiff, squared shoulders said otherwise.

"Questions must have occurred to you since you agreed to my offer. Shall we start with those?"

"Yes, of course." Susannah felt, but could not explain, the uneasy tension that fell between them. "Will your wife interview me as well?"

"My wife died three years ago. My girls are motherless."

"I am so sorry."

"While I was . . . away . . . the children lived in Massachusetts with Aunt Cellie, my mother's sister."

Happy to hear he had northern ties, Susannah nodded her understanding. "So you have Yankee blood as well."

He hiked a dark brow. "Is that important to you?"

Defiant in her denial, Susannah angled her chin a notch higher. "No, not at all."

"My aunt has been caring for the children for far too long. She is getting on in years and deserves a rest. Finding a wife during the war was not a priority," he explained woodenly. "I was otherwise occupied. But now that I have been recruited into the new United States Navy, I expect to be stationed in Annapolis for quite some time."

"Do you like Annapolis, sir?"

"Very much. But I did not think I would be fortunate enough to return."

"Return?"

His eyes sparked momentarily with the light of treasured memories, though he did not smile. "I was a student here. I graduated from the Naval Academy in eighteen fifty-five."

Despite his brooding countenance, Susannah considered Lieutenant Reardon a handsome man. She found his sculpted dark hair, aquiline nose, and sun-leathered skin attractive. A lusty strength simmered beneath his surface, and she sensed a noble nature.

"The academy is fortunate to have you," she replied. "Undoubtedly you are a navy officer to the core."

"To the core," he repeated. "And now that I am in one place for a while, it is time that I look for a woman to mother my daughters. Having a governess to care for them while I fulfill my duties at the academy and engage in the pursuit of matrimony will be helpful."

Lieutenant Reardon's detached tone made it sound as if he were on a military mission to find a wife, rather than a search for love and happiness.

"What do you expect from a governess? Not all parents require the same things," she hastened to explain. "I should like to have a clear understanding of my duties."

Since she had no understanding at all.

"The usual. They must be well behaved and learn their school lessons as well as social niceties. I expect my girls to be kept clean and fed and entertained at all times."

A rush of relief spilled through Susannah. She could do those things. "I look forward to meeting your daughters, and I promise to be as helpful as possible to you in your pursuit of matrimony." Susannah completed her pledge with a reassuring smile.

"Did you know that there is a bird in the foyer?" The plump woman who bustled into the room in a swirling of deep purple skirts and swoosh of silk directed her question to Reardon.

"A bird?"

" 'Tis mine. He, he's mine," Susannah admitted haltingly. If Reardon did not like birds, he might think again about employing her. "Bilge was left in my care by . . . a Yankee . . . sailor."

"A bird named Bilge?" With a barely disguised look of surprise, the woman turned to address Susannah.

"He is a cockatiel. I promise he will not cause any trouble."

"Aunt Cellie, this is Susannah Partridge."

The lieutenant's aunt's dark eyes shifted to Susannah, who rose to greet her. Aunt Cellie extended her hand in greeting. "My apologies. I did not see you immediately," she said.

"I have asked Miss Partridge to serve as governess to the girls. At least until I find a wife," he added. "They tire you too much."

"A governess, are you?"

Being that she could not claim to be a governess with complete honesty, Susannah merely smiled.

"Miss Partridge, this is my Aunt Celia Stuyvestant."

"It's a pleasure to meet you, Mrs. Stuyvestant."

Unfortunately, Reardon's aunt did not appear to be pleased to meet Susannah. With just a hint of a smile, the regal elderly woman skimmed Susannah's figure in rapid, cool assessment.

"Welcome to our household."

"Thank you."

"I only hope you are up to the work that looking after four young girls requires."

"I am used to hard work."

Aunt Cellie appeared to be quite robust for a woman of advanced years. A natural bloom lingered on her cheeks, belying the strands of silver streaking through her ebony hair. She wore her hair pulled into a bun and encased in a net spotted with deep amethyst-colored beads. Judging from the intense gleam in her dark coffee eyes, Susannah suspected that the older woman missed nothing that went on about her.

In accordance with the latest fashion, voluminous crinolines held the skirt of Aunt Cellie's deep purple moire gown what appeared to be several feet out from her body. Susannah felt quite shabby beside her.

"I am afraid the children are sleeping," Cellie said. "I suggest that you wait until morning, when they are fresh, to meet the darlings."

Susannah fervently hoped Reardon's daughters were indeed darlings. "I look forward to the moment."

"The faculty quarters are smaller than we would like. I fear you will have to sleep in the small sitting room off the girls' chamber."

To have a roof over her head and a pillow beneath her cheek suited Susannah just fine. Sharing a chamber with her charges would do nicely. "The sleeping arrangements will help me become acquainted with the girls more quickly."

"I have every confidence my daughters will take to you at once."

Susannah wished that she possessed the same confidence. But the trepidation she'd felt upon entering the Reardon residence seemed to be slowly slipping away.

Since their meeting over broken crystal, she had yet to see the southern officer smile, and she found his tall, rigid figure slightly intimidating.

Susannah hadn't always been a servant, but she'd heard the stories about what went on between the master of the house and those who served him in many of the fine mansions of Rhode Island. Why should Annapolis be any different?

"As the girls are asleep and I would rather not wake them, have Jane prepare the spare chamber for Miss Partridge."

"I shall fetch Jane at once." Aunt Cellie headed for the door and stopped. "Isn't it a bit too warm for a fire?"

"No, Aunt Cellie. You are the only one who feels warm."

She nodded, shrugged, and went on her way. Silence descended.

At last the lieutenant cleared his throat and spoke. "Would you like to familiarize yourself with our home? It might be useful to know your way around tomorrow when the girls are awake. Grace sometimes likes to play hide-and-seek just at the times that you wish she wouldn't."

"I see," Susannah said, suppressing a smile. Grace had won her heart already.

"This is my study, of course."

"And a very"—she paused, searching for the correct word—"serviceable, serviceable study indeed."

"Except for cleaning, nothing has been done to the house since we moved in a few weeks ago. Aunt Cellie has been busy with the children."

"I understand."

"Follow me then."

Susannah followed. Once in the corridor, the lieutenant turned right and opened the door to the chamber at the front of the house. "This is the parlor."

A rather large dining room lay directly opposite the parlor and, behind it, a spacious indoor kitchen. Reardon led her up the back stairs to the second floor. "The spare chamber, as well as Aunt Cellie's the children's, and mine," he said, pointing to each door, "are on this floor along with the indoor bath."

"An indoor bath!" She had seen her first indoor bath at the Devonshires'. The academy housing also boasted the new gas lighting. She'd come a long way from the cottage in Newport.

"Adam and Jane, our butler and housekeeper, are married and have a chamber on the third floor. They came with Aunt Cellie from Lowell, and I fear they will leave with her."

"Is your aunt leaving?"

"As soon as I find a wife. My aunt has never left New England before. I do believe she's quite homesick."

Susannah would never have guessed.

"New Englanders are staunch people," he explained as if he'd read her mind. "They never wear their hearts on their sleeves."

"I'd heard as much."

At that moment the shy housekeeper and Cellie emerged from the chamber the lieutenant had pointed out as spare.

"There are fresh sheets on the bed and a fire simmers in the fireplace, Miss Partridge," Aunt Cellie reported. "I regret that we have been using the chamber for storage, but I believe you will be able to make your way about."

"Thank you." Susannah could not suppress her happy smile but managed to stifle any sign of the excitement she felt. Quite by accident, she had found a temporary position with good people. She meant to do everything in her power to be a proper governess until her business in Annapolis ended. Unfortunately, she only vaguely understood the duties of a governess, but she would learn.

"Your bird and bag are waiting in the chamber," Jane added softly.

"Thank you." Susannah shot a grateful smile at the girl.

"If there is anything you might need, please let me know," Aunt Cellie said, fanning herself.

"You are most kind, Mrs. Stuyvestant."

"I do try. Happy servants are hardworking servants, as Edgar always says."

"Edgar?"

"My dear husband."

"And my uncle." The taciturn lieutenant said before dipping his head. "Good night, Miss Partridge."

"Good night."

She looked after him as he quickly disappeared down the stairs, returning to his office—to his work, she assumed.

"You shall need all your energy in the morning." Cellie said cheerfully. She smiled like the proverbial Cheshire cat. "Good night, Miss Partridge."

Alone in the spare chamber, Susannah leaned

back against the door and heaved a sigh of relief. There were moments recently when she thought she had forgotten how to be happy. But in this warm chamber, with its canopy bed and the thick oriental carpet beneath her feet, she felt her heart flutter as if she were in love.

Dodging tables and chairs, she made her way to the bed, where she collapsed in a cushion of down comfort. Seizing one of the pillows, she hugged it close to her body.

She'd been rescued from an uncertain fate by a tall, dark and . . . distant man. Perhaps he still grieved for his wife or his way of life in the South. Whatever distressed him, she felt certain it could be overcome. If she could help the lieutenant as well as his children, so much the better. He had shown himself to have a good heart.

"Bail! Bail!"

"Hush, Bilge." Susannah reluctantly left the thick, soft bed to adjust the drape that had slipped off her bird's cage. "No need to bail, we are no longer on a sinking ship. As a matter of fact, I believe we have landed in safe harbor."

Effectively silencing the cockatiel, Susannah undressed down to her chemise. After a difficult day she looked forward to a good night's sleep. As she turned down the light, her thoughts returned to her new employer. Intelligent and handsome, Reardon would have no trouble finding himself a wife.

Susannah might have considered herself a candidate . . . if she hadn't been already married.

# CHAPTER 2

The soft rays of early morning sun filtered through the lace curtains of the spacious dining room.

Trace sat at the head of the table. Emily, his oldest daughter, sat to his right, next to Grace, the youngest of the four girls. The twins, Alice and Amelia, were seated to his left. At the opposite end of the table, a place had been set for their new governess, who had not yet joined them for breakfast.

His daughters ate their meals in the same rigid fashion of the midshipmen at the academy mess hall; shoulders back, chin up. Trace believed discipline to be essential in the raising of children. He felt he'd never received enough discipline as a boy. His parents had had neither the time nor the inclination.

Except for an occasional slurp by the youngest, his daughters spooned their breakfast of porridge in silence.

"Sit up, Grace." Trace prodded. He expected good posture as well as good manners at the table.

Grace's big eyes fixed on his, eyes that blended

the startling blue of her mother's with his mellow gray. The result was an unrelenting silver-blue gaze that sometimes proved disconcerting.

"We want to make a good impression on Miss Partridge," he explained, "who will be joining us shortly." *If she truly desires to retain her new position. She's fifteen minutes late!*

"Who is Miss Partridge, Father?" asked sandy-haired Emily. The oldest, and boldest, of his daughters, she questioned him, though with the greatest respect, when the others hesitated to do so.

"She is your new governess. And I expect you to obey her in all matters."

"Is Miss Partridge to take the place of our mother?"

"No. No one can take the place of your mother, Emily," he replied in a quiet, reverent tone. "I have employed Miss Partridge temporarily to assist you—and me—until I find a mother for you. And a wife for me," he added hurriedly. "A wife and mother. I don't know how long it will take me to find such a woman, and I feel that in the meantime you should have a female influence."

Emily immediately objected. "Aunt Cellie has always taken care of us."

"And she has done an admirable job. However, Aunt Cellie is not of an age to be caring for four young children. This is the time in her life when she should be spending idle hours in the garden and . . . napping."

"And playing faro," Amelia said. "Aunt Cellie likes faro."

"She will not leave us, will she?" cried Alice, tugging at one midnight pigtail.

"No," Trace assured them. "Aunt Cellie has no plans to leave at the moment. Now, finish your breakfast."

Trace knew his aunt wished to return to Lowell as soon as possible. She urged him incessantly to find a wife even though she knew very well a wife was the last thing he wanted. He simply required a mother for his girls. Life would be so much simpler if he could have the one without the other. But Aunt Cellie would never approve of that arrangement. She would remain in his household until Trace grew old and bent if he didn't marry again.

He glanced up at the grandfather clock in the corner of the dining room. Time being of the essence to a military man, some sort of clock occupied every room in the house. Punctuality was important to Trace and Miss Partridge was now seventeen minutes late to breakfast. If she did not appear within the next five minutes, he would send Jane for her.

The girls exchanged worried glances that he ignored as he took another swallow of the strong, steaming coffee that he ordered to be served at every meal.

A loud, shrill squawking pierced the tranquillity of the breakfast setting. Startled, Trace tensed and then watched transfixed as a stone gray, yellow-plumed bird flew into the dining room. The hysterical creature circled the room flapping his wings and screeching until he at last landed on the chandelier above the center of the dining table. Black and gray feathers floated down to rest on the lace cloth.

Alice screamed.

Grace giggled.

Emily huffed in outrage.

And Amelia squinted up for a better view. She caught a feather on her finger.

"Bilge! Come back here, you naughty bird!"

Miss Partridge had arrived.

Carrying an open cage high in front of her, Trace's newly hired governess dashed into the dining room holding her skirts up with the other hand.

"Oh, I'm sorry, so sorry," she mumbled, as her gaze darted about searching for the bird.

His young daughters regarded the strange woman with wide-eyed wonder. Or was it alarm?

Trace leaped to his feet just as Susannah Partridge spotted the flyaway pet. "May I be of help?"

"He usually will hop into his cage if it's presented to him," she said, wiggling between Grace and Emily's chairs to get closer to the bird. "Does anyone have any fruit?"

"No, we have no fruit," Trace replied tersely, his eyes on the winged devil. When he'd hired her, he had no idea the woman had a pet. She hadn't mentioned she owned a bird, nor asked permission to bring it with her.

"He likes fruit," Miss Partridge explained, stretching on her tiptoes to lift the open cage door closer to the bird. " 'Tis easier to tempt him back into the cage with a piece of fruit but not to worry, I shall manage."

Trace hadn't realized he should be worried.

The petite governess changed her tone to a persuasive singsong. "Come into your cage, sweetie bird."

And that's when Trace took charge. "I believe that I can raise the door right to him if you will stand back, Miss Partridge."

"Oh, well, all right."

As Susannah turned to pass the empty birdcage to Trace, she stumbled and the white wooden coop struck him in the face.

"Oh my! I am *so* sorry."

Trace heard a smothered giggle from Grace. "No harm done." His nose smarted.

The bird backed up onto its newfound perch. "What's its name?"

"Bilge."

"Bilge?"

"It wasn't my choice," she said. "He's not even my bird. But I promised to take care of him."

"For how long?"

"Until the war was over."

"The war is over."

Amelia pulled on Trace's jacket. "Here's a piece of apple, Father."

"Apple is wonderful!" Susannah exclaimed. "What a resourceful young lady you are."

The dark-haired twin beamed.

"If you will place the bit of apple in the cage, Lieutenant Reardon, I am certain Bilge will hop right inside."

The bird went for the bait just as Miss Partridge had predicted. Trace breathed a sigh of relief as he snapped the cage door shut and handed the contraption to her.

"Thank you," she said, bestowing a smile brighter than a room filled with gaslights.

"Do you think you can keep him confined?" Trace asked. He didn't mean to sound stern, but he'd been very nearly blinded by Miss Partridge's smile, a smile that could melt a weaker man's resolve.

He had no time to care for pets in his household. His daughters consumed every free moment at home. Had he known Miss Partridge came with a bird, he would not have hired the cheeky woman. His impulsive gesture already had come back to haunt him.

"I will make certain Bilge is confined from this moment on," she promised Trace earnestly, having no idea of the second thoughts he was entertaining. Placing the cage in the corner, she responded to his gesture and took her place at the table.

"Thank you."

"The little devil escaped while I was putting new water in his little dish."

Trace straightened in his chair. "Just see that it never happens again."

"There shall be no more accidents, for today marks a new beginning." She turned her lovely smile on the girls. "I apologize for disturbing your breakfast. My name is Susannah Partridge, and I am to be your governess."

Trace caught Emily rolling her eyes and sent her a quelling glare. "Introduce yourself, girls. Name and age."

Miss Partridge shot him a puzzled look from her end of the table. He returned a frown.

Aware of his military bent in all matters, she saw that he seemed not to be able to put his training aside at home. His failure to make requests instead of giving orders made it doubly important to have a female influence on his daughters. Without a woman they would soon become little midshipmen or—heaven forbid—mutinous sailors.

"Yes, do tell me your names," Miss Partridge coaxed. "I am so glad to meet you. I have been anticipating our meeting since last evening."

The new governess's enthusiasm surprised Trace, though he did not know why it should. He did not know her well, after all. Aunt Cellie would have to stay until he could be certain Susannah Partridge would be a suitable substitute. Or until he gave in and found a mother for his girls—and a wife for him.

She wore the same threadbare black dress from the day before but without the apron. Not a hair on her head appeared out of place this morning.

Every pale golden strand had been pulled into a bun at the nape of her neck and there enclosed in a plain black net. The severe style displayed to perfection fine, high cheekbones and a heart-shaped face molded in porcelain. Her amber eyes shone with undisguised delight as she regarded each child.

"My name is Emily, and I am the oldest. I'm eight years old."

"Emily, you have such beautiful hair. It's the shade of sand under the midday sun."

Emily almost smiled.

"I'm Alice, and I am seven."

"I'm Alice's twin sister, Amelia."

Of all the girls, Alice and Amelia resembled Trace most closely, with their smoky-silver eyes and raven hair. "How fortunate you both are to have your father's most distinctive eyes."

Did that mean Miss Partridge found his eyes attractive, Trace wondered?

"My name is Grace." His youngest daughter held up five fingers before turning to the empty space beside her. "And this is my friend Twinkle."

Grace's invisible friend did not appear to faze the governess. "I am most pleased to meet all of you, including you, Twinkle." Smiling sincerely, she addressed the empty space directly.

"Grace believes she has a fairy friend," Emily scoffed.

"I am certain she must, then, or she wouldn't believe it."

In response, Emily rolled her eyes.

Grace gave Miss Partridge a wide, conspiratorial smile.

The bird might be back in the cage, but Trace felt more uneasy than when Bilge was on the wing. Something intangible had passed between the governess and her charges. Something he was not a part of and that he could not understand.

Unreasonable irritation scraped at the ragged edges of his spirit. "Emily, it's time to take the girls to school now."

Miss Partridge jumped up. "Oh, I would like to accompany the girls to school this morning."

"Its Emily's task," Trace informed her brusquely, thinking he would have to have a long talk with the overly zealous governess. Miss Partridge must understand her place. "A task that I have given her as the oldest in order to instill a sense of responsibility."

"Emily appears extremely responsible," Miss Partridge responded. Emily raised her chin proudly and shot her governess a grateful grin.

Trace stood, raising himself to his full height, an intimidating tactic that worked well with his students. "My daughters benefit from the discipline I see fit to impose."

Casting an extraordinarily beguiling smile his way, Miss Partridge replied swiftly. "They are fortunate to have a father who takes an interest in their raising."

Slightly disconcerted, Trace still could not help feeling pleased that Miss Partridge recognized his efforts.

"But if you wouldn't mind, I should like to know the location of your daughters' school and meet their teacher."

He'd been bested. Holding his tongue rather than replying too sharply to her in front of his children, Trace turned his fiercest frown at the woman, who waxed on with enthusiasm.

"I only suggest this in case my presence should be required one day at school," she said.

Miss Partridge had a point. He couldn't afford

to be called away from the academy on family business. Every moment of the day, Trace had to prove himself, to prove to students, officers, and instructors alike that he belonged there. Serving in the Confederate Navy at his father's insistence had almost brought his career to an end.

Proving his love and loyalty to the navy came second only to educating his students. Considered an expert in submersibles and torpedoes, he conducted classes in the Gunnery Department. His students were midshipmen born and raised in the northern states, young men disciplined to hide their contempt for the southerner that Trace's drawl declared him to be. A handful of the civilian faculty were not as well disciplined.

Trace surrendered to Miss Partridge. Knowing full well he could win any battle over how his children should be reared, he allowed the governess a small victory. "Very well. You may accompany the girls to school, Miss Partridge."

" 'Tis funny that you have a bird and your name is Partridge," Grace blurted, oblivious to the tension that stretched between her father and her governess.

"Yes, it is. And I shall tell you all about this naughty cockatiel on the way to school." Flashing Trace a disarming smile, his new employee bid him good day.

As the girls and their governess trooped from the dining room, he felt a sense of relief. When she understood what was expected of her, Miss Partridge would serve well. She seemed to have taken to his daughters at once. If she won them over quickly, it might not be necessary for him to find a wife as soon as he'd been thinking.

But first he would have to set her straight about some things.

*  *  *

Before leaving for the school, Susannah carried her bird up to the attic. Not for the first time, she wished she could add him to a thick, bubbling stew.

"I'll return for you, you naughty bird," she admonished him once again as she pushed, pulled, and tugged at a nearby window until it opened. If she could have lived with it on her conscience, she would have opened the cage door as well. In a matter of moments she ran down the stairs to the foyer, where the girls waited for her.

It was a fine day for walking. A slight nip in the air proved invigorating as she led Lieutenant Reardon's daughters past the academy's main gate and into the small city of Annapolis. Susannah had adored the girls at once, but she worried the lieutenant's strictness might be building resentment in them. Acting as a buffer between father and daughters, she believed she could definitely be helpful—even though she did not know much about being a governess.

She'd come to Annapolis in hopes of finding her husband. He'd gone off to war three years before and hadn't been heard from since. The features of his face had begun to fade from her memory. She had no ring; there had been no time nor money to purchase one. And he'd made her promise not to breathe a word of their marriage. He hinted he had enemies who might do her harm. She hardly felt married at all and constantly pushed worrisome thoughts about her husband to the far recesses of her mind. Was he alive? Did he still love her? Did she love him?

Susannah enjoyed the walk and the diverting chatter of the girls as they traveled the cobblestone streets up East Street toward the Capitol building with its beautiful wooden dome. According to the children, the redbrick school was located on East, midway between the Capitol and Prince George Street. They made haste as the loud gong of the school bell beckoned.

Below them was a sight Susannah had yet to tire of: sailboats bobbing in the bay while oystermen tonged the harbor beneath the sun and blue skies.

Grace claimed a tummy ache as soon as they reached the schoolhouse. She clung to Susannah's hand and hung back behind her skirts. Jeremiah Dawson, the single-room schoolhouse teacher, promptly excused Grace, explaining to Susannah, "I tried to tell Lieutenant Reardon that Grace is too young. Not everyone is ready for school at the same age."

"I understand," Susannah said. She guessed the young man was not more than two and twenty. He confessed that he had been a midshipman for a short while but had not the strength nor the will to endure the constant rigorous challenges of the naval academy. He'd left school and, rather than face disgrace at home in New Hampshire, he'd chosen to stay in Annapolis as the schoolmaster.

By the time she took her leave with Grace, Susannah felt confident that the rest of the Reardon girls were in good hands. Although she could not be certain, she thought the now and then skip Grace took on the way home signaled a speedy recovery from the child's tummy ache.

Aunt Cellie had not yet emerged from her room when they entered the house, so Susannah, with Grace in hand, proceeded directly to the attic. While the rest of the house boasted gas lighting, the attic had only the natural light that streamed through dust-streaked windows.

"Why are we here?" the girl asked.

Susannah surveyed the large attic with dismay. Old furniture, drapes, trunks, and odd items cluttered almost every inch of space. "I intend to carve out a small area for myself in which to sleep. A wide-open room of my own."

"Why?"

"Because I don't think it proper to impose myself upon you."

In reality her decision had more to do with the room adjacent to the girls' chamber being small and closed. No bigger than a box, the room had no windows and little space to move around in. The walls in the cramped area seemed to threaten to crush her. She'd developed an aversion to small spaces early in her life.

"But what if we get sick? Aunt Cellie always sleeps with us when we get sick."

"But you are sick."

Grace frowned, remembering the excuse she'd recently made. Lowering her eyes, she rubbed her belly. "It's not so bad now."

"Good."

"But what if it were?"

"I would fix a blanket for you to lie upon near me."

Grace nodded sagely. Again Susannah admired the small five-year-old's wide silver-blue eyes and gleaming hair, the same midnight shade as her father's. Apart from her apparent delight in her invisible friend, Twinkle, Grace seemed far too somber for one her age. Susannah meant to change that.

"Ah!" Susannah exclaimed with more excitement than she felt. "Look at this old screen. With a dusting, it will serve nicely to partition off an area for a cot."

"We sleep on featherbeds."

"I know." Susannah felt as if she'd been sleeping

on a soft cloud the night before. She had thoroughly enjoyed the oversized bed complete with plump down pillows, but this was a new day.

"Do you wanna move a bed up here?"

"I don't think we are quite strong enough. Come, Grace, let's look in this trunk."

"Blocks!"

The trunk was filled with toys yet to be unpacked from their recent move.

"Would you like to play with them while I work?" Susannah asked.

"I played with them when I was four years old."

"It's all right to play with them at five." Susannah sank to the floor to sit beside Grace. "Perhaps we should see how many there are."

"One."

Susannah took two from the trunk. "Two."

Grace took another and placed it beside the other three blocks.

"Now, how many do we have?"

Grace frowned and stared at the blocks. "One, two, three, four, five."

"You know your numbers!"

Grace's midnight curls bounced on her shoulders as she shook her head, smiling broadly. "I can read words, too."

"What a smart girl you are." It occurred to Susannah then that perhaps Jeremiah Dawson just wasn't the right teacher for Grace.

The grandfather clock in Trace's office chimed nine times. He pushed aside the papers he'd been reviewing. Apparently only a few members of his class had ever heard of torpedoes or mines—outside of those that produced gold and silver.

Although delighted to be back at the academy

as an instructor, Trace was disappointed that he'd been given only two classes to teach within the Gunnery Department.

Superintendent Porter had charged him with the responsibility of a controversial new project, an athletics program for the midshipmen. Under Trace's supervision, a ten-pin bowling alley and gymnasium were under construction. He suspected that he owed this most inglorious assignment to having served in the Confederate Navy. In order to regain the trust of faculty and students he must waste his hard-won experience on what many of his fellow officers considered a frivolous experiment.

Leaning back in his chair, Trace rubbed his chin, the feel of the prickly stubble of his beard somehow comforting. An hour ago, when he'd returned home, Aunt Cellie had reported construction of another kind, this in his own household.

A fresh streak of annoyance shot through him. Trace hadn't granted permission for Susannah Partridge to make changes in the house or in the sleeping arrangements. Although tired, he realized that if he did not straighten this out immediately, the amber-eyed, golden-haired girl might continue to break his rules, a pattern she'd begun by bringing in the blasted bird.

Leaving his study, he climbed up the flight of stairs to the second floor and called up the steep steps leading to the attic. "Miss Partridge, are you there?"

"Yes, I am."

"May I come up?"

A slight pause weighed in the air before she responded. "Certainly, sir."

He climbed the rickety wooden steps to find himself in a circular area that had been cleaned and cleared of clutter. In a short amount of time, Miss Partridge had converted a portion of the attic to a comfortable living space.

With grudging admiration, Trace surveyed the area. It was lighted by two oil lamps; lace curtains draped the window, and a faded oriental carpet covered the floor. The cage containing the cockatiel rested on a trunk. A washbasin and pitcher stood on a table beside the tall looking glass.

Susannah rocked in the lone chair. "I hope you do not mind that I have taken the liberty to make a space for myself."

"You have created a sitting room."

"Yes. But everything you see was here in the attic already."

Curious, he poked his head behind a screen dividing the area and found a cot.

"Without a fireplace are you not afraid of being cold up here?" he asked.

"Heat rises. I shall be kept warm from the other fireplaces in the house."

"You are supposed to sleep in the chamber by my daughters."

"I . . . I felt they needed a bit of privacy, as well as I."

"It was not a request that you remain with the children. It was an order. It is a rule. When I was a child, my governess rarely left my side and always slept in the adjoining chamber."

"The girls know that if they should become ill or frightened they will be welcome to sleep up here with me. I shall insist upon it. As it happens, the attic holds several cots."

She had an answer for everything.

Folding his arms across his chest, Trace narrowed his gaze on her. "Miss Partridge, when an admiral or a captain gives an order he expects his order to be obeyed. His orders are for the well-being of his men. In this case my orders are given for the safety and well-being of my family."

"But Lieutenant Reardon, a family is not a battalion."

"The principle is the same."

"You said your governess slept in an adjoining room."

"Yes."

"I would if that were possible, but as wonderful as this house is, the chamber is too small. You must have grown up in a large house."

"Yes. We lived on a plantation. Magnolia Bluffs. It was a spacious old house by the river with stately columns and high, impossibly high ceilings." Trace slipped into a long forgotten memory. As a boy, his shouts would echo as he ran through the manor.

"Magnolia Bluffs," she repeated. "Even the name is lovely."

"But it's gone now. All that remains is the foundation."

"I'm sorry."

"What of you? Is your home still standing?"

"I have not really had a home since my parents died. They were in a carriage accident eight years ago," she told him softly. "We lived in a small cottage in Newport. Rhode Island. Our home was cozy and cheerful. I slept in the loft with my sister. My father was a preacher."

Her wistful smile touched a spot within him that Trace had thought untouchable up until this moment. His heart warmed.

Her lips, pale peach and sweetly tempting, parted slightly. But savoring that peach was unthinkable. He'd been raised a gentleman in Magnolia Bluffs. An officer did not dally with those employed in the house.

"A preacher's daughter," he repeated. Another excellent reason for keeping his distance from the temporary Yankee governess.

"Yes."

"Yes, well . . . will you keep that bird up here where he cannot create havoc?"

"I am indeed sorry about the broken glass in the hall clock. He must have flown into it on the way to the dining room. I shall repay—"

What broken glass? The hall clock? His favorite? He hadn't even noticed. Miss Partridge was dammed distracting.

"Never mind," he grumbled. She'd warned him she was cursed. "As long as you keep the bird in the attic and are at the girls' side whenever they need you, I shall allow you to remain secluded up here."

"Thank you. You are most kind, Lieutenant Reardon."

"Because I have allowed you a modicum of privacy, do not be thinking you can have lovers sneaking up the back stairs, Miss Partridge."

She shot up out of the chair, her golden eyes blazing with indignation. "Why would you say such a thing?"

Because he'd known the bitter taste of betrayal at the whim of a beautiful woman. And he'd vowed never to be fooled again. But he felt the slings of Susannah Partridge's outrage. Even knowing that he was well within his rights to demand certain behavior from those in his employ, he suddenly felt like an insensitive bully. Confused by his confusion, Trace nonetheless could not back down.

"Simply as a warning. Be warned, Miss Partridge."

Turning on his heel, he beat a hasty retreat.

# CHAPTER 3

There would be no lovers sneaking up the back stairs to see Susannah even if she condoned such behavior—which she did not! She was a married woman. To her shame, the memory of Patterson Harling and their spur-of-the-moment marriage had begun to fade.

Her good-looking young husband had left to fight for the Union Navy after only four days of marriage. Before departing, Patterson had warned Susannah against using her married name until he returned from the war. He told Susannah that married women whose husbands had been captured by the enemy were in more danger than their single counterparts.

Although she did not understand his reasoning and knew nothing of military matters, she obeyed. Without a wedding band, using her maiden name, and showing no interest in men, she had prompted the gossips of Newport to proclaim her a certain spinster.

Worse, three years later, her husband had not yet returned. Unable to wait any longer, Susannah embarked on the search to find him. If she did not find Patterson here in Annapolis, and as yet she'd had little opportunity to look, she must search elsewhere. He lived. She felt it in her bones. But she'd had little time to dwell on her missing husband.

During the two weeks since joining the Reardon household Susannah had settled into the rhythm of her days as governess. At first the girls were a handful, testing her at every turn. Practicing patience and giving them lessons sprinkled with laughter, she rather quickly earned their acceptance.

Susannah had just returned from walking the older girls to school when Aunt Cellie descended upon her in the foyer.

"Miss Partridge, you must be outfitted at once with a wardrobe befitting the governess of a wealthy man."

Although Susannah had been under the impression that Trace had lost his plantation in the war and most likely all that he had owned, she could hardly question his aunt. If Cellie said Reardon was a wealthy man, he must be.

"I'm afraid that I do not have the funds to—"

"You are not required to furnish your garments. I shall."

Fearing this meant a uniform of some sort like the one Clara Devonshire had demanded she wear, Susannah protested. "While I am grateful, I cannot accept your generous offer."

Resting her hands on her barrel-round belly, Aunt Cellie regarded Susannah steadily, a threatening gleam in her dark cocoa eyes. "It's not an offer. It's a requirement. I shall not have my friends whispering that we have not the funds to keep up household appearances. Grace will stay with the housekeeper while we are gone."

"I don't want to stay with Jane," Grace piped up.

"Nonsense," Aunt Cellie declared, sailing out the door.

Grace had attached herself to Susannah early on, rarely letting her out of sight. Leaning low, Susannah whispered in the little girl's ear. "We won't be gone long. And when we return I shall bring you taffy from Lulu's sweet shop."

The five-year-old could not be bribed. "I shall tell Twinkle on you!" she warned with a stormy glare and a pretty little pout. Whirling about with skirts flying, Grace raced up the stairs to her chamber.

Unable to follow and soothe the girl as she wished, Susannah hastened to Aunt Cellie's side. It was all she could do to keep up with Trace's aunt as she hurried up Main Street. Shops and taverns lined the steep cobblestoned street. Fishing boats and sailing craft bobbed in the bay below. The autumn blue sky and crisp breeze proved exhilarating, but Ceila Stuyvestant gave Susannah no time to enjoy the weather. Although overweight and elderly, the woman moved like a young, robust midshipman.

"I don't know how a woman survives with only two dresses," Aunt Cellie fussed, as they neared Rebecca Morton's dressmaking establishment. "It seems I have more than a marriage to arrange before returning to Lowell."

"I have never needed more than two dresses," Susannah explained quietly. She could never afford more than two dresses, and those she had stitched herself.

"My nephew's position is such that everyone in

his household must be beyond question. You know, he never wished to fight for the Confederates. His mother was my sister, born and bred in Lowell. A true Yankee was Sarah. Trace's father insisted he throw in his lot with the South, and now you see the result. He is barely tolerated at the place that he loves most."

Aunt Cellie's ill-considered comments came as a surprise to Susannah. The lieutenant had not wished to fight for the South? He was barely tolerated at the academy? She would never have guessed. He certainly did not behave like a persecuted man—nor like a man disgraced, for that matter.

Although she found Reardon rather arrogant and mired in rules and orders, she'd expected those very characteristics would be favored by his colleagues at the academy. Not for the first time, Susannah felt a niggling fear that the Civil War would never end, that it was destined to be fought repeatedly in the minds of otherwise intelligent men.

For the first time since he'd saved her from Clara Devonshire's wrath, Susannah's heart went out to her taciturn employer. She resolved to wear whatever Aunt Cellie ordered for her with good grace.

"Lieutenant Reardon shows great courage to work among those who regard him as an enemy still," she offered, uncertain whether she should express an opinion.

"Courage or foolishness? My husband grows old and weary and has offered Trace the opportunity to manage our textile mill. But, no, my stubborn nephew insisted on resuming his military career. He told Edgar that he'd always dreamed of returning to Annapolis one day."

Susannah nodded, embarrassed by the confidences Aunt Cellie shared. But she had learned that the woman loved to talk—often to herself. It was common for her to prattle on around the house even though no one was listening. The bits of knowledge the sharp-eyed woman indiscreetly gave away today about her nephew were important to Susannah.

The lieutenant plainly did not intend to reveal much about himself to Susannah. She still did not know what made the man smile, laugh, or feel anger or disappointment. He guarded his thoughts and emotions. At least through Aunt Cellie, Susannah had learned Reardon was a man who followed his dreams. She respected that characteristic. She had it herself. And she told herself that the better she knew Lieutenant Reardon, the easier it would be to get along with him.

Reluctant to take sides in the family debate about business versus military life, Susannah chose her words carefully. "Things happen for the best. My father, who was a preacher, always said as much."

"And I have said *too* much." Seeming to have suddenly come to her senses, Aunt Cellie stopped in mid-step. Drawing herself up to her full five feet, she became Mrs. Edgar Stuyvestant and shot Susannah a deep frown. "Pay no attention to the chatter of an old woman." Then, seizing Susannah's elbow, she started up the street again.

While Susannah might not understand Reardon's love of military life, she did understand his fondness for Annapolis. She'd instantly been captivated by the picturesque setting. In many ways the seafaring port reminded her of the small Rhode Island village where she had spent most of her life.

A tinkling bell announced their arrival in the dressmaker's shop.

"Rebecca will outfit you properly," Cellie pronounced.

After greetings were exchanged and introductions made, the tall, lanky dressmaker led Susannah into a curtained area in the back of the shop to take measurements. Cellie stayed in the main shop area to consider fabric swatches.

"Mrs. Stuyvestant said you need five gowns and one for special occasions."

Susannah stepped up on the platform. "It seems so much."

"You have an admirable hourglass figure," Rebecca noted as she circled the platform, studying Susannah's body. "I shall make you beautiful gowns."

The dressmaker set to work quickly and quietly. Even the bell announcing another customer did not deter her. The conversation that ensued outside the curtain could be heard clearly. Susannah hoped eavesdropping might prove more entertaining than the silent fitting.

"Celia!"

"Maude! What a pleasant surprise. We do not often see each other outside of our faro afternoons."

Reardon's aunt gambled? Another bit of information she would never have guessed.

" 'Tis sad but true," replied Maude. "If only you were not the busiest of women, settling your nephew's home and caring for his children."

"Fortunately, we are settled now, and he has lately hired a governess for his girls," Celia announced.

"That is good news."

"Yes. I shall have more time for cards."

"We will have a game soon," Maude promised. "What brings you to Rebecca's shop?"

"I am purchasing gloves for my niece. She has come for a visit, and tonight we must attend the Baldwins' dinner party. She insists that she cannot attend without proper gloves."

"I wasn't aware that you had a niece." Aunt Cellie's voice took on a strange quality, one Susannah had never heard before. "Forgive me for asking, Maude, but is your niece married?"

"No. So many young men her age were killed during the war. I don't know what a young girl is to do nowadays."

Cellie's answer came quickly. "My nephew is only thirty years old, a young man yet."

"Is he looking for a wife?" her friend asked.

"Yes. The lucky woman who lands Trace will have herself a brave, handsome husband."

Susannah noted Mrs. Stuyvestant neglected to mention the four children that came with this prize of a brave, handsome husband. Neither did she mention that Trace had never been known to smile—at least since Susannah had been in residence.

"I have not met your nephew, you know." Maude's tone held a hint of suspicion, as if she thought Trace Reardon might have three arms. "Will he be attending the Baldwins' dinner party?"

"No, I am afraid Trace's social life has taken a back seat to the demands of his work. But we would enjoy having you and your niece to dinner later in the week."

"I shall accept right here on the spot. Molly is eager to meet any and all eligible bachelors."

Co-conspirators in a pleasant plot, the women giggled like young girls.

Susannah's stomach did a slithery somersault. She sensed trouble brewing. Although she did not know Trace Reardon well, he did not appear to be a man who would happily suffer matchmaking, even from his well-intentioned aunt. Susannah could not imagine this trained leader of men, capable of making snap judgments, relinquishing control of his private life any more than he would relinquish control of the men under his command—or, as she had discovered, control of his daughters.

Before she excused herself, the dressmaker finished the measure of Susannah from waist to ankle, shoulder to wrist, and all other conceivable variations. "Excuse me. I shall return in a moment."

Obviously Rebecca had been eavesdropping on the conversation as well and knew instinctively that the time had come to sell Maude the gloves.

Susannah merely nodded, her thoughts with Reardon. She wished she could warn him what was afoot. After his visit to her attic retreat, she hadn't been able to lose the feeling that beneath his gruff, brooding exterior lived a man with a sensitive soul.

Perhaps, given time, she could free him.

Trace had endured a rough day.

The carpenters constructing a gymnasium on the second floor of the old Fort Severn structure had installed the ten striking bags too close to one another. Almost every bag would have to be removed and their stands rebuilt. Whereas he had hoped to deliver the finished gymnasium ahead of schedule to Rear Admiral Porter, he now would be hard-pressed not to fall behind schedule.

He'd just digested this bit of unsettling information when Elliot Conroy, a civilian instructor in the Seamanship Department, had cornered him for the sole purpose of taunting him. The burly expert in knots and shrouds cursed Trace for being a Confederate coward who had no business among loyal Unionist midshipmen.

Trace strode away from Conroy with a terse "Good day." An hour later he'd faced several students in his torpedo class who objected to the idea of working with explosives. Trace suspected their real objection might be to having a former Confederate naval officer instructing them. He'd arranged to meet privately with the midshipmen on the following afternoon—a delay necessitated by Aunt Cellie's dinner party. Given time, he felt certain he would win the boys over.

But he couldn't be late for dinner. His aunt had made that quite clear. Before she returned to Lowell she felt it her duty to present him with several candidates for wife and mother. In an effort to hasten his aunt's return, Trace felt obligated to meet the young women who had earned Cellie's approval by either birth or beauty.

Trace had not had a woman in many months. Romantic encounters proved too difficult. He'd been badly burned in the *Sultana* explosion, and disfiguring scars blanketed his right side and back. The scarlet, puckered expanses of once-scorched flesh were not a pleasant sight. Loathe to be seen without a concealing garment, he presented a strange bed partner, never removing shirt or nightshirt.

Trace's pride could not risk seeing revulsion or, worse, pity in a woman's eyes. To his deep remorse, he knew he would never again feel the excitement of a woman's breasts against his bare skin.

After bathing and changing into a fresh uniform, Trace emerged from his chamber physically refreshed but still not in the best of moods. He would rather be reading a book by the fire than putting his best foot forward to entertain a stranger in hopes that she would become his future wife—a wife he had no wish for, but sorely needed to mother his girls.

A burst of laughter rang out from his children's chamber, as if they knew he was thinking of them. They should have been sound asleep at this hour. Quietly crossing the hall, he opened the door a crack.

Susannah sat on the floor. Emily, Amelia, Alice, and Grace sat cross-legged in a semicircle around her. Dressed in their white linen nightshirts, his beautiful daughters presented a lovely vision, a gathering of angels—though at times he'd known them to behave as if the devil possessed them.

None noticed his presence. Enraptured, they paid fascinated attention to the gray- and yellow-plumed bird perching on Susannah's finger.

"Just like others in the parrot family, a cockatiel can talk," Susannah told them. "He can even mimic other birds and sounds."

"Can we hold him?" Amelia asked.

"No. Absolutely not," Trace growled, marching into the room. Not only did he startle the girls and their governess, he startled the cockatiel as well. The damn bird flew at him—and out of the room.

"Oh no!" Susannah leaped to her feet.

"I'll get him," Emily cried, scrambling to give chase.

"No. It's my fault. I'll go. Say good night to your father, girls." She turned to him with wide eyes and whispered, "Will you shut off the lights?"

"Wait for me in the corridor." Trace could hardly contain his anger.

"But Bilge—"

"He won't go far."

"But your aunt's dinner guests will be arriving at any moment—"

"Wait for me in the corridor," he repeated between his teeth. The insolent woman was adding to his irritation by attempting to argue with him. Finally, she exhaled with a huff and, with her chin held to a defiant angle, silently glided from the room. His daughters, attempting to suppress their laughter, had hopped into their beds and were pulling up the covers. Trace gave each a kiss on the forehead before shutting off the gaslights.

As he reached the door, a small voice spoke from the darkness. "I didn't know birds could talk, Papa."

"Good night, Grace."

"Birds talk just like fairies."

Amelia and Alice giggled.

He shut the door.

Miss Partridge paced in the dimly lit corridor. She wore a sage green silk dress. Her voluminous skirts swished each time she turned on her heel. Although Trace knew that his aunt had intended to outfit the governess in gowns more befitting her station than those she owned, this was the first he'd seen of the new wardrobe. He liked what he saw. But he wouldn't be diverted.

"You promised not to allow the bird to escape again," he said in his sternest tone of voice.

Miss Partridge abruptly stopped her pacing. He was diverted.

Trace couldn't be certain whom to compliment: his aunt, the seamstress, or the golden-haired woman before him whose curves were so enticingly displayed. The high-collared, buttoned bodice hugged Susannah tightly, revealing the outline of full, firm breasts and a waist the size of a teacup.

"Bilge did not escape," she retorted. "I brought him to the girls' chamber as a bedtime lesson. They know nothing about birds—or any other kind of creatures, for that matter."

"Eventually they will learn what they need to know. It is not your job to teach. I do not expect you to give my girls lessons."

She raised her gaze to his, light amber eyes sprinkled with gold dust. Eyes that appeared open to her soul, eyes to melt a man's heart. If the man was not vigilant.

"Please forgive me," she snapped. "Perhaps I do not understand my duties as well as I should."

Mesmerized by her wondrous eyes, Trace experienced a moment of rare weakness. "You have been governess for a short time. Mistakes happen."

"You will see no more of Bilge, Lieutenant Reardon."

But hearing the scream come from below, Trace knew he would see the bird at least one more time.

With a small cry of alarm, the governess dashed to the stairs. Trace seized her hand to hold her back. And regretted it at once. For all her spunk, he felt her vulnerability. Susannah Partridge's hand, small and warm within his, sparked an inexplicable connection. Her hand trembled; her eyes met his in a question.

Unable to release the governess's hand, or tear his eyes from her luminous amber-jewel gaze, he felt a bolt of searing heat rock his body. An impulsive move, a simple touch had left Trace as dazed as a man struck by lightning, as confused as a man who's had too much to drink and wakes up in the bed of a strange woman.

Clearing his throat, he let go of her dainty hand. "I think it would go better for you with my aunt if I took care of the matter. I'll return Bilge to the attic."

"Please, don't let anyone hurt him," she begged.

With a curt nod, Trace hurried down the stairs to find the ill-behaved cockatiel perched on the shoulder of a young woman who could only be Molly Spriggs. Molly being the young woman Aunt Cellie considered a likely candidate to be Trace's future wife.

Molly could not seem to stop screaming.

And help was not forthcoming. Both Molly's Aunt Maude and Trace's Aunt Cellie appeared immobilized. The women regarded the yellow-crested miscreant with wide, fear-filled eyes.

Bilge ruffled his feathers. Molly moaned.

Extending his hand, Trace held his index finger toward the bird, chanting silently. *Come to me, Bilge. Come to me, Bilge.*

Tears streamed down Molly's eyes as the bird flapped his wings.

Bilge squawked. The piercing sound was followed by a command that could only have been made by a bird once owned by a sailor. "Blow the man down. Blow the man down."

Trace didn't know why he felt like laughing. Plainly Molly was terrified, and the older women remained transfixed. Nevertheless, he could feel the laughter welling up in him, about to burst forth like oil from a newly tapped well.

Laughter wouldn't do at all. He hadn't laughed in months, and now was not a good time. In hopes of forestalling a show of bad manners, he pressed his lips together and scowled at the bird.

*Come to me, Bilge. Come to me.*

"Get it off me! Get it off of me!" the frightened dinner guest pleaded before swooning.

As she went down, Bilge went up.

Trace made it to Molly's side in time to save her from falling to the floor. The cockatiel flew from the room, squawking furiously.

There would be no dinner party tonight.


Susannah was amazed, but relieved, to see Bilge fly back up into the attic and directly into his cage. She snapped it shut.

"You naughty bird!" she hissed, vexed beyond measure.

She might well be out of yet another position, this time through no fault of her own. If the lieutenant had not barged into the room, all would have been fine. Bilge would not have taken a fright and flown off, and the girls would have been enlightened as well as entertained.

The screaming had ceased. That would have been encouraging if the house hadn't become eerily quiet. In the stillness of her attic lair, Susannah's heart thudded in dread. Anticipating dismissal, she listened for Lieutenant Reardon's footsteps in the corridor below and then upon the ladder leading to her attic retreat. None came.

"Bail! Bail!"

Susannah threw up her hands. "I cannot bear to be in the same room with you, you . . . trouble-making bird!"

She tossed a cloth over the cage, clasped a shawl around her shoulders, and made her way down the back stairs and into the garden. A strong wind whistled within the garden walls and caused her skirts to billow. Swirling leaves rustled as they fell from the two giant poplars, spotting the garden.

When Susannah removed the hairnet so as not to lose it, she inadvertently removed pins as well. Unleashed from its severe style, her hair swirled around her shoulders. Pale wisps swept across her face. Seeking warmth, she tightened the black wool shawl around her.

She felt more alone than ever sitting on the cold stone garden bench.

Losing her position as governess in the Reardon household was unthinkable. The lieutenant paid her well for caring for his daughters. And Emily, Alice, Amelia, and Grace were delightful young ladies, each in her own way.

But Susannah yearned for a family of her own. She was no longer a young woman, and the war already had robbed her of some of her best childbearing years. If she was not reunited with her husband soon, she would remain childless, a governess and spinster aunt. Her younger sister, Mabel, had already given birth to five children.

The need to find Patterson grew urgent. Susannah's long dreamed of family was just that without him—a dream. She must find Patterson soon, and the search required funds. If Reardon dismissed her, she would be lost. A small flame of hope still burned within her. She refused to think the worst, that Patterson had been killed in battle.

Her gaze fixed on the slender crescent moon. A black velvet sky stretched out endlessly above her. She wondered if somewhere Patterson looked up at the same sky tonight. She wondered if he had engaged in battle with the Confederate Navy often and if by chance Patterson and Trace Reardon had fought against each other. 'Twas a chilling thought.

She must go inside. But as she stood, Susannah heard the door open and close. She held her breath.

"Miss Partridge, are you out here?"

Lieutenant Reardon. Her stomach constricted. She was about to be dismissed.

"Yes. By the rosebushes." Though they were bare but for thorns.

His dark brows were gathered in a frown as he strode up to her. "What are you doing in the garden? Are you not cold?"

She had expected him to say, "You are dismissed." She hadn't considered that he might be concerned about her.

"Yes, but it is quite . . . quite refreshing." If she kept talking, he'd have no opportunity to end her employment. "Look, how the moon shines and the stars appear close enough to reach up and touch."

" 'Tis only a sliver of a moon."

"But it is still beautiful," she said, swiping the hair from her face. In light of their strained conversation, she might not be able to delay her dismissal much longer.

"I thought to find you in your chamber," he said.

*To dismiss her!*

"Whenever possible I prefer to be outdoors," she replied blithely.

"Even on a chilly eve?"

Although his face was in shadow, Susannah could hear the puzzlement in the lieutenant's voice. He stood no more than two feet from her. She could feel the heat of his body, inhale the spicy, lusty male scent of him. Shameful thoughts for a married woman!

Susannah took a step backward. "Do you think it's chilly?"

"It's too cold to stay in the garden. You'll catch your death, and then what will happen to the children?"

"Oh no," she replied, resisting. "I'm not cold." As soon as she denied the truth, her teeth chattered.

"What was that?" he asked.

" 'Tis invigorating," she answered stubbornly.

Through the heavy cloak of darkness she could feel the lieutenant's gaze, studying her as he might a rare creature that he could not understand. Susannah shifted nervously from one foot to the other. With her luck, Reardon would dismiss her for being mad as well as owning a misbehaving bird.

"We did not finish our discussion begun in my daughters' chamber," he said at last.

"Perhaps in the morning—"

The lieutenant interrupted. "You seem to have no regard for the rules—"

Susannah interrupted. "Bilge was frightened by the sound of your voice. He never would have flown away otherwise."

She shot him a wide smile and batted her lashes. It could not hurt to flirt with him in order to win a reprieve. 'Twas not quite right for a married woman, but Susannah was a desperate married woman.

"I do not refer to your evil bird—"

"He is not my evil bird. As I mentioned before, I am only keeping him for a . . . for a friend."

"I expect you to follow the rules as well as my daughters. Their bedtime is seven o'clock, not eight o'clock."

"But once in a while—"

"No," he interrupted again, holding up a hand to stop her argument. "There is no 'once in a while' in the Reardon household. Rules and routine must be maintained."

Her stomach knotted in frustration. Although Susannah could not apologize for doing what she felt was right, she could defer. Especially since he did not seem inclined to dismiss her. Still, she dared not breathe a sigh of relief yet.

"Lieutenant Reardon, I shall do my best to maintain the routine."

"I'll be most appreciative," he drawled.

A soft tone, a southern drawl that sent a warm, tingly sensation from the region of her heart straight down to her toes.

He began to unbutton his jacket. Tall and striking in his military best, the handsome lieutenant must surely have won the heart of his guest tonight at first glance. Any woman would be drawn to his smoldering eyes, the essence of power that shimmered from his broad shoulders. His southern drawl.

Despite the cockatiel's interference. What sort of woman would not overlook a bird's play to win the lieutenant's favor?

Or was Susannah just drawn to men in uniform?

He'd removed his jacket while she mused like a schoolgirl.

"What . . . what are you doing?"

"If you insist on walking in the garden on the coldest night of the year thus far, Miss Partridge, you shall have to wear my jacket. Your shawl is not made for this wind."

"But shouldn't you return to the party?"

"Thanks to your bird, the party is over, Miss Partridge."

To her surprise, she caught an amused twitch of the lieutenant's lips as he moved closer to help her into his jacket.

Susannah smiled. Trace Reardon had given her a glimpse of the man she would like to know. The man he'd been and could be again. Dallying in the dark garden alone with Lieutenant Reardon suddenly did not seem wise for a married woman.

"I'm sorry," she said.

"I'm not," he replied softly.

The musky male scent of him permeated his jacket, the heat of his body remained imbedded in each fiber to warm her. Her heart raced as if she were locked in his embrace.

"On . . . on second thought, you may be right, Lieutenant. It's much too cold to linger in the garden. I should not wish to . . . to disappoint the girls by becoming ill."

Susannah slipped out of his jacket before she lost her head to the moon and the stars and . . . the man.

"Very well. Good night, Miss Partridge."

Did she hear disappointment in his voice? No, she could not credit it. She started toward the house.

"I like it when you see things my way."

She halted and turned. The lieutenant grinned at her, full out, unabashed. Her heart skipped like a schoolgirl's.

Susannah sounded quite breathless when she was finally able to speak. "Good night, Lieutenant Reardon."

# CHAPTER 4

A fainthearted woman like Molly Spriggs would never do for a man like Trace. He regretted that she had been frightened by Bilge. But if one small bird on the wing proved too much for her, he could not imagine what four young children might mean to her health. He must move on in his search for a wife and mother.

To that end, the following evening, as he dressed for the weekly academy hop, he attempted to focus on his personal priorities—a difficult task since usually his military career consumed most of his waking thoughts.

Since he was already surrounded by females in his household, the thought of adding another, in the form of a wife and mother, disturbed Trace. As it was, he felt extremely uncomfortable among so many skirts. As a naval officer he was accustomed to the company of men. He knew what to expect from his own sex. He understood aggression and territorial instinct.

Trace believed a man should feel like a king in his castle—not the odd man out. Like any man, he found the idea of having a son to carry on the family name greatly appealing, but, given his history, he feared that more daughters would result from any union. And as much as Trace loved his girls, four were enough. He once knew a man who had fathered seven daughters before he gave up and rolled over in his bed at night.

The woman Trace married must be content to remain childless. He realized finding a woman who met all of his criteria might prove difficult. He'd all but decided to determine his strategy and draw up a battle plan, just as he would in a military campaign. Winning a woman might be likened to winning an important port in time of war. And until he'd found and won the woman, he would be at the mercy of Susannah Partridge's eccentricities.

Clearly, it was in his best interest to spend more time on acquiring a wife. He knew that Aunt Cellie would not leave until she was certain a wedding was near.

He'd volunteered to chaperone the Saturday hop tonight in hopes of meeting young women from town. Annapolis maidens flocked to the weekly academy dance with a mind to meeting and capturing the eye of a midshipman. Midshipmen became officers, and officers led a good life. Many a poor woman dreamed of a secure future as the wife of a naval officer. Trace expected his status and rank as a lieutenant to increase his opportunities with the young ladies—at least with those who would not be put off by his southern accent.

Trace arrived at Recitation Hall not long after the hop had begun. Overcrowded and warm, the hall buzzed with excitement and energy. The musicians, a group recruited from the midshipmen's band, did not always arrive at the same key at the same time. But observing the smiling faces and coy flirtations, and listening to the laughter, Trace realized that no one gave a fig about the shortcomings of the violin player.

With a dozen officers or more in attendance, some accompanied by their wives or women friends, the midshipmen were well behaved. To his knowledge they had not even spiked the punch bowl—a favorite trick.

Now that he was here, Trace ambled along the periphery of the dance floor, unable to concentrate on his mission. He would rather be home creating a design for a submersible that would operate as conceived. A submersible with hidden explosives capable of taking the enemy by storm. Explosives bound to the end of a pole such as they had used during the war were dangerous and provided no surprise on attack.

But he would never be able to give himself completely over to the work he loved without a woman at home to care for his children. So he had to keep his mission here in mind. Just when he was beginning to think this night a loss, Trace spotted a likely candidate at the punch table. Forcing a smile, he approached the young dark-haired woman.

"May I pour a glass of punch for you?"

She raised wide, startled eyes to his and then after a momentary hesitation nodded.

"Allow me to introduce myself," he said, as he ladled the pink punch into the glass. "I'm Lieutenant Trace Reardon."

"Pleased to meet you, sir," she replied in a barely audible voice.

Blushing, she lowered her head, regarding the punch as if it were a suspicious substance. Her plain, pale face and thick brows did not discourage him. Trace had been married to a beautiful woman who had drawn too much attention, far too much attention, from other men. A plain woman would suit him just fine.

"Might I ask your name?" Trace inquired when the shy stranger did not offer her name.

"Beatrice."

"Beatrice is a lovely name." The old southern charm that once came so easily in the company of women, almost eluded him now.

"Thank you."

"Do you live in Annapolis?"

"Yes sir."

"And what brings you to our hop?"

"I like to dance, sir."

This was agony. The inner tick-tick-tick of impatience had begun. Trace became easily frustrated. Patience had never been one of his virtues. How could a man expect to win a woman's heart when he must pry the most innocuous information from her?

Conversation was not the key to Beatrice.

"Would you give me the pleasure of this dance?" he asked.

The musicians were doing their best with "Beautiful Dreamer" when Trace whirled Beatrice onto the dance floor. He'd heard the new Stephen Foster tune before, a truly beautiful melody when played by talented musicians.

And while Beatrice might enjoy dancing, she unfortunately possessed neither rhythm nor grace. Trace did his best not to trounce on her feet. He stood a full foot above the mousy young woman and before too long found himself surreptitiously scanning the hall for his next dance partner. And that's when he spotted Susannah Partridge sweep through the door.

What was his governess doing here? She'd been

retained to care for his daughters, not to go out dancing on Saturday night.

The boredom he had felt a moment ago evaporated, replaced by equal parts of indignation and curiosity. The emotions collided in the pit of his stomach.

Miss Partridge was beautiful. Heads turned as the diminutive creature with the golden curls made her way toward the punch table. From across the crowded hall she did not appear to be a dangerous woman—which Trace had begun to suspect she was. Since that night in the garden, she'd begun to creep into his thoughts when least expected. Just yesterday her smiling face, in radiant detail, had sprung to his mind in the middle of a lecture.

The music changed abruptly. "Oh, Susannah" rang through the hall, and Trace's shy partner backed away from him.

"I do not care for the rousing dances," she explained in a whisper.

But Susannah obviously did.

As Trace escorted Beatrice back to the punch table, he watched as Susannah accepted an offer to dance with a handsome first-class midshipman. Within seconds she was whirling around the floor. Her eyes were alight with merriment as she gazed up at the good-looking young man who had chosen her as his partner.

The skirt of her azure blue silk gown billowed about her, threatening to expose her ankles. The skin-hugging bodice featured a neckline that plunged unseemingly low. Miss Partridge's creamy, quite voluptuous breasts formed a deep, seductive valley as they rose and fell in a soft, transfixing rhythm. The severe bun she usually wore at the nape of her neck had been replaced by a cascade of flaxen curls falling from her crown. Curls that beckoned a man to twirl them about his finger, feel their silky softness.

Warmer than he had been only moments ago, Trace ran a finger around his collar, striving to loosen the thing and ease his breathing. Riveted to the spirited figure of his daughters' governess, he wondered that Aunt Cellie could have approved the purchase of such a revealing gown for Miss Partridge. It was plainly a gown designed to attract unwary males.

Even he, standing impatiently on the sideline of the dance floor, could not drag his eyes away from her. As an observer, Trace was torn. One minute he beheld her in rapt admiration, and in the next he chafed with inexplicable irritation. Perhaps he should have a word with her. After all, Miss Partridge had not asked him for permission to attend.

He ambled about the floor so that when the music stopped, he stood close enough to seize Susannah's elbow.

"Lieutenant Reardon!" she exclaimed.

Flecks of burnished gold glistened deep within her large amber eyes.

"Miss Partridge."

"Shall we dance?" she asked, effervescent as newly uncorked champagne.

"Immediately."

Trace carefully gathered Miss Partridge in his arms, keeping her at a respectable distance.

She felt warm and fragile in his arms. For a moment he likened himself to a knight of old, the protector of the most precious princess in the kingdom. Holding her, he warmed. His pulse beat faster. The indefinable energy and joy-of-being that she exuded washed over Trace, refreshing his weary spirit.

"I didn't expect to see you at the hop," he said, in a vague search for explanations. "I don't recall you mentioning the dance."

"Should I have?" She gazed up at him as if he might be feverish. Her eyes weren't smiling anymore.

Barnacles felt bigger than he did at the moment. He did not mean to spoil her happiness. He attempted to recover. "No. No, but who is watching my daughters?"

"The girls are asleep. They've been sleeping for hours. Good gracious, it's ten o'clock."

He glanced at the clock. "So it is."

"Aunt Cellie assured me that if any one of them woke up she would attend to her needs."

"Aunt Cellie gave you the evening out."

When Miss Partridge nodded, her curls bounced. "Yes. She apologized that you had not given me any time to myself. I have been employed for more than two weeks, and she thought I might be entitled to time of my own."

With so much to do at the academy, Trace had lost all track of time. "Has it been over two weeks?"

"Yes. But I did not complain to your aunt," she hastened to add. "And I would not complain to you. The girls are delightful. I enjoy being with them."

"I have been remiss," he said. In a strange way it seemed as if Miss Partridge always had been a part of his household.

"Tonight I felt the need for a bit of entertainment."

"Accept my apologies. From now on you may spend each Sunday as you wish. I insist that you take one day away from my demanding daughters, else you should grow tired before your time."

He did not wish to lose the services of Miss Partridge. The girls seemed to have taken to her quickly.

"Sunday," she repeated with a troubled purse of her lips.

Trace gazed at her lips. Full and moist, shining like dew-kissed peaches. Succulent. Delicious.

He sucked in a breath, and his heart launched into an uneven beat.

"Does that mean I shall not be able to attend the Saturday night hops?" she asked.

He tore his gaze from her tempting mouth and looked straight into her extraordinary eyes. His throat went as dry as a barrel of sawdust. Could he not regard her without suffering some sort of strange physical reaction?

Trace swallowed hard in order to reply in a steady voice. "You shall have free time from Saturday night until Sunday night."

"Thank you, Lieutenant Reardon."

Caught up in her enchanting smile, Trace found it difficult to move.

But his thoughts took flight. His governess had joined the ranks of the town girls seeking a potential officer as a husband. If she married, he would lose her. Did she not realize she was much older than the other young Annapolis women? Her chances of finding a midshipman to wed were dim.

No sooner had that thought flashed across Trace's mind than a tall, gangly midshipman from the second class approached. The perfect gentleman, he bowed respectfully, first to Trace and then to Susannah. "Miss, may I have this dance?"

Susannah looked to Trace. "Lieutenant, would you mind?"

"Certainly not. Enjoy your dance, Miss Partridge."
He stepped back, feeling the sharp edges of irritation prick an erratic path beneath his skin.

Apparently some of the young officer candidates were oblivious to her advanced age.

For the remainder of the evening, Trace occupied himself observing Miss Partridge, who danced every dance, with a different midshipman each time. As he was unable to carry on a flirtation with another woman while looking out for his popular governess, the evening ended dismally. Even Beatrice had disappeared.

Susannah awoke on Sunday morning to the sound of children whispering at the bottom of the steps. What a pleasant sound! Would that the children were hers.

Stretching, she slipped from her single mattress to look out of the window. The autumn sun shone through the remaining red and gold leaves, shedding a lovely dappled light.

Although a bit bodily weary, her mind felt refreshed. And relieved. For a few moments last evening, Susannah had feared the lieutenant would forbid her to attend the Saturday night hops. Ever since arriving in Annapolis she had attended the dances in hopes of meeting a midshipman or an officer who might have seen Patterson Harling or who knew of his whereabouts. Last evening proved to be just as disappointing as previous nights. No one that she met or danced with knew of Patterson.

At least she enjoyed the dancing. But Susannah had been surprised to see her formidable employer there. She'd never seen Lieutenant Reardon at one of the dances before. But she enjoyed her single dance with him. She would have liked another.

Susannah planned to put the precious time of her free day to good use in finding Patterson. Now that she earned a good salary, she could pay an experienced person to search for her missing husband.

Soft steps on the ladder were accompanied by a small voice. "Miss Partridge. Are you awake?"

"Yes, I am. Come up."

Susannah grinned at the little girl as Grace peered up at her. She scooched down to be eye level with the youngest Reardon. "Good morning, Grace."

" 'Morning."

After a few minutes of silence during which Grace aimed her child's gaze directly into Susannah's eyes, Susannah finally spoke. "Is there something you want to ask me? Or tell me?"

The dark-haired child nodded. "It's my friend's birthday today."

Emily, who'd come up behind her little sister huffed in a haughty fashion. "An imaginary friend. A fairy!"

"A fairy? How wonderful!" Susannah exclaimed. "How old is she?"

Grace held up five fingers. "Same as me."

"And what is her name?"

"Twinkle."

"Well, we shall have to give Twinkle a party."

Rolling her eyes, Emily spun away. But Grace beamed.

The children didn't realize that Sunday was Susannah's free day, and she had not the heart to disappoint Grace. Besides, there had been precious few such celebrations in the Partridge household when she was a girl. Her father had preached that celebrations in the form of parties and dances were the first steps toward an afterlife in hell.

Ever since she had been on her own, Susannah had taken every opportunity to celebrate. Giving a birthday party for a fairy named Twinkle seemed a delightful thing to do on a Sunday afternoon. She bid the girls to join her in the garden directly after attending church with their father and Aunt Cellie.

The small garden off the indoor kitchen had gone to weed during the war. While the academy grounds were slowly being restored to their former beauty, this spot still showed the years of neglect. But the sun warmed the garden on an otherwise brisk fall day, and the scent of burning leaves drifted on the mild breeze. Susannah deemed it a perfect place for a tea party.

When the girls returned from church, all was ready for their party. Susannah sat on the ground with Reardon's daughters. Spreading their skirts about them, they formed a circle. Grace announced that Twinkle danced inside the circle.

Emily rolled her eyes. Alice squirmed, and Amelia stared squinty-eyed at the spot.

They sipped tea, ate molasses cookies, and discussed what sort of gift was appropriate for a fairy.

"A flower," suggested Emily, reluctantly taking part.

"A ribbon?" Amelia asked Susannah.

"I'm certain Twinkle would believe those gifts very sweet."

"Can we sing to her now?" Grace asked.

Emily and Alice moaned.

Smiling, Susannah tugged at one of Grace's braids. "What a splendid idea. And then we'll play—"

She was interrupted by a deep, resonant rumble, the polite interference of a throat being unnecessarily cleared. Knowing it could only be one person, Susannah raised her eyes to the porch and met Lieutenant Reardon's cold, granite gaze.

Her heart gave an uncertain skip. As the lieutenant was tall, commanding, and darkly handsome, Susannah thought it only reasonable that she should find him attractive. Reasonable—and wicked, for a married woman. "Good afternoon, Lieutenant."

He beckoned her with a crooked finger. "A word, Miss Partridge."

Oh dear. "I'll return directly," Susannah said to the girls as she pushed herself to her feet. "Carry on with your song."

Advancing toward the glowering lieutenant, she thought once again that she'd never known such a splendid figure of a man. If he could only learn to smile more frequently, women would be flinging themselves at his feet.

"Miss Partridge. Did we not agree that Sunday would be your free day?"

"We did indeed. But something came up."

"What?"

"Grace wished to have a birthday party."

His dark brows furrowed into a perplexed frown. "It's not her birthday."

"No," Susannah paused, smiled, and cast him a warning glance. "It's her friend's birthday."

Missing her unspoken message, the lieutenant frowned. "What friend?"

She tried again, batting her eyelashes as if she might signal a more urgent warning with them. "Grace's imaginary friend," she whispered.

His frown grew deeper.

"Every youngster has an imaginary friend."

He regarded her whispered explanations with undisguised suspicion. "I never had an imaginary friend. Boys are not as—"

"As creative as girls?" she asked, purposefully interrupting the mule-headed man before he inadvertently wounded one or all of his daughters.

Reardon stared at Susannah as if she were deranged.

Grace intervened, standing to issue her own invitation. "Can you stay at our party for Twinkle, Papa?"

"Twinkle?"

"She's a fairy," the child explained.

Lieutenant Reardon's eyebrows shot up in alarm. He regarded Grace as if she'd informed him that *she* was the fairy. But Susannah knew he could not be angry with his youngest daughter.

She was a different matter, however. When her taciturn employer turned to her, sharp, silver fury flashed in his eyes. His silent anger sparked the space between them. 'Twas a lethal look he shot her. Susannah raised her chin, deflecting his furious glance with an air of proud defiance. She dared him to disappoint his sweet little girl.

"Papa?"

"Yes, Grace. I'll stay."

His reply brought grand smiles from all of his daughters. Susannah understood by now that Reardon did not spend much time with his girls and felt awkward talking with them. He was a military man through and through.

Today, however, he did not look like one. Dressed in civilian clothes, he wore black trousers and waistcoat with a white shirt left unbuttoned at the collar. The sleeves of the shirt had been rolled back to reveal corded forearms dusted with dark hair.

While the compelling widower emanated a quiet strength of character, which Susannah had recognized the moment they'd met in Mrs. Devonshire's hall, for some reason the evidence of Reardon's physical strength jarred Susannah.

As she resumed her place, he folded his long frame to join them on the blanket, grimacing only slightly. Grace handed her father a child's china teacup, and Susannah poured her employer a swallow of the watered-down brew, all that his cup would hold.

"I was about to mention to the girls that at the first sign of spring, they might wish to plant a herb garden right here. Herbs would add so much to their meals, and they would have the satisfaction of watching the plants grow."

"You know a lot about herbs, do you?" Reardon asked. His tone held a sardonic edge.

"As they relate to cooking," she replied, undaunted. "I am an excellent cook—or so I've been told."

"Do fairies like to hide in the herbs?" Grace asked.

"I believe they do," Susannah answered before anyone else had the opportunity. Emily had already begun to roll her eyes. "Most herbs have wonderful fragrances which I'm certain the fairies appreciate."

Reardon was having none of the fairy talk. "Where did you learn to become such a knowledgeable cook, Miss Partridge?"

"My mother taught me. As my father was a preacher, we were rather poor. By using various herbs like sage and basil, my mother was able to make the simplest meal a tasty one."

"You must demonstrate your skills by cooking for us one evening."

She forced a smile. If her employer had thought to call her bluff he was in for a surprise. "I would be quite happy to do so."

"May we help?" Amelia asked. An inch taller than her twin sister, she exhibited endless curiosity. Although Alice possessed gray eyes as well, Amelia's were even more like her father's in that they shone with intelligence.

"Yes! We shall all of us spend a day in the kitchen and prepare a meal for your father, the likes of which he has never tasted."

"That is what I fear," Trace Reardon responded dryly.

Later that evening, Trace sat with his aunt in the parlor. Cellie had summoned him. His daughters and their governess had retired for the evening. Except for the steady tick of the shelf clock, an occasional crackle from the simmering fire, and the click of Cellie's knitting needles, all was quiet.

Beneath the glow of gaslight, Cellie rocked in her favorite chair, knitting something that appeared to be a scarf. He waited.

"Were you successful at meeting a nice young lady at the hop?"

Trace shifted in his plum-colored wing chair, folding one long leg over the other and paying particular attention to the crease in his trousers. His civilian ankle boots were polished to a military sheen.

"As a matter of fact, I did meet a sweet young lady," he said. "Unfortunately, she proved to be too shy." Unlike Susannah, who had made her presence known the moment she'd arrived at the weekly dance.

"An officer's wife cannot be shy," Cellie responded, telling Trace what he already knew. "And she must be tutored in the graces of socializing. I doubt you will find such knowledge in a town girl."

"Social graces can be quickly learned."

"Perhaps one of your fellow officers might have an eligible sister?"

"My fellow officers will never introduce their sisters to a man who served in the Confederate Navy."

"You had no choice in the matter. It was all your father's doing. I never liked him, you know."

Aunt Cellie had voiced her dislike of his father ever since Trace could remember. It no longer bothered him. "The reason that I served in the Confederate Navy makes no difference to my colleagues, only the fact that I did."

The truth of the matter was that he had not done it for his father. He had done it for his country.

"Perhaps we should take a journey into the South," Aunt Cellie suggested. "A great many southern widows would be pleased to find a husband as kind and as handsome as you, Trace." Before he could respond she asked, "Do you think it would be safe to travel south?"

"Aunt Cellie, I have no time to travel. The superintendent has charged me with providing a program of athletics for the students, and that is in addition to the classes I teach."

"The superintendent expects too much from one man."

Rear Admiral David Dixon Porter was a personal hero to Trace. Porter's exploits had begun thirty-seven years ago when he served in the Mexican Navy as a youngster. By the time he was fifteen years old, he'd help quell a mutiny and had been held prisoner aboard a Spanish prison ship.

Trace revered this man, who had gone on to distinguish himself during the Mexican and Civil Wars. If he could earn one ounce of the respect the superintendent commanded from his men, Trace would consider himself a successful naval officer.

But he didn't disagree with Aunt Cellie often. Not aloud anyway. He cleared his throat and prepared for a skirmish. "I must disagree. Superintendent Porter is giving me an opportunity that I am most grateful to have. The Union victory cost most southern naval officers their careers."

"How shall you find a wife, then?"

"Perhaps by chance."

"You cannot leave such things to chance. And I will not return to Lowell until you are happily wed," she vowed.

Trace stiffened. His aunt's declaration, while not unexpected and certainly well-meaning, served to dishearten him. Although he didn't know what he would have done without her help, the time had come for her to loosen her hold on him and his daughters.

In a mild state of annoyance, he rose and began to pace. "Aunt Cellie, there's no need for you to stay now that we have Miss Partridge. The children seem to like her well enough."

"She is much too pretty to be a governess for long. She will be leaving soon, if you ask me."

Which he hadn't.

"Susannah will find a husband before you find a wife," his aunt added.

Another distressing thought. His aunt seemed determined to upset him. "Do you think so?" he asked.

"A woman like Miss Partridge attracts men like bees to honey."

It was true. He'd seen it himself at the hop. She was like honey to a horde of hungry, lusty young bees.

"Why should Susannah care for your children when she might marry and have children of her own?" his aunt asked.

Trace didn't know, but he offered an answer. "My impression is that Miss Partridge is an honorable woman who would not up and marry and leave us without giving advanced notice."

"Being a man, your impression cannot help but be founded on Miss Partridge's physical attributes."

And being a reasonable man, Trace considered his aunt's accusation, which sounded like some sort of indictment against his gender. Had he, in fact, been blinded by soulful amber eyes and a voluptuous figure? Had he been distracted by Susannah's determination and spunk?

No.

"No, that's not true, Aunt Cellie."

"Then prove it to me. Get on with it. Find yourself a wife."

"My time is limited—"

"Now that Miss Partridge is caring for the children, I have free time I shall be glad to offer in your pursuit of wedded bliss."

Trace quit his pacing. Confronted by the bright, challenging eyes of his staunch aunt, how could he refuse her?

He shrugged. "Do whatever you like."

Beset by spiky frustration, Trace turned to the side cart to pour himself a brandy. He disliked being bested by a woman.

*Thrump. Thrump. Thrump.*

He stopped in mid-step. The noise had come from outside the parlor and sounded like someone falling. Someone falling down the stairs. Aunt Cellie threw down her knitting and jumped up from her rocker.

The fear that it might be one of his daughters sent Trace sprinting from the room. A picture of Emily lying in a broken heap flashed through his mind. Anger followed. He had employed Miss Partridge to keep watch on his girls and prevent just such an accident.

He came to an abrupt halt in the hall.

In a cloud of crinoline, a tangle of skirts, and a tumble of long golden curls, Miss Partridge lay in a twisted heap at the foot of the stairs.

# CHAPTER 5

Susannah had fallen down the stairs like a drunken sailor.

Sprawled on the floor, bruised and aching, she counted to ten before gingerly raising her head. She lived! Albeit in a blurry world.

But with one look at Lieutenant Reardon, she wished she were dead. Or at the very least, capable of disappearing like Grace's fairy friend.

Two wavering side-by-side versions of her apparently immobilized employer regarded Susannah with the same open-mouthed alarm. What must he think?

Her back felt as if she'd been lying on a bed of spikes, and piercing pain shot through her left ankle, again and again. Both body and ego were sorely wounded.

"Miss Partridge, are you all right?" Reardon rushed to her side.

She struggled to right herself. "I . . . I think—"

"No, don't move," he warned as he knelt beside her. "Let's make certain you've not broken any bones."

"Oh, I be . . . believe that I am intact," she stammered. Even her voice seemed to rattle.

"Dear me," Aunt Cellie bustled up behind her nephew. "What happened?"

"Miss Partridge fell down the stairs."

"Only the last four steps or so," Susannah hastened to correct him. "My slipper caught in the hem of my gown, and I lost my footing."

"But you might have been seriously injured," Aunt Cellie said, clasping her hand to her chest as if she might give way to the vapors. "Shall we call the doctor?"

"No, no, please. I've just had the wind knocked out of me. I shall be fine in a moment. Allow me time to breathe normally." She inhaled deeply, demonstrating that all was well with her breathing apparatus.

"Do these sorts of accidents happen to you frequently?" Reardon asked. His eyes darkened as his rugged features folded in a wary frown. She could tell he suspected the worst.

"I have no more accidents than most," Susannah assured him. Which was not quite accurate. "This could have happened to anyone."

"Is something wrong with one of the girls?" Aunt Cellie asked, quickly overcoming her initial concern over Susannah.

"No, no. The girls are sleeping. I was on my way to the kitchen for an apple."

"An apple before bedtime?" Cellie inclined her head, studying Susannah as if she were an odd duck. It was a look Susannah was becoming accustomed to seeing from Reardon's aunt.

"Yes. I sleep better on a full stomach," she explained, thinking that more than likely the pain in her ankle would prevent her from getting any sleep tonight.

"I should die if I ate before bedtime," Cellie remarked.

Grimacing, Susannah reached down beneath her petticoats to rub her throbbing ankle. Her foot was bare. Her slipper had come loose and been knocked away in the tumble.

Reardon's gaze followed her movement. "How badly does your ankle hurt?"

"It may be sprained," she acknowledged.

"Or broken." He frowned.

"Sprained. I like to expect the best," she said, forcing a smile.

Cellie clicked her tongue and heaved an exasperated sigh. "I shall get you an apple."

"Mrs. Stuyvestant, I truly appreciate your kindness, but I would not have you wait upon me."

"I shall always be needed around here," Cellie said as she bustled toward the kitchen.

"My aunt *needs* to fetch you an apple," the lieutenant said with a droll twist of his lips.

"I understand, though I have lost my longing for one now."

"May I look at your ankle?"

"I . . . I guess that would be all right." He was her employer, after all.

She slowly pulled her gown up and away from her injured limb. 'Twas a scandalous thing she did. Quite likely her father was rolling over in his grave at this very moment. There! It was done. Susannah had exposed her ankle like a common trollop. She'd purchased her ticket to Hades.

But her fear of spending the hereafter with a horned beast was forgotten as she gazed at her formerly dainty ankle. A bright shade of scarlet, her left ankle had swollen to the size of a grapefruit.

Reardon nodded his head as if he were an experienced physician accustomed to seeing this type of injury. "Just as I thought."

"What is it?" she asked anxiously.

"An extremely severe sprain." His gaze slowly slid from her ankle down to her bare toes. "I wouldn't advise putting any weight on that ankle, Miss Partridge."

"No, of course not. Not right away. But I am certain it will be fine in the morning. Do not worry. I shall be able to take care of the girls."

"I'm not worried about the girls at the moment," he said quietly. His silver ash eyes met hers with startling impact.

Susannah's heart came to a dead stop—or so it felt. Locked in the velvet dusk of his eyes, she replied by rote. "I . . . I regret having been the cause of any concern."

His gaze never left hers. "I shall have to carry you to your chamber."

She stared, uncertain she was breathing any longer.

Without waiting for her acquiescence, he scooped her into his arms. Cradled in the lieutenant's arms like a babe, she felt the power and strength of him become as real as the rocky cliffs of Newport. He carried her up the stairs with ease, as if she weighed less than his scabbard and blade. Against the steely, muscled wall of his chest, Susannah felt the calming beat of his heart, felt the confident stride of his steps, and for the first time in her life knew the elusive feeling of security. Susannah felt safe in his arms.

The delicious, faint scent of bay rum, spicy and male, proved far more soothing than any salve from the apothecary. The heat of his body triggered warm waves of pleasure that coursed through her like a rushing river. She should not be having these feelings, but she didn't know how to stop them.

He came to a halt just short of the children's door. "Miss Partridge, I cannot carry you up to the attic."

"I understand."

Oh no. He expected her to sleep in the small, closed room off his daughters' chamber. Impossible.

"Miss Partridge, while I dislike—"

Even though the door was closed, Susannah placed a finger over her lips. "Please, do not wake the girls," she whispered.

He immediately appeared contrite. Lowering his voice, he continued. "I do not wish to vex you at a time like this, while you are in pain. But I must mention the fairy business." His frown deepened. "Lest I forget."

How did he expect her to think of fairies at a time like this? His closeness filled her senses, warmed her, stirred a curious aching.

"The fairy business?" she repeated.

A lock of thick, midnight hair fell to his forehead. Would he think her bold if she reached up and brushed it back? He held her closely enough in the dimly lit corridor. His finely etched features were shadowed, but his lips were only a breath away. So close. So tempting.

"Yes," he said in a strangely husky timbre. "The fairy. I would not have you encouraging Grace to believe in such foolishness as fairies."

"Do you not believe in magic?"

She felt him take an uneven breath. "Certainly not."

"Well, I do." Susannah wasn't afraid to admit it. "We should never lose the magic in our lives. It's a true blessing to have the ability to believe in fairies and other miracles."

The lieutenant's expression was inscrutable as he gazed at her quietly. Could he not feel the magic of this moment?

"I've . . . I've never experienced a miracle," he said at last.

Susannah smiled. Her eyes met his. This whispered conversation in a darkened hallway felt like a miracle to her. Unfortunately, he was not the man she should be sharing the miracle with—it should be her husband.

"Then I promise you a miracle soon, Lieutenant Reardon."

How could she promise him such a thing? Had she lost her mind? No! She would help him find a wife! She would give him the miracle of love.

Susannah felt his body stiffen as he shifted his gaze to a spot over her shoulder. "You may believe what you like, Miss Partridge, but please do not fill my daughters' heads full of foolishness. If I hear Grace or any of the others mention a fairy again . . . you shall need to find other employment."

"But Grace has believed in Twinkle, her fairy friend, for quite some time. It would be wrong to take that away from her. She will outgrow the notion in her own time."

"See that she does."

"Yes sir."

"I must set you down now so that I may open the door. Be careful not to put weight on your left foot."

"I shall be very careful." Should she tell him she could not sleep in the tiny chamber? Would he laugh at her weakness, or challenge her?

"When I lower you, step only on your right foot," he said. "Do not put any weight on the left ankle."

"Lieutenant, I cannot sleep in there."

"What? Why?"

Susannah lowered her head and spoke over the wedge of pride stuck in her throat. "I . . . I have an aversion to small spaces."

"Hmm." He thought a minute before coming up with an answer. "Then you must sleep in the guest quarters until you can climb the ladder to the attic."

She was relieved that her earnest employer neither mocked her nor displayed the slightest contempt. And for a moment longer, Susannah enjoyed the iron-sure embrace of Trace Reardon.

But as soon as he gently deposited her on the large four-poster bed in the guest chamber, the warmth she had felt in his arms became a chill that spiraled through her like a child's top.

He loomed above her, darkly handsome and fiercely noble. "Is there anything else I can do for you?"

*Oh yes!*

"No, thank you."

For the first time that she could remember, Susannah heartily regretted that she was a married woman.

The following day, Trace stood on the ground floor of the old Fort Severn building, overseeing construction. The ten-pin bowling facility would be ready for the midshipmen in record time. Workmen labored over the last lanes with admirable speed.

Even with the smell of fresh shaved wood in the air, the scent of lilacs lingered in Trace's memory. The scent of a woman pure and untarnished, the scent of Susannah Partridge.

An unbidden image of disheveled golden curls

and wide amber eyes sprang to his mind. Puzzled and disgruntled by the intrusion of a woman into his workday thoughts, he pushed the vision to the back of his mind.

"Johnny Reb."

Trace turned toward the door. It wasn't the first time he'd been the object of the slur. But not on the academy grounds. No matter what they might think privately, officers were gentlemen and beyond demeaning their fellow officers. Only one man derided Trace with the term.

Elliot Conroy limped toward him. Most likely his heavy limp resulted from a wound received during the war. Very few men had escaped without injury. Trace's own scars were hidden.

When introduced at the first faculty meeting several weeks ago, Conroy had made no attempt to hide his contempt for Trace. Steering clear of the man did no good. The civilian instructor sought Trace out solely to taunt him.

"Will the midshipmen be playing games here soon?" Conroy asked, peering about as if searching for defects.

"Yes. I expect they shall be learning the art of athletic competition before the month is out."

"Do you suppose games were the only thing they'd trust a reb like you to do?" he asked with an unconcealed sneer.

Rather than fall for the bait and be drawn into a useless argument that would lead to fisticuffs if Conroy had his way, Trace kept his silence. If it had been anyone else but the burly seaman, he might have pointed out that he taught a valuable class on submersibles.

"What can I do for you, Conroy?"

"I heard you were at the battle of Mobile Bay."

"Aboard the ironclad, *Tennessee.*" Trace had

served with Franklin Buchanan. The Naval Academy's first superintendent had cast his lot with the South. Promoted to admiral in the Confederate Navy, Buchanan was placed in command of the naval defenses of Mobile Bay.

"My brother died at Mobile Bay."

Buchanan had ordered the *Tennessee* into the midst of the Union fleet and singlehandedly engaged three monitors and fourteen man-of-wars ships at point-blank range before he was forced to surrender. Many men had died that day.

"I'm sorry for your loss," Trace said. The dispassionate tone of his voice belied the resurfacing of painful memories of his own.

He'd been sent to a prisoner-of-war camp following Buchanan's surrender. There were many times as a Confederate in a Union prisoner-of-war camp that Trace thought dying in Mobile Bay might have been preferable.

Hatred honed to a razor edge glittered in Conroy's eyes. "You killed my brother."

"I did not kill your brother, Elliot."

"How do you know?"

Trace couldn't know for certain. "The chances are unlikely."

"Someone's got to pay for my brother's death."

"The entire South is paying for your brother and thousands like him."

"This time the murderer has a face, and your face is as good as any Johnny Reb."

"Mr. Conroy, I fought for the Confederacy out of respect for my father. What's done is done and in the pas—"

"It'll never—"

"Don't interrupt me again, Mr. Conroy," Trace ordered through clenched teeth. Never long on patience, whatever he had left hung by a thread.

With his fists balled at his sides, he unleashed his anger in a low, well-enunciated rumble of warning.

"I have a deep sense of duty to our country. Not a duty to the South, nor to the North, but to this nation as a whole. The United States is a young, growing country yet in the process of healing. But it will heal. And we will come together one day to become the greatest, strongest nation in the world. In part because of the values we instill in our young men here at the Naval Academy."

"Those are mighty fine words, but words can't change what you did," Conroy spat back. "Southerners don't belong here."

"We all suffered during the war," Trace argued. "It's time to put the death and destruction behind us. It's time to build as one nation."

But Elliot Conroy wasn't listening. Deaf to idealism and blinded by hate, he raged on. "My mother hasn't been the same since Ray died. Do you know what the Bible says? An eye for an eye."

"Your misfortune cannot be denied."

Fury flashed in the civilian instructor's eyes as he took a threatening step toward Trace. "That's what you call my brother?" he rasped. "My only brother buried in some unmarked grave is a . . . misfortune?"

"Mr. Conroy." Trace drew a deep breath, determined not to lose his self-control. "I think it's time to bring this conversation to a close." He turned on his heel. "Good day."

Conroy seized his arm. "I think what's needed here is some man-to-man combat. I'll be the North. You be the South."

Blood at the boil, body tight with tension and jaw clenched, Trace spun around, reacting instinctively. Drawing back his arm, he plowed his fist into Conroy's jaw.

The stunned seaman fell to the deck.

*Damn, that felt good.*

Bracing himself on his elbows, Conroy rubbed his hairy jaw and snarled, "You're gonna pay for this, Reardon."

Narrowing his gaze on the fallen knots-and-shrouds expert, Trace issued a terse warning. "Don't ever touch me again."

Turning quickly, he strode away, but not before hearing his venomous colleague swear beneath his breath, "I'll see you in hell, Lieutenant. You're goin' to the brig."

A definite possibility. By losing his temper, he had played right into the hands of the man who most wanted him ousted from the academy. Knowing he could ill afford to allow impatience to overcome intelligence at this stage of his career, Trace chastised himself. *Damn.*

Two days following her accident on the stairs, Susannah joined Cellie Stuyvestant and Trace Reardon in the foyer. The lieutenant and his aunt had come to an impasse.

"We are all going to the church potluck supper?" Trace asked his aunt, in a tone that conveyed his disbelief in what he'd just heard. "Don't you think that a group appearance might discourage any young women who might otherwise wish to make my acquaintance?"

"Susannah will be with the girls. You will not be identified as their father immediately."

"Susannah can hardly walk," he protested.

"I'm fine," she said, realizing he'd spoken her given name for the first time.

She was determined to go to the social. In the search for her husband, she could not afford to leave any possibility unexplored. Patterson might be anywhere. Although she felt it highly unlikely that she would find him at church, she could not reject the notion out of hand. During their brief time together he'd given no indication that he was a God-fearing man, but the war had brought many men back to their faith.

In just a few days, she would receive her salary from the lieutenant. She planned on using the money to hire a detective. Every penny she earned would go toward finding Patterson. At this point, she could barely remember what he looked like and feared she would not recognize the sound of his voice. He'd possessed the swagger of a rake, she recalled that much, but he was a naval officer, no rake. For all Susannah knew, her young husband might be dead, and even with the aid of a detective, she might never know for certain what became of him.

Lieutenant Reardon hadn't budged. "I can't say I like this idea, Aunt Cellie."

Anxious to be on their way, Susannah dared intrude. "If you don't mind me expressing my opinion, I think your aunt has taken a wise notion. If a woman will not take on your family, you will know from the start that courting her would be in vain. If time is of the essence, you will not waste any."

He stared at her for a moment and then gave a curt nod. "Call the girls, Susannah, and we shall be off."

Emily ran down the hall steps, holding a crooked branch. "Look, Father. I fashioned a walking stick for Miss Partridge."

"You made that yourself?"

Emily beamed. "I found the stick, and Adam helped with the carving."

Her father tousled her hair, bringing forth a giggle.

"Take my hand, Miss Partridge," Grace instructed in her small voice. "Twinkle and I will help you down the front steps."

Each of the girls—Grace, Emily, Alice, and Amelia—had been extremely sweet and solicitous of Susannah since her fall. With her ankle still swollen and painful, she had avoided any undue movement until now. Relieved to learn they would ride to church in the carriage, she let go of Grace's hand and leaned on the lieutenant's arm as he helped her into the shiny vehicle.

Although he rode his horse to the church, upon arrival at the church, he again was at Susannah's side to help her.

"No sense being a stubborn Yankee, Miss Partridge. Lean on me until we get inside. Putting weight on your ankle might delay the healing process," he added, almost as an afterthought.

"My nephew is right," Aunt Cellie chirped. "You must be back in good form as soon as possible."

Susannah smiled. Her injury had interfered with Cellie's afternoon faro games.

"Once we are inside, I shall help watch the girls, so you may be sociable, Trace," his aunt continued. "Now, are you not glad that I did not hurry back to Lowell and Edgar?"

"Extremely, Aunt," he replied drolly.

Susannah lowered her head to hide her smile.

She had attended many a church potluck supper while her parents were still alive, but never in a silk dress. As she entered the hall, she discovered a large gathering, which she should have expected in a bustling port city.

Not knowing anyone in attendance, Susannah

decided to pass the time by keeping an eye out for any man who might resemble Patterson Harling, as best she could remember him. But first she watched the lieutenant launch his pursuit of a future wife. He began by pacing the perimeter of the hall, scouting prospects.

Susannah longed to advise him. Just as she had required her employer's help moments ago, it was clear that he needed hers now. She'd made a list of the qualities the perfect wife for the lieutenant must possess: patience, intelligence, understanding, spirit, social poise, and grace. Coincidentally, she herself possessed all but the last.

Clasping his hands behind him, Reardon stood near the center of the hall looking about as if he were searching for a particular person—which Susannah knew that he wasn't. How astonishing that a good-looking man like Trace Reardon should not be besieged by women. He looked particularly handsome dressed in his dark blue uniform emblazoned with three gold stripes and a star at the sleeve.

Susannah ached for him as she regarded the lieutenant's obvious procrastination. Aunt Cellie came to his rescue by ushering a young woman to her nephew's side. Emily, Amelia, Alice, and Grace were dispatched to Susannah.

"Would you like a glass of punch?" Emily asked as the girls gathered around her.

"That would be lovely."

Alice squinted at the dishes lining the table where Susannah sat. "I see nothing I like to eat."

"Do not worry. We shall find you something delicious."

Amelia, who had been standing behind Susannah, leaned over to whisper in her ear. "Do you see the lady talking with Father?"

"Yes, I do." She hadn't taken her eyes off the loquacious woman who seemed never to stop talking.

"She sounds like Bilge when he squawks."

"Twinkle doesn't like her," Grace added.

Susannah felt it her duty to remonstrate, but she did so mildly. "You must not judge another by appearances."

But they were right. She did sound like Bilge.

"Why must Father have a wife?" Emily wanted to know.

"Men and women were meant to be together," Susannah replied.

"Then why don't you have a husband?" Amelia, the ever-curious, asked.

"You could marry Papa!" Grace exclaimed excitedly before Susannah could answer her sister.

"Don't be silly, Grace. Miss Partridge is an old maid," Emily declared.

Startled, Susannah was about to deny Emily's assertion, but hesitated. She very well might be an old maid! If it happened that she was a widow, there would be little opportunity for her to meet a man to love and marry again. It was well known that a shortage of eligible men in the country existed.

And, deep down in her heart, she feared that she might have been abandoned by her husband. Perhaps Patterson hadn't returned to Rhode Island for her after the war because he believed he'd made a mistake. He hadn't loved her, after all. If either case were true, she was doomed to a childless life alone. A lump lodged in her throat, too bitter, too large to swallow.

"Uh-oh, Father is heading our way," Amelia warned.

"She didn't last long," Emily said, giving voice to Susannah's observation.

"Remember your manners," Susannah cautioned.

"Are you quite bored, Miss Partridge?" the lieutenant asked upon reaching them.

"No sir." She had found some amusement in watching Reardon extricate himself from his aunt and the chatterbox.

At the far end of the hall, the preacher called for all the children to form a circle about him for a round of songs.

The girls scampered away, and Susannah was left alone with Reardon. An uneasy silence fell between them.

"That may keep my children diverted for a few minutes."

"But only for a few. Your daughters are quite intelligent, you know."

"Are you finding them to be a handful?"

"No. They are lively, spirited young ladies. I enjoy their company."

"A preacher's daughter would not fabricate in order to tell a father what he most wished to hear?"

"I speak the truth. But do not worry about me. This is a perfect time and place for you to find a wife."

"This is not where I shall find the proper wife," he responded stubbornly.

"Surely, there must be a saint of a woman set upon doing good deeds in the hall? There always is."

"I have not met one. Miss Fancy did not pause for breath, and Miss Ruth Reynolds had no use for a man with a southern drawl," he held a hand up so that she could not deny the hostility that he encountered. "I recognize the problem when I am faced with it."

" 'Tis a pity. But they are only two out of how

many women in the hall—fifteen, twenty? Carry on, Lieutenant. They dare not come to you, you know. Think of securing a wife as launching a military-type campaign in which you must capture the enemy. Your weapons will be charm, rank, and—"

"You sound eager for me to find a wife," he interrupted. "Have you grown weary of the girls in such a short time?"

"No. No."

"Launch a campaign. You make it sound so simple," he muttered as his dark brows gathered in a frown. "But it would not be the first time that I thought of women as the enemy."

"No!"

"Yes. Why must you all be so baffling? A woman only pretends to know what she wants. A woman believes she wants to marry an officer because of his dashing uniform, and then when he is away doing his duty, she grows restless and takes a lover."

His dour expression made Susannah wonder if the scenario he'd described had happened to him. If it had, she could not be surprised that he did not feel eager to marry again.

"It's true, some women do not know what they want," she allowed, answering carefully. "But many more know their minds exactly. Those women make faithful and loving wives."

"I don't believe I am capable of distinguishing one type from the other."

"Your aunt appears to be a good judge of character. I'm certain she will assist you—just as she is doing now."

Aunt Cellie advanced upon them with another young girl in tow.

"Trace, I should like you to meet Millicent

Witherspoon. Poor Millicent lost her husband during the war and since becoming a widow has worked as Doctor Trumbull's nurse. Millicent, this is our governess, Susannah Partridge. I have told Mrs. Witherspoon about our darling girls."

Millicent dipped her head. "It's a pleasure to meet you. Your daughters are very attractive young ladies, Lieutenant Reardon."

"Thank you."

"Come, Susannah," Aunt Cellie tapped Susannah on the shoulder. "We must round up the girls and find a place at the table."

Reardon cast a glower at his aunt. "Miss Partridge can't walk."

"Yes, I can," Susannah assured him. "I have this fine walking stick which Emily made. The Reardon sisters are clever girls," she told Mrs. Witherspoon.

In the end, Trace dined with Millicent during the potluck supper, much to the chagrin of his daughters. And after seeing his family into the carriage, he walked the widow Witherspoon home.

The girls sulked as they prepared for bed.

"Father has behaved rudely."

"Hush, Emily. Your father is attempting to find a mother for you, and he will be forced to forgo the social niceties upon occasion."

But Susannah sympathized with his daughters' ill humor. She felt out of sorts as well. A man should always leave the party with the woman he brought.

A sharp streak of suffocating jealousy attacked her, taking her by surprise, forcing her to gulp air. Good gracious!

She had no right to feel spurned in favor of another. The lieutenant hadn't brought Susannah to the church supper. He'd escorted his aunt and governess. That's all she was to Trace Reardon—

his daughters' governess. And she must never forget it.

It was all she could be.

In the morning, Susannah planned to see a solicitor. She had to know what had become of her husband. No matter that she felt little but curiosity when she thought of Patterson now; she'd promised to be his wife until "death do you part."

She would honor her vow. But one way or another she meant to discover if Patterson Harling was dead or alive.

# CHAPTER 6

Grace in hand, Susannah limped down Main Street to the Sugarplum Sweet Shop. Although her ankle still felt tender, she had no more time to waste. Every penny of her newly received wages was tucked inside her reticule. She had repaid Clara Devonshire for the broken vase and had no more debts. Today she meant to commission a solicitor to find her missing husband.

Mr. Walter Holtsmutter had been recommended by her friend Lulu, owner of the pastry shop where Susannah stopped with Grace every day after walking the older girls to school. They shared cocoa and hot cross buns, often with Twinkle, and always with Lulu. The shopkeeper had offered to watch Grace today while Susannah talked with the solicitor, whose office was only two doors away.

Grace was happily chomping on a gooey cinnamon bun when Susannah prepared to depart, promising her silver-blue-eyed angel that she would return within a few minutes. Deliciously occupied, Grace merely nodded her head.

A bell dangling from the inside doorknob of Mr. Holtsmutter's office rang sharply when Susannah opened the door. Turning to a stranger for help in finding her husband seemed shameful. Feeling embarrassed, she hung back.

The dirty plank floor creaked with each halting step she took. Filtered rays of sun poured through the grimy front window, providing the only light in the long, narrow office. At first glance it was obvious that Mr. Holtsmutter didn't care for cleaning and had no wife to do it for him.

A wiry man peered up at her over round spectacles lodged beneath the bridge of his nose. Uneven stacks of paper took up almost every square inch of his desk.

"Mr. Holtsmutter?"

"That is I." He rose to greet her, extending his hand in a jerky gesture. "Have a seat."

"My name is Susannah Partridge. Lulu suggested that you might help me."

"What kind of help are you needing?"

Susannah took a deep breath. "I wish to discover if my husband is alive."

"He's gone missing?"

"Yes. He was a midshipman when the academy was in Newport. But before he was graduated, Patterson went off to the war and I never heard from him again."

Mr. Holtsmutter leaned back in his chair and wrung his hands. "It's a familiar story. One I've heard many times before, and I'm happy to say that I can help you."

The solicitor made Susannah nervous. His movements were choppy, and his speech came in staccato bursts. Most unsettling of all, his squinty eyes never left hers.

Susannah perched tentatively on the edge of

the chair. "As I am certain that you can imagine, for a woman not to know if her husband is dead or alive is a terrible thing."

"Can't get a new husband if the old one's still alive."

" 'Tis not the way of it, Mr. Holtsmutter," Susannah snapped, wondering how the solicitor could be so insensitive. "My husband might have been maimed or wounded. What if he cannot remember who he is or even that he has a wife? If he is alive, I should be at my husband's side honoring my wedding vows."

Holtsmutter removed his spectacles and wiped them on the sleeve of his shirt. "I have a fellow who tracks deserters down for me."

"Patterson is not a deserter," Susannah declared, jumping to her feet. At least she fervently hoped not.

"Otherwise brave men have been known to commit cowardly acts during a war."

Susannah did not find comfort in his philosophizing. "Will you take my case, Mr. Holtsmutter?"

"How much can you pay?"

"I can give you three dollars a month."

The solicitor scratched the top of his bald head. "What's your husband's name?"

"Patterson Harling."

"Harling?" he repeated, squinting at her. "Didn't you say your name was Partridge?"

"Yes. But Patterson told me that I must use my maiden name while he was away at war. He said that it might be dangerous for me and for him if it were known that he'd taken a wife."

"He said that, did he?"

"Yes. He hinted that he would spy for the Union Navy. He was anxious for my safety if he should be captured by the enemy."

Holtsmutter raised his gaze to the ceiling and sighed. "Do you have a likeness of him?"

Many were the times that Susannah wished she owned a likeness of her young husband. But Patterson had none to give her, and there had been no time to sit for a daguerreotype before he left for the war.

"No," Susannah replied, "but I can describe him for you."

"Go ahead."

"Patterson is tall, with auburn hair and a broad nose. But not too broad." She could no longer visualize her husband. It had been three years since she'd last seen him, and Patterson's image had all but faded from her mind. "His eyes are blue."

"Has he got all his teeth? Any scars?"

"He possessed all of his teeth, the last I saw him. And I do not recall any scars."

"Where's his home? Did he tell you that?"

Mr. Holtsmutter barely hid his disdain. For some odd reason, he clearly disliked a man he had not even met.

"Of course he did," Susannah said coolly. "Ohio. Patterson has family in Ohio."

"Where in Ohio?"

"I . . . I'm not certain."

"Did he plan to stay in the navy?"

"I . . . I don't know," she said ruefully, as shame seeped through her veins.

Lowering her head, Susannah reproached herself once more for not learning more about Patterson before she married him. But it had been a whirlwind courtship in a time of war, and time had seemed of the essence. She'd been quite infatuated with Patterson Harling. However, Mr. Holtsmutter's questions pointed out that she had not known as much as she should have about the man she married.

"I need more information, Miss Partridge."

"We weren't married for long before he left for war."

"Where was he last time you saw him?"

"In Newport. He was shipped out to Philadelphia."

In another jarring movement, Holtsmutter jerked up out of his chair. "This isn't much to go on, but we'll do our best. Come back in two weeks."

"Two weeks?" Although she knew it to be unreasonable, Susannah had hoped that with a professional search for Patterson, she would have news sooner. While she took great pleasure caring for the Reardon girls, her desire to cradle her own babies had intensified daily as a result.

"Mrs. Harling, or should I call you Miss Partridge?"

"Ah . . . Partridge, Miss Partridge, if you please. No one knows me by—"

"Rest assured your secret is safe with me."

"It's not so much a secret."

But it was. She'd not confided in anyone. Only her sister knew she had married Patterson; only Mabel knew how concerned Susannah had been when Patterson didn't return.

"It may take months to find your husband," Mr. Holtsmutter told her, adding quietly. "And then we might find him in a grave."

The bottom dropped from the pit of her stomach. "A year," she repeated in a faint rasp.

"I don't want you to get your hopes up."

A dense fog of disappointment settled on her shoulders. Nodding her understanding, she stood to leave. "I'll appreciate any news."

Slightly dazed and completely dispirited, Susannah left the solicitor's office with her head lowered. She didn't see the man, couldn't avoid the collision. She ran into a wall of iron that rocked her back on her heels.

An arm went out to steady her. "Whoa! My apologies, ma'am."

Susannah looked up and discovered the wall of iron belonged to a roughishly handsome man, a midshipman much older than most.

"No, no, I am the one who should apologize," she said. "I wasn't watching where I was going."

"Are you hurt?" he asked.

"No." In truth, her ankle injury throbbed anew.

"It isn't every day that I run into a beautiful woman. Literally." His blue eyes twinkled, a mischievous grin hovered about his mouth as he removed his cap. "Midshipman First-Class Rand Noble at your service."

Susannah inclined her head and smiled at the academy student. "Midshipman Noble."

"And whom have I had the pleasure of running aground?"

She wasn't certain she should give him her name. But then, the midshipmen were duty bound to be gentlemen at all times. "Susannah Partridge."

"Perhaps I should escort you to the doctor's office, Miss Partridge."

"Thank you, but that won't be necessary."

"Ah, but perhaps we should make certain that I have broken no bones." He flashed a disarming smile, a smile that would melt a heart of stone.

"You are most kind, but I do not require the services of a doctor. However, I shall watch where I am walking in the future," she assured him.

"Allow me to watch where you walk as well. I shall see you home."

The charismatic midshipman was nothing if not

persistent. Stuck by his carefree manner and charm, Susannah could not feel annoyed with him.

"Thank you, but I need no assistance," she demurred softly.

"In that case, I shall take you to the Sugarplum Sweet Shop for tea." Slanting an irresistible smile toward her, he offered his arm. "To assure myself that no harm has been done."

Laughing, she tucked her hand through his arm. "As a matter of fact, I was on my way to the Sugarplum."

The autumn day held a cool, crisp breeze and the scent of burning leaves. Whitecaps bobbed on the bay beneath a vivid blue sky while shrimpers and oystermen plied their trade. Artists dreamed of such a vibrant harbor scene to capture on canvas.

Trace emerged from the tobacco shop just in time to see Susannah take Rand Noble's arm. The oldest midshipman ever to attend the academy, Rand had earned a reputation as a notorious rake. What was he doing with Trace's governess? More important, where was Grace?

Striding across the street, Trace raised his arm in greeting, "Hello, there! Wait up!"

Susannah turned and her eyes went wide.

A smooth smile glided across Rand's lips.

After an exchange of salutes, Trace addressed the twenty-five-year-old midshipman. "Do you have permission to be off grounds, Noble?"

"Yes sir. And I can assure you that this isn't what it looks like."

"What does it look like?"

"It might appear as if I am out for a stroll with a pretty woman."

"And what are you actually doing?" Trace wanted

to know. Noble had already earned seventy-five of the two hundred demerits allowed annually, and the school year had hardly begun.

"Miss Partridge and I collided. I'm accompanying her to the Sugarplum Sweet Shop to make certain she has not been hurt. But I fear that she's been injured. She's limping."

"She's been limping for two days, Midshipman."

"I appreciate your concern, Midshipman Noble," Susannah interjected. "But Lieutenant Reardon is my employer. I am the governess to his children."

Attempting to keep his impatience in check, Trace turned to Miss Partridge. "Speaking of my children, what have you done with Grace?"

"She is with Lulu in the Sugarplum Shop."

As Rand Noble took his leave, the twinkle in his eyes never faded, much to Trace's consternation. The dashing student aimed his smile solely at Susannah. "I can see that my services are no longer needed. But I should like to call upon you, Miss Partridge. When you are healed, of course."

Susannah smiled as if she might be willing, but she said nothing. As the midshipman strode away, however, Trace caught and recognized the light in her astonishing eyes. She found the academy's oldest midshipman attractive!

"May I ask why you left Grace with Lulu?" Trace asked, feeling more annoyed than reasonable.

"I had personal business that I cannot attend to on a Sunday."

"I do not pay you to conduct personal business."

To his surprise, Susannah turned on him. Her usually soft as velvet eyes blazed with shards of glittering, golden anger. "By all means, deduct thirty minutes from my wages!"

Trace immediately backed down. His daughters

adored Susannah. He didn't know what he would do if she left at this point. "I shall do no such thing," he replied calmly. "Not this time. But in the future, should you have pressing business, notify me in advance so that we may make proper arrangements."

"I made proper arrangements. Grace has been happily occupied."

"You left her in a sweet shop? Sweets are not good for children. I would have thought you knew that."

Trace couldn't explain why he felt so angry with Susannah for what amounted to a minor transgression. She hadn't left Grace alone, after all.

One hand went to her hip. "Are you going to dismiss me?"

"No. I shall escort you to the Sugarplum Shop."

What personal business had she? And with whom? Trace wanted to know, but he had no business asking. If he possessed one-tenth the charm of Rand Noble, she would tell all without being questioned. But he hadn't. Once a natural, skillful practitioner of southern charm, he'd grown cynical and lost the will to exercise the art soon after marrying Louise.

The fragrance of cinnamon and sugar filled the Sweet Shop. Trace spotted Grace at the same instant that she saw him. Lulu, the proprietor of the shop, sat next to his youngest daughter.

Grace jumped down from her chair and ran toward him, her mouth covered with sticky white icing. Apparently unwilling to part with it for even a moment, she clutched a cinnamon bun in her hand. "Papa!"

Descending to sit on his heels at Grace's level, Trace opened his arms.

His daughters were his greatest joy, especially in

moments like this. He worried often that he did not give them the same delight that they brought to his life.

"Want some of my cinnamon bun?"

"Grace, I don't—"

"Your father would love a taste," Susannah interrupted. "What a sweet, generous girl you are to share your bun."

He shot the interfering governess a scowl to which she responded with a brilliant smile, a smile that uncannily served to warn him not to disappoint his daughter.

"Yes. Yes, I would," he said. "Thank you, Grace."

"But don't you think we should sit at the table so we don't leave crumbs for Lulu?" Susannah asked.

"Of course," he allowed. When had Miss Partridge begun to give the orders?

They were soon seated at a cozy table.

"Miss Partridge bought me a cinnamon bun and hot cocoa, Papa."

"Miss Partridge is extremely thoughtful."

"She had to see a man."

Trace frowned.

"That is not exactly as it sounds, Lieutenant Reardon. I required the . . . opinion of a solicitor," Susannah explained.

"You went to see Walter Holtsmutter," he stated, taking an educated guess. Holtsmutter's office was the closest.

"Yes, I did."

"While Miss Partridge was away, Twinkle kept me company. I gave her a piece of my bun."

"Twinkle," he repeated. The fairy business again. Trace shot Grace's governess a wordless threat and clamped his jaw tightly to prevent himself from saying the words he longed to say, but not in front of small ears.

Miss Partridge smiled but did not reply. Instead, her gaze flickered to his shoulder. Apparently she did not wish to take up the Twinkle matter in front of Grace, either. He would reprimand her again later. Days ago, he'd given orders for her to put a stop to the fairy nonsense.

Like a man sorely burdened, Trace heaved a sigh. "If you required a solicitor, Miss Partridge, you should have come to me. I would have been happy to refer you to mine. My solicitor is extremely knowledgeable in all things legal."

"I did not wish to bother you with a small matter. I am satisfied that Mr. Holtsmutter will do nicely," she replied, still staring at his shoulder.

"Is something wrong with my uniform?"

"You have icing on your shoulder."

He started to groan, but Susannah cut him off quickly. " 'Tis a mark of distinction. Not many officers have been able to share a sweet with their daughter this morning."

"Yes. I . . . I am a very fortunate man."

"Can we do it again, Papa?"

"I shall try and arrange to have midmorning sweets with you and your sisters very soon."

"One at a time would be lovely, too," Susannah said, as she withdrew a handkerchief from her reticule and dipped one corner in a glass of water. "Each of the girls deserves your undivided attention occasionally, don't you agree?"

"Quite." He hadn't thought of it before. She was right.

Susannah rubbed at the icing on his shoulder with her wet hanky. For an instant the sweet smell of her lilac fragrance overpowered the delicious bakery scents. He inhaled deeply.

With the exception of his aunt, and long ago his

mother, no one had fussed over Trace in this manner for many years.

"There, now. Not a smidgen of icing left," she said, again with a smile that outshone the sun. "You look as good as new."

As good as new. Never.

Her eyes met his. The bright smile faded from her face as his gaze locked on hers. Wistful. Wondering. Wanting. An intangible connection so fleeting that he could not grasp nor fully understand it passed between them, slipped through his fingers like a bayou breeze. But he knew it had more to do with man and woman than with employer and governess. Inexplicably, his heart grew tight within the walls of his chest.

As good as new. If she knew. If she only knew.

Trace would never be good as new. The burns on his body had left angry red, pitted scars. While his memories of what he'd endured in the Union prison camp might fade, the scars that ravaged the right side and back of him would never diminish. He would remember the explosion of the *Sultana* until his dying day. But unlike many who were maimed and wounded during the conflict, Trace's scars were concealed.

Any woman of fine sensibilities seeing him unclothed would surely feel revulsion and swoon. A well-bred woman would refuse to touch him. What he could ignore playing the courting game would be impossible to overcome in the marriage bed.

No matter how large his personal fortune, or what rank he achieved in the navy, Trace would never be the man most young women of privilege desired. His uniformed appearance was deceiving. Despite his aunt's insistence on finding him the perfect woman, Trace felt the futility of it all. Perfect women did not settle for imperfect men.

His only solution was to find a wife who would be happily married in name only. A marriage of convenience to a woman who would mother his children and attend social events with him. A partnership without intimacy.

Trace required a woman who did not care to have children of her own. But where was he to find such a woman?

"Lieutenant Reardon?" Miss Partridge regarded him with a puzzled expression.

"Yes, thank you, Miss Partridge. My uniform is as good as new." He took one last sip of tea and stood. "I must return to the gymnasium now. I shall walk you and Grace to the academy grounds."

Susannah Partridge wiped the corners of Grace's mouth. "Now you are as good as new, too," she declared with a wink.

The child looked from Miss Partridge to Trace and back. "Can we bring sweets to Alice and Amelia and Emily, too?"

"What a wonderful idea!"

"You shall be responsible for their teeth rotting away," Trace growled in Susannah's ear.

"I doubt that very much. The girls haven't had a sweet to eat since I have been their governess," she said, fumbling in her reticule.

Trace stayed her plunging. "Please, Miss Partridge, this shall be my treat."

Grace clapped her hands as he paid Lulu. His youngest daughter's eyes sparkled with delight as she skipped ahead out of the Sugarplum Sweet Shop. "Won't my sisters be surprised, Twinkle?"

It wasn't the fairy that Trace heard answer. It was Susannah.

"Indeed," she said.

"If one of my girls loses a tooth—"

"There are times when we all need some sweetness," she interrupted.

She meant him. He knew she meant him. He purchased an extra bun for Miss Partridge. She was right again. Trace had once been able to sweet-talk with the best. Perhaps the time had come to relearn the social skills that used to be second nature.

Susannah had limped out onto the street ahead of him and waited there with Grace.

Blue skies had given way to gray. Thick, purple-gray clouds rolled overhead, concealing the sun. The crisp autumn air had grown damp and chilly. Susannah drew her shawl tightly around her as she watched the fallen leaves swirl over the uneven cobblestones and catch in the hem of her gown.

As they made their way down Main Street and back to the academy grounds, Reardon walked stiffly beside Susannah, holding Grace's hand.

The lieutenant was angry with her again, she thought. But she could not help but speak her mind. She found it impossible to stand idly by when it came to the children. It was sad enough that the girls were motherless, but to bear a tense, distant father only compounded the situation. Neither could she credit the mothering skills of Aunt Cellie, who longed to relinquish her time with the girls in favor of long afternoons playing faro.

Owing to Susannah's opposition to the lieutenant's wishes upon occasion, and the possibility that Holtsmutter might discover Patterson alive and well, she might not be in Reardon's employ much longer. Clearly, in whatever time she had left in the household, she must do her best to make certain father and daughters grew closer. Although

Reardon often seemed tentative around his daughters, she believed that he loved them very much. And while the girls sometimes appeared intimidated by the lieutenant, they loved their father dearly.

The solution was simple. The family must spend more time together. Later that afternoon, as soon as she met the older girls at school, Susannah put her family plan in action. She ushered the brood to the old Fort Severn building where the academy's new gymnasium and ten-pin bowling allies were under construction.

Susannah noticed that the moment Lieutenant Reardon saw his daughters and governess approaching, his body stiffened. But his frown, his wary gaze focused on her alone. No doubt he suspected trouble.

She smiled, intending to put his mind at ease.

His frown deepened.

Apparently, *she* frightened him.

# CHAPTER 7

"Surprise!" Grace yelled, her lilting child's voice echoing in the hall.

Reardon hiked a dark brow.

It wasn't exactly a scowl that followed his frown, darkening his rugged features. But as he strode toward them, Susannah silently questioned whether this visit had been such a sterling idea after all. It would take more than a smile to put the lieutenant at ease.

They met in the center of the bowling alley and shooting galleries. Fortunately, Susannah thought, with wry humor, they stood closer to the bowling alley than the shooting galleries. While the lieutenant might like to shoot her, he couldn't do it with the children in attendance and the weapons out of reach.

"Good afternoon, Lieutenant Reardon," she said, greeting him cheerfully.

Her forced cheer did not win a smile from him. His voice rumbled like thunder. "Good afternoon, Miss Partridge."

Towering over her, the lieutenant presented a

powerful, intractable presence. The object of his somber scrutiny, Susannah felt small and vulnerable, much like a meadow mouse being considered as dinner by a hungry panther. His eyes, now darkened to charcoal, snapped with impatience.

"We are on our way to the parade ground," she explained hastily. "I hope you don't mind, but I thought it would be . . ." She paused for inspiration, and it struck. "I thought it might be educational for the girls to see where you work and what you are doing."

"Wel—"

"This appears to be a ten-pin—" she interrupted him nervously.

"Bowling alley."

"Do you know how to bowl, Father?" Amelia asked raising her curious gray gaze to his.

The impatience slid from his eyes, granite gray softened to a softer shade of smoke. "Yes, Amelia, I do."

"Will you teach us?" Emily, the lieutenant's eldest daughter asked, her eyes alight with the possibility.

"The alley is for midshipmen, Emily."

"Certainly there will be times when the boys are not about?" Susannah suggested helpfully.

The look Reardon shot her indicated he did not desire her help. "Yes, but—"

Nevertheless, she would give it. She proceeded to interrupt him once again. "I see no reason why girls cannot hit the pins as well as boys."

His dark brows gathered in a frown above the bridge of his noble nose. "The ten-pin balls are too heavy for girls."

"We . . . girls and women are stronger than you might suspect," she insisted, unfazed by his silent reproach.

"I rather doubt that my girls could lift the balls, let alone roll them down the lane."

"But they might enjoy the attempt," Susannah countered, with a smile.

The lieutenant stepped aside and beckoned her with a finger. "Miss Partridge, a word."

"Of course," she replied brightly, obediently following him to a spot out of the girls' hearing.

"Allowing my daughters to see where I work and what I'm doing is one thing. To fill their heads with impossibilities is another."

"I believe that nothing is impossible, Lieutenant."

"How could I have forgotten? You are the woman who believes in fairies."

Refusing to allow his remark to disturb her, Susannah pretended that she hadn't heard. She turned to the children. "Girls, would you like to see the second floor?"

She knew they would. They responded in unison and rather boisterously.

Jaw clamped tightly, Reardon led the way up the steps. Susannah found the lieutenant attractive even in anger. The strong, square cut of his jaw suggested raw masculinity and physical strength. Certainly, other women must find him as appealing as she. His inability to find a wife became more puzzling. A scowl could be overlooked, and most women did not quail before the prospect of raising another woman's children. She came to the conclusion he simply wasn't trying. To her knowledge, Reardon hadn't seen the widow Witherspoon since the church supper.

With sure, quick strides, he led Susannah and his daughters into the second-floor gymnasium. It was still under construction, and the scent of fresh sawdust permeated the hall. Vaulting horses and mats were stored along one wall, climbing ropes and rings fell from the ceiling, and striking bags stood off in the far corner.

"What will the boys do here, Father?" Amelia asked.

"Among other things, they will learn how to box and wrestle. In the process the superintendent expects the midshipmen to develop a keen competitive edge."

"You see, girls, there are important goals to be met here," Susannah added. "We have learned something, myself included. The gymnasium is not only for entertainment."

The lieutenant nodded. His body appeared more relaxed than it had a moment ago. "Not at all. Like Miss Partridge says, the gymnasium will serve important purposes."

"Do you know how to box, Father?" Alice asked.

"I have held my own in boyish fisticuffs," he admitted with a sheepish smile.

She went a step further. "Have you wrestled?"

"I have. But I am a far better pugilist."

"You can do anything," Grace declared, her eyes shining with awe.

Trace Reardon smiled then, warmly, at his daughters. "No, I cannot do everything," he replied modestly.

Much too modestly, in Susannah's opinion. With his broad shoulders and a chest wide enough to hold a bevy of medals, she judged the lieutenant capable of turning back the tide.

Knowing this sort of thinking could lead to wicked thoughts, Susannah tore her gaze away and raised it to the ceiling. "What fun it would be to swing on a trapeze."

"No, no, Miss Partridge. Do not consider it even in jest."

"I wasn't jesting."

"With your predilection for accidents, I shudder at the thought of you flying through the air."

"It would be like flying!" she exclaimed, increasingly warming to the idea.

"Women possess a delicate nature and are not meant to swing from a trapeze."

The presumption that all women possessed a delicate nature had been fostered by a few who did. Susannah wasn't one of them. "Do you have a net?"

"Miss Partridge, you are not swinging from my trapeze in any circumstance."

"Reardon!"

Susannah turned at the sound of the ragged call. A tall, heavyset bearded man swaggered toward them in an uneven gait. He wore a smile more sardonic than pleasant.

With his gaze locked on the approaching figure, Reardon issued a quiet, urgent order. "Miss Partridge, take the children home. I have business to attend to with Mr. Conroy."

Unpleasant business, she guessed. "We shall be at the parade ground if you find that you can join us," she told him before hustling the children away.

Only two workmen labored in the gymnasium. Without the children, only the sound of sporadic hammering echoed in the hall.

Elliot Conroy came to an abrupt stop not more than two feet from Trace. "How's the playground coming?" he asked, scratching behind his left, tattered ear.

Trace gritted his teeth. "It's not a playground."

Conroy smirked.

"How's your jaw?"

"Not a bone broke."

"I expected you to report me."

"Did you now?" Conroy hitched his thumbs beneath the waistband of his dark trousers. "Well, I ain't a man who needs someone else to fight my battles for me."

"I don't have any quarrel with you, Conroy."

"But I've got one with a Johnny Reb who's building an indoor playground."

"The gymnasium is about discipline and creating officers with physical strength. Men with stamina and a competitive spirit."

"Lofty words," Conroy sneered.

In fact, Superintendent Porter had reported student morale had increased solely in anticipation of the opening of the facility. He'd made it clear to Trace at the beginning that improving student morale was a priority.

"Physical development will become an important part of the academy curriculum," Trace replied firmly, but his heart waffled. While the other officers taught military skills necessary for survival, his contribution seemed insignificant in comparison. While Trace built a gymnasium and ten-pin lanes to boost student morale, the navy worked on inventor Oliver Halstead's new twenty-two-foot submersible, the *Intelligent Whale*. He ached to be in on the development, to open the midshipmen's minds to the future of the navy in a new world beneath the sea.

"So swinging from a trapeze is goin' to be as important as knowing your knots, is it? Sounds to me like yer spittin' into the wind, Reardon."

Because he'd had almost identical thoughts, Conroy's taunt slammed like a fist into Trace's gut. Each encounter with the scornful civilian instructor seemed more menacing than the last.

"I don't have to justify my position to you. I follow orders."

Elliot's gaze narrowed on Trace. "Those your children I saw leavin' here?"

He couldn't very well deny it. "Yes."

"All girls? You fathered all girls?"

Trace gave a tight-lipped reply. "Yes."

"And the beautiful little lady, is she your wife?"

Conroy's questions were off the mark. His interest in Trace's family posed a new and dangerous threat. "Why are you asking?"

"You've got yourself a fine family is all," he said. Cocking his head, he shot Trace a derisive smile. "What you need are some boys to make things perfect. From the looks of her, yer wife will be giving you sons before long. She's built for it—"

"Don't say another word." Trace spoke his warning slowly and deliberately. His hands curled into fists.

Elliot Conroy ignored the warnings. "My brother would have liked to have had a family like yours. But he's dead. My brother died before he had a chance to live."

"Conroy, I've said it before, I'm sorry about your brother. But I'm not personally responsible for his death. We all lost friends, brothers, and fathers. We have to put the past behind us."

"Wouldn't you just like that?"

"Maybe if we got to know each other, have a drink together some ni—"

"I wouldn't be caught dead drinkin' with you," Conroy growled. His dark brows furrowed in a frown so deep, his eyes very nearly disappeared.

"Lieutenant Reardon!"

Trace looked up. It was Rand Noble again, striding across the floor, grinning.

Seaman Conroy grunted, "Another fool. Looks like this navy will let any fool be an officer."

Before limping off in the opposite direction of Rand Noble, Elliot Conroy leveled a parting snarl that said more than words. Watching him leave,

Trace wondered if the embittered man was stupid enough to seek revenge upon him. Perhaps it was time to consider taking steps to ensure his daughters' safety, and that of Susannah Partridge as well.

"Lieutenant Reardon."

Shaking off his disquiet, Trace turned to Noble. "How can I help you, Midshipman?"

"I thought I should officially ask your permission to call upon Miss Partridge."

"You don't need my permission."

Noble shook his head. "This morning I distinctly had the impression that your permission was required."

"Susannah is the governess to my children. As I am not her father, my permission is not required. Sunday is her free day."

"Then you have no objections if I call upon her on Sunday."

What could he say? "None."

"You realize that she is older than you."

"Miss Partridge possesses a spirit kin to my own."

A spurt of true alarm bolted through Trace. "Are you under the impression that Susannah Partridge possesses a spirit akin to yours?"

"Yes, I felt it instantly."

Of course. Rand Noble would be the first midshipman to swing from one of the trapezes. "Are you aware that she is the daughter of a preacher?"

"No. But I do not see how that matters. Does he preach here in Annapolis?"

"He's passed on," Trace replied.

Rand flashed a triumphant grin. "Then it matters not at all."

"Call upon her if you will."

"You have no interest in the lady?"

Frowning, Trace squared the set of his jaw. "Of course not."

"I thought I detected—"

"Nothing. You detected nothing," he barked. Realizing he might be protesting too much, Trace lowered his voice and managed a semblance of a smile. "Susannah is an admirable governess, and my girls are quite fond of her. That is my only interest."

"I am not surprised your daughters are fond of her."

"Have you checked the rules of conduct? Are you quite certain that it is not against the rules to be courting a woman while still attending classes?" Trace asked.

The rakish first classman appeared surprised by the question but answered smoothly. "I'm in my last year at the academy, and, as I understand it, my free time can be spent as I choose. I choose to form a friendship with Susannah Partridge."

"Very well."

"The gymnasium appears almost ready for use. I think I can speak for the entire student body in saying we're looking forward to using the facility."

Rand Noble had the political instincts of a general. "You won't have long to wait," Trace assured him.

As supervisor on the unlikely project, Trace had made record time. The civilian carpenters had worked speedily and done a good job. He expected the project to be complete within ten days. Perhaps then he could devote himself once again to submersibles and torpedoes.

"Excellent." Noble saluted Trace with military precision and a stern expression. An expression that rapidly softened to what some might consider a mocking smile. "Perhaps I shall see you on Sunday when I come to call on Miss Partridge."

More than his smile, the mischievous twinkle in Noble's eyes disturbed Trace. "Perhaps."

With a thought to warning Susannah against Rand Noble's charms, he watched the aged first classman stride away. Noble's reputation was worse than the one Trace had once enjoyed, when he was young and carefree—before the war, before his marriage to Louise. He felt so old now. How had he grown so old in just a few short years? For a moment he longed to feel young and on the prowl again.

Dress parade was held every fair evening during the spring and fall on the flat strip of land beside the Severn River. Stately old maple trees lined the field at either end, some with barren branches, some with scattered leaves of crimson and gold. At the west end of the site a white gazebo had been constructed for spring concerts.

Led by the newly outfitted and enlarged Naval Academy Band, the midshipmen marched as smartly as military veterans.

Trace spotted Susannah and the girls before they noticed him. Standing near the gazebo, two of his daughters were stationed on either side of Susannah. Emily and Alice to her left. Grace and Amelia to her right.

Beneath the murky late afternoon sky they braved the biting wind to watch the parade. The female fivesome might have been mistaken for a mother and her children rather than a governess and her charges, just as Elliot Conroy had supposed.

Grace marched in place, her little hand to her temple in a child's salute to the flag.

Emily appeared infinitely bored, barely concealing a yawn behind her gloved hand.

Alice looked as if she were seeking friends among the onlookers.

Amelia gazed dreamily at the river.

Susannah's amber eyes fixed on the flag, her

chin raised proudly. The skirts of her lavender dress billowed and slapped against her with each gust of wind. She appeared oblivious to her wind-blown appearance. And how charming it was—from the red tip of her nose to the rosy luster of her cheeks. The unrelenting breeze had blown buttermilk strands of silky hair that had escaped from her bonnet across her face—strands he would brush away, if only he could.

Petite, and resplendent in her beauty and misty-eyed patriotism, she stood out among the women observing the parade. Anyone could see at a glance that Susannah was a proud, indomitable woman—a woman who offered comfort and refuge. Susannah Partridge was like the anchor that stayed a ship in a stormy sea. She took his breath away.

As he was considering this strange and astonishing feeling, Trace caught a flash of movement from the corner of his eye. A large, shaggy mongrel dog weighing well over sixty pounds bounded in hot pursuit of a small, swift cat. A little boy scurried to remove himself from the animals' path. The route of the cat toward the trees behind the gazebo would take the chase directly into Susannah and his children.

Engrossed in the music, the flag, and the parade of smart midshipmen, Miss Partridge had no inkling that she was in danger of being swept off her feet. And not in the romantic sense. Making a mad dash to her rescue, Trace sprinted through the crowd. He was too slow and too late. The over-sized, shaggy dog knocked Susannah off her feet.

With a cry of surprise and a great billowing of lavender and white skirts, she went down like an anchor. Short of breath, Trace reached her side before his immobilized children could act.

Her eyes were closed. He kneeled down beside

her fearing the worse. His accident-prone governess had hit her head on the hard ground. She very likely had suffered a concussion.

"Father! Miss Partridge was hit by a flying dog!" Emily informed him in a horrified tone.

Grace began to wail.

"Miss Partridge will be fine," he assured his daughters as he gathered Susannah's limp body into his arms. "Won't you, Miss Partridge?"

Silence. Nothing. Nothing but the sweet scent of lilacs promising spring and rebirth.

Enveloped in his arms, her body felt fragile and warm, with a warmth that spread to Trace in some magical fashion. A warmth that ignited beneath his skin, pulsed and radiated through his body like fingers of fire. His heart beat in double time as a searing heat settled in his loins. His reaction both startled and disconcerted him.

Alice knelt by his side. "Is she dead, Father?"

"No." She could not be dead and have done whatever this was that she'd done to stir forgotten desire within him. "No."

"Do something, Father!" Amelia demanded, falling to her knees opposite him.

Trace loosed one arm in order to gently pat Susannah's cheek. Beneath his palm, her cheek felt satin smooth, soft as a pansy's velvet petal. "Wake up, Miss Partridge. Wake up, please. The children are worried."

Nothing.

"I shall run for the doctor," Emily volunteered.

Trace looked up. Emily's anxious expression cut to his heart.

"Let me try again," he said. This time Trace was not as gentle as he patted Susannah's cheek. He did not whisper her name this time; instead he commanded her to consciousness. "Miss Partridge."

"Look," Grace sniffled and pointed to Susannah's eyes.

Her long dark eyelashes, curling against her cheek, fluttered ever so faintly.

Trace leaned in closer. Smothered in the sweetness of lilacs, he whispered in her ear. "Miss Partridge, can you hear me?"

He held his breath as slowly she opened her eyes. Clearly dazed, she regarded Trace as if she'd never seen him before.

"You've had a small accident," he told her quietly.

Her lips parted in a warm, enchanting smile. She smiled up at him as if he were the only man in the world, an admiral, a legend, a god. His throat felt drier than the sawdust on the gymnasium floor. For an instant Trace was no longer aware of his hovering daughters or the handful of onlookers.

He did not hear the roll of the drums, the blare of the bugles, or the midshipmen's drill. Immobilized by her smile, for that moment in time, he felt as if he and Susannah were alone on the field.

"Hello, Lieutenant." Her soft greeting triggered a shot of relief.

"Hello," he replied in a strangely husky timbre. "An accident?"

He nodded. "Do you think you can stand?"

She nodded—just before her glazed eyes rolled back in her head. Not a promising sign, he thought.

"You may have reinjured your ankle."

"Are you going to carry me home?" She blinked her eyes open to saucerlike proportions in an apparent effort to focus.

As much as he would welcome an excuse to hold her again, in a crowd like this, more conventional methods to get Miss Partridge home were called for. "If you will lean on me, I think we can manage."

Trace carefully lifted Susannah to her feet. Wrapping an arm around her shoulder, he held her close to him and felt her tremble.

"Breathe deeply," he urged.

Standing on the windswept ground with his arm circling her dainty frame, he experienced a feeling of protectiveness that he'd not known before. A feeling of protectiveness for a woman who'd made it clear to him that she needed none.

"Are you going to be all right, Miss Partridge?" Emily asked in a halting voice.

"Oh yes." She cast a shaky smile at each of the girls. "I shall be fit for dancing by evening."

"You go too far," Trace whispered in her ear as she wobbled against him.

"Where does it hurt?" Ever-curious Amelia wanted the details.

"I fear that I have a lump on the back of my head, and my bottom feels a bit sore," Susannah duly reported, making light of her injuries. "Nothing serious."

"Twinkle will help you home," said Grace, whose cheeks were marked with tearstains.

"Are you ready?" Trace asked.

The plucky governess nodded.

"We'll take it nice and slow," he soothed.

And when he looked up from her eyes, from the pain he saw there despite what she had told the girls, he recognized the broad, sloping shoulders of Elliot Conroy in the small pocket of onlookers turning away.

# CHAPTER 8

A bit battered but determined, Susannah marched through Walter Holtsmutter's door the following morning as soon as the solicitor opened for
business.

"Have you no news for me?" she asked, perching uneasily on the chair opposite his desk. "I must
find my husband immediately."

If not sooner. Yesterday afternoon, when she
woke to find herself in Trace Reardon's arms,
locked in the endless depths of his eyes, she knew
she was in trouble. Her thoughts were none that a
married woman should be having. Overriding the
aches and pains of her body, the warmth in her
veins and the thrumming of her heart were symp-
toms of something else entirely. The delicious sensations she'd experienced while lying bruised and
short of breath had nothing to do with being
knocked down but everything to do with the man
who held her.

The lieutenant's silvery eyes had reflected concern. In that brief, unguarded moment she had
glimpsed a ravaged man's soul. A man who pro-

tected his heart at all costs. And yet, without meaning to, she'd managed to breach his defenses, if only for a breath in time.

If she was in danger of losing her heart to Trace Reardon, the need to know whether Patterson Harling was alive or dead became more imperative than ever.

Holtsmutter sliced the air with one choppy movement of his arm. "As a matter of fact, I received a message late last evening. I intended to send word to you this morning as my first order of business."

Unable to conceal her skepticism, Susannah raised a brow.

"My man believes he may have located your husband."

Her beleaguered heart leapt into a frenzied beat as she sprung to the edge of her seat. "Where?"

"If it's the same fellow, he's alive and living in Baltimore."

"Living in Baltimore?" she repeated, stunned to learn that Patterson might be so near.

"This fellow doesn't go by the name of Patterson Harling, and he's lived in Baltimore for over a year, long before the war ended."

The Confederate states had formally surrendered only six months ago. When had Patterson left the navy, and why? Nothing made sense. Susannah had waited for her husband, written to him every week, but most often her letters were returned with no explanation.

Had he been released from service early? Why had he gone to Baltimore instead of returning to her in Newport? If indeed this man was her husband, there could be but one explanation. Amnesia. Patterson could not remember that he was a married man. He'd been wounded and lost all memory of her.

Holtsmutter slid a daguerreotype across the desk toward her. "Is this your husband?"

Susannah stared at the grainy likeness. The photograph had been taken from some distance. The lone dark figure might be anyone.

"I . . . I can't be certain."

"He goes by the name of Harling Patterson."

"He has reversed his name?"

"It would appear so." Walter Holtsmutter shifted in his chair as if the information made him uncomfortable.

The daguerreotype showed Patterson without his uniform. She'd never seen him without his uniform. Susannah stared at the picture, waiting for a light of recognition, a rush of excitement, to feel prickly goose bumps or the excited rush of her heart.

But she felt none of those things. She merely felt the slightest twinge of pity for a man who had once dreamed of becoming a naval officer and instead had become a man who could not remember his own name accurately.

"If . . . if my husband is no longer in the navy, how does he earn a living?"

"My man reports that Mr. Patterson is buying property in the South."

"Has he become"—she paused to lower her voice, for no other reason than the shame of what she was about to ask—"has he become a carpetbagger?"

"We believe that to be the case."

Susannah nodded, took a deep breath, and straightened her shoulders. "I shall go to Patterson this Sunday. Where can I find him?"

"He resides at the Kirkwood Boarding House."

If it had been possible, she would have departed at once for Baltimore. But she could not leave the children on short notice. Aunt Cellie had disengaged herself from her grandnieces and would require gentle persuasion to stay with them instead of going out to play faro. Heaven knew what the lieutenant would require to allow her to run off on the spur of the moment.

To think that the search for her husband might come to an end in a city only hours away seemed incredible. Her mind spun with a dizzying tumble of scenarios. She felt quite light-headed but dared not linger. Grace waited for Susannah in the Sugarplum Sweet Shop and might eat herself sick.

With as much dignity as she could muster, Susannah stood and paid the solicitor. She had barely enough of her hard-earned wages remaining to make the trip to Baltimore. "Thank you, Mr. Holtsmutter."

Before she'd even left his office, she began to make her travel plans. She would need more than a day. She must shore up her resolve and ask Lieutenant Reardon for additional free time away this very evening.

Trace left the gymnasium early. The facility would be completed long before Admiral Porter's deadline. He'd neither seen nor heard anything more from Conroy, and it was a perfect day for a sail about the bay with his daughters—and their governess. There was no reason why Miss Partridge should not be included in the outing. He enjoyed her company. He enjoyed holding her even more. But most importantly, he found peace of mind in the way she doted on the girls.

For the first time since receiving his orders to Annapolis, his spirits were high. He even whistled as he walked the winding paths of the academy grounds. An uncommon sense of well-being gave a lightness to his step. It felt good to be alive, to fully appreciate the beautiful Indian summer afternoon. A bright sun splashed on the harbor where the Severn River met the Chesapeake Bay. The brackish water glistened beneath its rays as in an artist's seascape.

Trace had been taken aback to realize how much his daughters enjoyed the tour of the ten-pin lanes and gymnasium. While he'd known all along that he should spend more time with them, he hadn't fully understood the pleasure their happiness would give him. Determined to make a favorable impression on the superintendent, he'd put the construction of the gymnasium ahead of his family. He'd been unfair to them and meant to make up for his lack of attention starting now.

As soon as he walked through the door of his home, he called out an exuberant greeting. "I'm home!"

Aunt Cellie came bustling from the kitchen, "Oh, my dear." Dressed to go out, she pulled on her gloves as she approached him with a dark-eyed frown. "Trace, are you ill?"

"No," he assured her, although he couldn't blame his aunt for assuming as much. He couldn't remember the last time he'd come home this early in the afternoon. "I found some extra time and decided to take the girls sailing."

Her dark coffee eyes widened. "Oh?"

"I've not spent enough time with them since we moved to Annapolis."

"Yes, that's true." She still appeared puzzled. The crevices in her pale, wrinkled brow deepened.

"Were you on your way out?" he asked.

"Yes, and I—well, I planned to play faro this afternoon."

"Please don't let me stop you." Trace gave her an encouraging grin before asking, "Are the girls in their chamber studying?"

"Uh. No. They are . . ." Aunt Cellie hesitated and then completed her explanation in a rush. "They are in the garden with Miss Partridge. Good-bye, dear."

His aunt scurried away. Obviously, she had no intention of telling him what the girls and their governess were doing in the yard. Trace experienced a nervous stomach lurch as he moved to satisfy his curiosity. He was astounded but not dismayed by what he saw.

They were washing a dog. And they were all wet.

The big, ugly dog that had knocked Susannah over at the parade ground sat in a wooden tub in the center of the garden. The tongue-lolling canine appeared to be in his glory, surrounded by gleeful girls and one laughing woman.

Engrossed in their formidable task, his daughters and their governess did not realize that Trace stood on the porch observing. His rollicking, boisterous girls and their equally ebullient governess were covered with more soap and water than the black and white, shaggy animal of uncertain heritage. Perhaps a bit of buffalo, he mused.

Long tendrils of Susannah's hair, wet and limp, framed her face. The bodice of her sage green gown was soaked, but the joy in her smile and the sparkle in her laughing eyes made her one of the loveliest sights Trace had ever seen. She put sky-wide rainbows and golden sunsets to shame.

Trace chuckled. The exhilaration, the lively fun

that filled the air, against the backdrop of the shaggy dog's unflinching patience, proved contagious.

Susannah heard his chuckle. Her gaze flickered to the porch. Her smile gave way to a startled expression, which slowly faded to one of apprehension and then was quickly replaced by one of false cheer. "Hello, Lieutenant!"

The girls immediately stopped what they were doing. The laughter ended abruptly. All eyes, seemingly as large as ships' hatches, were on him.

In the silence, Trace realized that this was his moment. He could be a hero, or not.

"Do you need some help?" he asked.

A chorus of laughter, giggles, and five vastly relieved expressions answered his question.

Tossing his uniform jacket aside and rolling up his sleeves, he strode down the steps and fell to his knees at the washtub opposite Susannah. "Good afternoon, Miss Partridge."

Her eyes were wide and wary, her smile tenuous. "Good afternoon, Lieutenant."

The shaggy dog wagged its tail, splashing everyone.

Emily wiped the suds from her face with her forearm and made the first faltering justification. "He followed us home from school, Father."

"And he was stinky," Grace added.

"We decided he must be a stray, and it might be nice to give him a bath," Susannah explained with a glance Trace interpreted as one begging forgiveness.

"It would be even nicer if he could stay," Alice allowed.

Trace released a mock sigh of resignation. "How did I know one of you would be suggesting that?"

"Please, Father," Amelia pleaded, her gray eyes

alight with tears, tears ready to be shed in a flash for her cause. "We have no pets, and Fred needs a home."

"Fred?" he asked.

"That's what Grace named him," Amelia replied quickly. "She said we couldn't give him a bath until he had a name."

It was the first time in his memory that Amelia had ever listened to anything her younger sister had to say. "We do have a bird. Have you introduced Fred to Bilge?"

Trace felt quite sure that given half an opportunity, Fred would have Bilge for lunch.

"Not yet. But Bilge is Miss Partridge's bird," Emily pointed out.

"We should have a pet of our own," Grace declared with a sweet pout.

"But, ah, this dog . . . Fred. Fred knocked Miss Partridge down," Trace reminded his daughters before turning to the silent governess. "How do you feel about keeping him?"

Susannah never hesitated. "I think he would make a fine pet for the girls. He'll serve as a companion able to protect and play with them."

"A watchdog," Intrigued by the idea, Trace shrugged. "I hadn't thought of it, but it might be a good thing."

Susannah took the inch he had offered and went the mile. "And I believe it would be a wonderful lesson in responsibility for the girls to take turns feeding and brushing him and making certain that Fred has his exercise each day."

Trace agreed. "Very well, then. Let's make Fred Reardon an official member of our family."

His daughters responded by cheering, crowding against him, and throwing their wet, soapy arms around his neck and torso and anywhere they could reach. Over their shoulders, Susannah beamed.

When at last the mongrel was bathed and rinsed, he smelled like a piece of fruit. Fred had been bathed with orange-scented soap. Trace was laughing as he dried his hands and bare forearms. His spirits soared. Washing the dog had been easy work and the first task he could remember sharing with all of his daughters. The memory of their laughter during their joint effort would linger with him for days to come. And someday, when he was an old man holding grandchildren on his knee, he would recall this afternoon with unparalleled fondness. He credited the golden-eyed governess for opening his eyes and his heart. She'd given his family a special gift.

"Miss Partridge, when you are dried, I would like a word."

"Oh?" She appeared startled.

"In my study, please," he said with a smile, attempting to put her at ease.

An hour later, Susannah left the girls to their studies. Fred, smelling like an orange grove, curled contentedly in the center of the chamber while Grace brushed him.

Being summoned to the lieutenant's office did not feel like a good thing to Susannah. Yet, she had never seen him as relaxed and happy as he had been when washing the dog with his daughters. Initially she had feared the prospect of taking in the big animal who would eat his weight and more daily, but she'd soon decided to fight for the girls' right to keep him. She had never thought to accomplish such an easy and happy victory.

She hoped the lieutenant would remain in the same cheerful frame of mind when she requested an extra free day to take care of her personal business. To aid her cause, she dressed with care to look her best. She chose a pale blue silk gown with a low, scooped neckline trimmed with lace. She smoothed her hair into a neat bun at the nape and secured the flyaway strands in a blue silk net.

When she reached the lieutenant's closed study door, she took a deep, bracing breath before knocking.

"Come in."

The small room, with its dark paneling and oriental carpets, felt warm, almost cozy. Two gaslights and a blazing fireplace spread a shadowy light across the chamber.

Trace Reardon leaned against the mantel. His towering, solid form filled the room. Susannah stood transfixed, riveted by his overwhelming masculinity. A sense of his potent virility spilled through the room, so strong she could almost taste it.

He'd changed from his wet uniform into a fresh white linen shirt and dark civilian trousers. The shirt, unbuttoned at the throat, allowed a glimpse of dark chest curls. This subtle sign of raw masculinity set Susannah's heart spinning. 'Twas a shameful reaction for a married woman. Surely, she would roast on a spit in Hades. There was no question that was where she was headed.

The fire crackled and sizzled. His eyes locked on hers. One corner of his mouth turned up in a devastating crooked smile. Susannah lost her ability to breathe.

Reardon still hadn't spoken as his gaze drifted down the length of her, pausing at her neckline. A sharp, silver light of admiration flickered in his eyes. She watched in wonder as the silver-gray deepened to a mesmerizing shade of smoldering ash, the color of clouds before a ravishing storm.

Her breath returned in a shallow rasp as his

perusal continued. But when his eyes met hers again, Susannah's knees buckled, causing her to grip the back of the nearest chair.

"You look none the worse for bathing a mongrel." The lieutenant's crooked smile widened to a teasing grin.

Her heart all but stopped. Although clinging to her composure by a hair, she managed a soft laugh. "Fred's bath truly provided more entertainment than a chore."

"For a woman with no experience as a governess, you have proven a boon to my daughters, Miss Partridge. They seem . . . not so sad. They smile more than they have since their mother . . ."

His voice trailed off, and he turned away. The fire hissed and spit as he poked at the logs. The flame burned higher, brighter.

"If I am making a difference in their lives, then I am happy. You have been blessed with fine, good girls, Lieutenant. And . . . and they must miss their mother."

"Yes." He set the poker aside.

The subject Susannah had been wishing to pursue had been opened at last. Because she wanted to do her best for the Reardon girls in whatever time she had left with them, she ventured forth on what could be a treacherous path. "How . . . how long did you say it has been since your wife passed away?"

"Three years. Louise has been gone three years." His gaze, hard, flat, and unreadable, met Susannah's.

Fearing she'd driven away his good mood, she spoke softly, giving encouragement. "It hasn't been that long since the tragedy, then. I'm certain that you will see more smiles from your girls as time goes on. Time heals."

"Yes, time heals," he murmured, wandering from the fireplace to perch on the edge of his desk. Only the chair that Susannah still clung to stood between them. Her senses tingled, filled with the thoroughly masculine scent of bay rum. The scent of him. He wore it always. He wore it well.

She swallowed hard. Had she said too much? Too little?

"But I did not ask you here to discuss my daughters."

"You didn't?"

"Nor Fred." He folded his arms across his considerable chest. While he did not quite cast her a frown, the furrows in his forehead deepened.

Susannah's palms grew moist.

"First Classman Rand Noble has asked permission to call upon you on this coming Sunday."

"Oh—"

"Before you decide, let me warn you that Noble is no ordinary first classman. He comes with a reputation as a womanizer. Although you may find him to be a handsome man, he is not the sort any mother desires for her daughters."

"I see—"

The lieutenant no longer hid his displeasure. His rugged features settled into a full-blown frown as he interrupted her once again. "I would suggest you refuse his invitation."

"Yes. I must."

"You must?"

"I . . . I must attend to some personal business."

Reardon's questioning gaze pinned her to the spot. But he did not speak. He simply stared as if the fact that she would have business other than his family had stunned him temporarily.

Rubbing her arms as if she were cold, Susannah turned and made her way to the fireplace, putting breathing space between them.

"I have family business that I must see to." She stared down into the fire.

"We have already agreed that you are free to do whatever you choose on Sundays."

"This business requires more than Sunday." Summoning a deep, steadying breath, Susannah turned her back to the fire to face the lieutenant. She looked him directly in the eyes. "I need another day. May I have Monday as well?"

"You wish to be away Monday as well as Sunday," he repeated, as if he were trying to understand what she had asked. He was no dull-wit. He'd never before had a problem understanding her.

Her hands moved down to press her stomach, press away the butterflies flittering there. "My business concerns a . . . a relative who has been missing since the war." Her heart hammered so loudly she feared Reardon could hear it.

Susannah could not bring herself to say "husband." The word stuck in her throat. And she didn't know quite why. While waiting for the lieutenant to speak, Susannah rationalized her omission. It was no business of Reardon's. Why should she mention a husband until she could be certain that she had one?

His eyes, his expression softened. "I didn't know."

"Normally I would not trouble you with my business, but there is reason to believe . . . believe my relative may be alive."

A gleam of what appeared to be compassion settled in the lieutenant's eyes. "Is that why you consulted Walter Holtsmutter?"

"Yes. The solicitor is connected to trained men who devote themselves to finding persons thought missing in the war."

Nodding his understanding, Reardon stood, towering over her, filling the small chamber with the overwhelming force of his maleness.

Waiting motionlessly for his answer, Susannah was startled when his head jerked and he sniffed the air. Sniffed deeply. His attention had drifted.

"Do you smell that, Miss Partridge?" he asked, frowning.

Susannah sniffed. "Yes. Yes, something is burning."

Her gaze darted about the chamber searching for candles.

The lieutenant's scrutiny ended abruptly when it reached the fireplace and Susannah. His eyes widened in horror.

"It's you!" He pointed behind her, to the hem of her gown.

Susannah whirled to see the back of her gown afire. She had stepped too close to the fire and the hem of the wide skirt had caught flame. Although a common hazard, she hadn't had to concern herself in the past. Unable to afford them, she'd never worn layers of full petticoats and voluminous skirts before coming to the Reardon home.

Immobilized in terror, regarding the licks of fire swallowing silk, she did not see nor hear Trace Reardon until he knocked her to the floor. Enfolding her in his arms, he rolled over and over with her.

When he came to a stop, the flames had been put out and he lay on top of her.

She could not feel his weight. She could not feel her own. Her heart thrummed and her pulse raced. And when shock gave way to feeling, it was her body that burned. Rivers of honey heat ran through her, ran deep.

Trembling, she met his gaze. Desire simmered in the silver shadows of the lieutenant's eyes. Unmistakable, heart-swelling, male desire.

Susannah could not look away. She could not still the delicious moist heat that pooled between her thighs. She could not ignore the wanton longing to wrap her arms around his neck and bring his lips down on hers.

"Miss Partridge, the fire is out."

The timbre of his voice sounded strangely hoarse. Despite his pronouncement, he made no move to remove himself. His breath warmed her cheek. Beneath the weight of him, engulfed in the musky male scent of him, Susannah's heart floated like a gossamer cloud. She yearned to run her fingers through the raven strands of the lieutenant's hair, strands that had come loose to frame his dark, sun-leathered face. How had this happened? How had she come to feel the way she did now? No man had ever seemed as necessary to her life as Trace Reardon.

She'd become a Jezebel!

She forced a somewhat uneven, rather breathless response. "Thank you, Lieutenant Reardon."

His gaze remained locked on hers. "Take as much time as you like. Take several days away if necessary, Miss Partridge."

A Jezebel, loving one man while wed to another.

Almost an hour after Susannah Partridge had hurried from Trace's study clutching the hem of her smoldering gown, he still stood by the window inhaling large gulps of cold air. He'd opened the window to chase the smoke from the room and to cool the searing need that ripped through him. Trace had never wanted a woman as much as he had wanted Susannah moments ago.

When he had come to a stop on top of her and felt the lush fullness of her breasts against his chest, his loins had exploded with an ache so harsh and primeval that he had come close to taking the innocent governess on the floor of his study.

Only the bewilderment in her eyes had stopped him. Poor woman had not even known enough to be afraid. She could hardly be afraid of something she'd never known: the lust in a man's heart and the raging desire that gripped his loins.

But was it Susannah who stirred his desire, or the long-suppressed need for a woman?

Trace slammed down the window and stormed from his study. Without pausing for a coat or jacket, he strode out the front door. He needed a long, cold walk—and a wife.

With nowhere else to go, he headed toward his home away from home, the old Fort Severn building, where his labor would end soon. He estimated that the bowling alley and gymnasium would be finished within two weeks.

With the midshipmen in their quarters studying and the officers at home with their families, the academy grounds were all but deserted. Only the marine guards, recently introduced to the academy, marched patrol.

Trace's body had just begun to cool when he rounded the corner and saw flames. Fort Severn and the ten-pin lanes were on fire.

# CHAPTER 9

Trace stopped in his tracks. Immobilized. Smoke billowed from the downstairs window of the old fort. Memories of that night just seven months ago came flooding back, crashing over him with the punishing power of a tidal wave.

It had begun as a simple journey north aboard the steamer *Sultana*. Eager to be reunited with his children following the end of the war, Trace chose the swiftest means of transportation. But shortly after midnight, the *Sultana*'s boilers exploded. The force of the blast catapulted Trace from his bunk.

Sections of the pilot house and cabin had been hurled high into the pitch-dark night. He heard the immense chunks fall back on the deck of the sidewheeler, chunks that buried passengers in the fiery debris.

He ran to the deck, to a sight he would never forget. Flames engulfed the steamer and passengers. Fire danced on the waters of the Mississippi. The cries of women and children too weak to swim the wide expanse echoed in the night.

Trace didn't think about what he did next. He acted on reflex. Driven by a desperate desire to save whatever lives he could, he dashed into the fiery inferno, first to rescue a mother and her two children, and then a Union soldier heading home. And when the fire beat him back, he jumped into the water, into the flames to find children who could not swim, to carry them across the river to shore.

He saved many lives that night but came close to losing his own. Badly burned, Trace spent the next four months in the hospital. He was disfigured for life, and the scars still pained him, still were healing.

Fear held him in its paralyzing grip as he faced this new fire. He hesitated to run into the flames. He knew what could happen. But if he did not, his military career would be over. Cowards had no place in the new navy.

"Lieutenant! Those are our bowling lanes!" Rand Noble shouted, running at breakneck speed past Trace toward the burning building. "Call the alarm!"

"Don't go in there, Noble," Trace yelled. Galvanized into action by the breakneck speed of the midshipman, he gave chase.

But Noble was ahead of him and didn't stop. A thick cloud of smoke billowed from the building as the reckless midshipman burst through the doors. Close on his heels, Trace could hear Noble coughing ahead of him. The smoke clawed at his throat, choking him as well. But he refused to turn back now. Racing into the ten-pin lanes, he discovered the fire contained to one spot beneath the window. An open window. A window he hadn't left open.

What might have been a catastrophe proved to

be more smoke than fire. Midshipman Noble had removed his jacket and flailed at the flames with it, attempting to smother the fire. Trace took up the battle while Noble went for help and water.

Thirty minutes later they stood over the smoking spot.

"Whew," Noble remarked, wiping his brow with the back of his arm. "Good thing I came along when I did."

"Yes, it is. I couldn't have put the fire out without your help." Trace paused, regarding the winded first classman with suspicion he hadn't had time for until now. "What were you doing out at this hour, Noble?"

"Ah. Well. I had been visiting a lady friend. I hadn't meant to stay as long as I did—"

"Do you have a pass?"

"Well. No."

Trace shook his head and chuckled. Rand Noble would never change.

Noble inclined his head as if he were trying to read Trace's expression in the darkened hall. "Are you going to give me demerits, Lieutenant?"

"No." Surprising the first classman with a comradely slap on the back, Trace smiled. "As a matter of fact, Noble, you'll be the first to play ten pins when the lanes open."

A slow grin spread across Noble's mouth. "Thank you, sir," he replied, executing a smart salute.

"Dismissed."

Trace watched the midshipman leave before turning his attention once more to the charred remains of rags heaped on the floor. The rags had been soaked with whale oil and purposefully set afire. If he and Noble hadn't happened along, the entire building might have burned to the ground.

Weeks of effort, planning, and overseeing the construction of the gymnasium, shooting gallery, and ten-pin lanes would have gone up in smoke. Fort Severn would have been just a memory.

For whatever reason, the arsonist had started the fire beneath the window, and the damage had been contained to a relatively small area. Trace figured repairs would delay the opening of the facility for less than a week.

While the fire might have been a student prank, it seemed unlikely that any of the midshipmen would participate in a stunt that might lead to the shame of suspension from the academy and would delay the opening of entertainment constructed especially for them. Trace regarded this incident as a warning—a personal warning to him from Elliot Conroy.

Tomorrow Trace would report to Admiral Porter and seek out Seaman Conroy.


Tomorrow Susannah would be on her way to Baltimore. She counted the hours. She could not find her husband too soon. Once in the arms of Patterson Harling, she would forget the lusty heat, the undeniable evidence of the lieutenant's arousal pressing against her last night. When Reardon's steely body had come to a stop atop her, she had feared she would swoon. Not from his weight, but from the desire burning in his eyes. He'd wanted her. And, dear Lord, she had wanted him.

He'd put out the fire in her skirts, but started another, a fire far more dangerous. Susannah quickly concluded that until the hour of her departure, she must studiously avoid the lieutenant. She had no doubt that he needed a wife. And Susannah needed her husband.

But once again she found herself on the floor, though this time in less threatening circumstances. She sat in the Reardon girls' chamber coaxing Grace to come out of the armoire.

"Grace, what are you doing in there?"

"I'm talking to Twinkle."

That the child would choose a dark, closed space to commune with her fairy friend seemed inconceivable to Susannah. Small spaces still frightened her. When she was a child, her natural curiosity occasionally landed her in trouble. Her mother had spared the rod in favor of discouraging Susannah's adventures by locking her in the root cellar.

Only four years old when these punishments began, she had been terrified alone in the small, dank cellar. Shivering in the dark, she had spent a good deal of the time listening, and holding her breath. With a child's vivid imagination, Susannah had envisioned the rats, spiders, and worms that shared her cellar space. One afternoon a furry creature had darted across her legs and she had wet her chemise.

With a shake of her head, she chased back the demons who hid deep in her memory in order to concentrate instead on Grace.

"Could you not speak with Twinkle out here where it is light?" she asked.

"Then you could hear me."

"Oh. Is that it? Do you and Twinkle have secrets?"

"Yes," the child replied in a small voice.

"It's all right to have secrets," Susannah assured the youngster quickly. Grace appeared to miss having a mother more than the other girls. Twinkle's existence might well owe itself to the dark-haired child's pain.

"We must go to meet your sisters now, Grace." Susannah's urging was met with silence. "You may walk Fred on his leash, and we shall make sugar cookies when we come home."

Bribery always worked. Especially with Grace. After a moment more of silence, the armoire door opened with a squeak. Grace grinned. Susannah opened her arms to give the child a long, sweet hug. The warmth and the little-girl smell of her tore at Susannah's heart. When the time came, as it soon must, it would be difficult to leave Grace and her sisters. She'd quickly come to love them almost as if they were her own.

True to her word, as soon as they returned home with Amelia, Alicia, and Emily, Susannah dismissed the cook and set to work in the kitchen. With Aunt Cellie off playing faro and the lieutenant not expected home for several more hours, it seemed a good time to break with their rigid schedule.

The girls routinely rose at six in the morning, ate breakfast at six-thirty, and were off to school at seven. When they returned home from school, they were expected to study until dinner at six-thirty. Following dinner they spent an hour in the parlor with Aunt Cellie to read, stitch needlepoint, or to play the piano. The regimen was too military to suit Susannah. They weren't midshipmen.

She set to work in the kitchen. Fred curled up by the warm stove, his languid gaze on the bird-cage. Bilge's cage had been set up on a shelf where he could oversee the operation, which he did with a good bit of squawking and shrill comments.

"All hands ahoy! All hands ahoy!"

The silly bird must liken the flurry of activity in the kitchen to the scurry of sailors on deck.

Despite wearing large white aprons folded as small as she could make them, by the time the first batch of cookies was ready for the oven, the girls were covered with flour and sugar. The ingredients were everywhere, smeared on aprons, hands, and faces. A liberal sprinkling of flour covered the floor, and streaks of lard and drying egg yolk decorated the table where they had mixed the batter.

"We shall have to clean up while the cookies are baking."

Emily shook her head. "Babette cleans up."

Babette was the cook that Susannah earlier had dismissed for the day.

"Babette is not here," she pointed out. "Come, with all of us working together the kitchen will sparkle in no time."

"With Babette gone who will make supper for us?" Alice asked.

"While you are studying, I shall prepare our supper."

"You can cook?" Emily's obvious amazement amused Susannah.

"Yes, I can," she replied with pride. And then gave a sigh. How could she leave when she had so much more she'd like to teach the girls. They should know how to bake more than sugar cookies.

Alice volunteered for cleanup without further urging. "I shall wash the bowls, Miss Partridge."

Amelia never allowed her twin to best her. "And I shall dry," she declared.

Susannah heard the front door open and close but, thinking it must be Jane or Adam, paid no mind until she heard Reardon's voice. "Is anyone home?"

Fred lifted his head and barked.

Avoiding the lieutenant was out of the question. Fleeing from the kitchen, which appeared to have been hit with snow flurries, was not an option.

Amelia's eyes rounded as her father strode into the kitchen. She looked as if she had been caught doing something forbidden.

"Hello, Father."

"What are you doing in the kitchen, girls?" he asked as he sniffed the air. "It certainly smells good—as sweet as the Sugarplum Shop."

"We did not expect you home this early," Susannah said softly. She found the lieutenant's new habit of coming home when least expected disconcerting.

"I needed to rest for a while," he explained, running a hand through his raven hair. "There was a fire at Fort Severn last night."

"Oh no!"

"Fortunately there was a minimum of damage, but I had little sleep."

"Have a cookie, Papa," Grace offered.

Smiling, Reardon took the warm cookie and bit into it. "Mmmm," he murmured. "This is very tasty. When did my girls become accomplished chefs?" he teased.

"Have another," Emily urged, smiling proudly.

"I'd like to, Princess, but I can't spoil my appetite before this evening's dinner party."

"Dinner party?" Susannah asked.

"Yes." His gaze searched the kitchen. "Where's Babette?"

Susannah nervously smoothed the sides of her head, though not a hair had fallen out of place. "Babette didn't mention a dinner party when . . . when I let her go for the day."

"Miss Partridge," he drawled. "A word."

"Yes, of course." She forced a smile. "Girls, it's study time."

Reardon's daughters left the kitchen, quite obviously relieved to escape the cleanup. Fred followed, tail wagging.

"Foul wind! Foul wind!"

"Hush, Bilge!"

Except for the crackle of tension in the air, silence descended upon the kitchen. With lowered eyes, Susannah wiped her hands on her apron. Her long, dark lashes fluttered against her cheeks. A patch of flour decorated her chin.

Trace found her incredibly beguiling. The scent of fresh-baked sugar cookies laced with cinnamon proved as seductive as any exotic aphrodisiac. For a moment his troubles evaporated.

He'd just come from meeting with Admiral Porter. While the superintendent regretted the fire in the bowling lanes, he insisted that the lanes and gymnasium must open as scheduled. Trace did not report his suspicion of Elliot Conroy as the culprit who started the fire. Instead, he speculated that one of the workmen might have been careless and tossed a lighted cigar on the floor near to the pile of discarded polishing rags. In fact, the carpenters laboring on the new armory beside the Fort Severn building might even have been at fault.

Trace was saving Conroy for himself. He meant to confront the civilian instructor man to man.

"Miss Partridge, why were my daughters baking cookies during their study time?"

She raised her chin, meeting his eyes with a steady gaze. "This afternoon the girls learned the importance of teamwork, something the boys at the academy learn on a daily basis."

A woman's way of thinking could be treacherous. Trace should have known that Susannah would have a perfectly reasonable explanation. He could not argue with what she had said. The woman never failed to impress him with her intelligence and quick thinking.

He pointed to the clock. "The rule is study first, before leisure. They're off to a late start with their books."

"Your daughters learned measurements today, a cup, a half-cup, and a quarter of a cup. Even Grace understands these concepts now. From time to time, I believe it's good to bend, or dare I say, break the rules."

"Break the rules?"

"We must become adaptable in order to deal with life's surprises. Some of them unfortunate."

"Is this something you have learned first-hand?"

Perching herself on the high kitchen stool, she nodded and said softly, "When my parents died suddenly, I became responsible for my younger sister. My dreams were put aside so that I could care for Mabel."

Taken aback by her quiet confession, Trace could only mumble. "I . . . I'm sorry for your loss."

Susannah spoke earnestly, her tone holding no hint of self-pity. "I was very young at the time, but I had already learned the value of being adaptable."

"My mother passed away when I was a boy, but I've always had a family to help see me through," he said, sharing his past with her, as they seemed to have at least one common thread. "Years before Aunt Cellie stepped in to take care of my children, she had done her best to be a mother to me. At least as much as my father would allow. And at the time, my aunt had not learned to love faro."

Her eyes were raised to his, luminous golden

eyes that promised treasure. Trace's gaze fell on her quiet smile, transfixed on her lips. The color of summer peaches, plump and moist with morning dew, Susannah's lips waited. For the kiss he'd come close to giving her last night?

She sniffed. A dainty sound. She frowned.

Trace smelled the burning odor then. "Are your skirts afire again?"

"Oh no!" Her gaze shifted to the stove. Smoke swirled from the oven. "The last batch of cookies is burning."

Susannah darted to the big, black iron stove and quickly removed a tin tray of cookies singed black at the edges.

While Miss Partridge was otherwise engaged, Trace stole a cookie from the platter already baked. The warm cookie fairly melted in his mouth, sweet, but not too sweet. Unable to stop at one, he snatched another.

"My aunt will be very upset when she learns Babette is not here to prepare dinner."

"I shall prepare dinner; have no worry."

The accident-prone governess was going to prepare dinner and he should not worry?

He hiked a brow.

"For a short time I earned my way as a cook. I'm quite good," she assured him earnestly.

Perhaps it was possible. His aunt had arranged for him to meet Mary Millbanks tonight. The mayor of Annapolis's niece was visiting from Virginia.

"Aunt Cellie will expect dinner to be served promptly at eight," he cautioned Susannah.

"And so it shall be."

He wondered if there was anything Susannah Partridge could not do. The last thing Trace heard as he strode from the kitchen was Bilge squawking, "Bail! Bail!"

\* \* \*

Susannah prepared a six-course meal that Aunt Cellie could not criticize. She often had the feeling that Reardon's aunt regarded her as a necessary evil in the household. Dismissing Babette without knowing the dinner plans had been a foolish thing for Susannah to do, but she refused to give Aunt Cellie cause for more disapproval.

Confining herself to the kitchen for the next four hours, she peeled, chopped, stirred, and baked. Promptly at eight, dinner was served. Babette could not have cooked a more satisfying meal than the steaming tureen of onion soup and the platters of codfish balls, roast chicken, and baked beans offered that evening at the Reardon table. Hot Maryland biscuits straight from the oven accompanied each course. Apples and pecans were offered for dessert along with a thick molasses pie, tea, and brandy for the lieutenant and the mayor.

Much to Susannah's relief, Jane had stayed to serve as she usually did when there were guests for dinner. It had taken some time, but the housekeeper was showing signs of actually appreciating Susannah.

Weary from the extra chores of cooking and cleaning up the kitchen, Susannah entered the girls' chamber later than evening limp with exhaustion. She'd come to make certain they were asleep. But when she discovered their beds empty and Fred nowhere in sight, a jolt of fresh energy shot through her body and took hold of her.

Initial alarm gave way to resignation. Knowing how curious Reardon's daughters were, she guessed at their whereabouts at once. And she found them exactly where she first looked. Emily, Alice, Amelia, and Grace sat on one of the highest stairs, out of sight of their father and guests in the drawing room but low enough to catch glimpses of those gathered through the banister rails. Fred lay on the landing keeping a watchful eye.

"You're supposed to be in bed," Susannah bristled, hands on her hips.

Alice put a finger over her lips as a signal. "We're spying," she whispered.

Amelia shushed her sister as Emily pulled Susannah down to sit beside her on the step. "Have you seen Miss Millbanks?"

"No."

"She's the tall one with the dark hair. Her laugh sounds just like a horse neighing."

"You must be jesting." But in the next instant, Susannah heard the laugh. Emily had not jested, nor exaggerated. Mary Millbanks sounded like a horse.

Leaning over the girl's shoulder, Susannah caught a glimpse of the woman. The mayor's niece looked as if she were going to a ball in an off-the-shoulder gown of deep purple velvet. The neckline plunged to embarrassing depths, but not a blush showed on Miss Millbanks's cheeks. She stood with the lieutenant near the fireplace, but not close enough for her voluminous skirts to catch a flame.

Lieutenant Reardon, splendid in his dress uniform, appeared quite taken with the young woman's abundant cleavage.

"How old do you think she is, Miss Partridge?" Emily asked.

"Oh, perhaps eighteen or nineteen." Susannah thought the young woman attractive, despite a turned-up nose and thin lips that one day would most likely appear pinched.

"Aunt Cellie says she would make a good wife," Susannah's oldest charge remarked with a note of melancholy. "She said Miss Millbanks might marry Father."

"We wanted to see what she was like," Alice explained.

Susannah strained to get a better look. "When your father is ready to take a bride, I feel quite certain he will introduce you to her first."

"He might if you ask him," Alice said. "He is different around you."

While she wished to ask what difference Alice thought she detected, Susannah let the remark go. Instead she sought the girls' understanding. "Your father is lonely. It's time for him to take a wife . . . of his own choosing."

Emily tossed her sandy curls. "It's only been three years since Mother left."

"Left?" Susannah repeated, believing she hadn't heard Emily correctly. "I thought your mother passed away."

"She did. She died when the ship she left in capsized."

"Oh, girls," Susannah gathered Emily in her arms. Her arms were not big enough to wrap around all of Reardon's daughters at once, but she did her best to enfold each one. "I'm so sorry."

"But she'll come back, someday," Grace said. "Twinkle has promised to bring her back."

Susannah understood now why Grace held so many private conversations with Twinkle. She was working out the terms of return.

"I am certain that your mother's departure had nothing to do with you girls," Susannah said as gently as possible. "You know that, don't you?"

"Mother wanted to go back on the stage," Amelia said. "I heard her tell Father."

"They argued a lot," Emily told Susannah, withdrawing from her arms. "Until he went to war."

So Reardon had married an actress who left him and her daughters. A betrayal that ended in her drowning. Susannah's heart constricted with pain. Pain for the girls, pain for Trace. It was no wonder that the lieutenant had no taste for marriage or for bringing more children into the world.

"I don't want to talk about Mother anymore." Alice's eyes shone bright with tears.

"We won't." Susannah ruffled the high-strung girl's hair. "We shall talk about Miss Millbanks. Do you not think she wears too much rouge?"

Emily agreed readily. "Yes. And listen."

Mary's little neighing laugh drifted from the parlor.

Susannah strained for a better look. The lieutenant appeared puzzled as he regarded his attractive guest.

"Come girls, it is not polite to spy."

And it was not right that she should feel envious of a woman who laughed like a horse.

"Mary will play the piano for us now." Aunt Cellie announced.

Susannah took one last look and experienced an odd sinking feeling in her stomach. She was not born to wealth and had none of the qualifications she knew Cellie Stuyvestant sought in a wife for her nephew. In addition, there was the inescapable fact that she was already married.

It wouldn't be long now. There were not many hours left. In the morning she would be on her way to Baltimore. Susannah would be in her husband's arms once again, and she would return to this house only to say good-bye.

# CHAPTER 10

*Kaboom.*

The thunderous blast rattled the windows of Fort Severn, where Trace was working this Saturday morning. More detonations would follow. The frigate *Santee* had been converted to a gunnery ship, and the midshipmen were firing practice broadsides into the bay. An agreement had been reached with the good citizens of Annapolis to allow the ear-splitting exercise on this one day of the week.

*Kaboom.*

Unfazed by the explosions, Trace continued his inspection. New flooring had replaced the fire-damaged portion in the ten-pin lanes. The soot had been washed off the lanes and the shooting gallery. After his approval of the work today, the floor would be finished and polished. He'd been fortunate. The civilian carpenters hadn't balked at working the extra hours required to make the repairs so quickly. Still, the ten-pin lanes and gymnasium would open three days later than planned. Instead of completing the facility ahead of time, the fire had caused Trace to miss his deadline.

There was no doubt in his mind that Elliot Conroy had purposefully undermined the project. Unlike the academy officers, the civilian instructor was not subject to the school's strict code of honor.

Because everyone knew that Trace had worn a Confederate uniform, he'd done his best to keep his reputation spotless since returning to the academy. Only one other Confederate officer had been invited back. Julian Spencer, a graduate of 1861, served in the harmless position of academy librarian. A fate even worse than building a gymnasium, in Trace's view.

If the case were brought before a hearing board, the cause of the fire would clearly be a matter of one man's word against another's. Since the odds of Trace prevailing with a board made up of former Union naval officers were not in his favor, he'd decided to keep quiet about Conroy rather than file a report.

Still, the fact remained that the furtive seaman had destroyed his attempt to finish the gymnasium in record time. And that failure ate away at Trace. He knew he wouldn't be able to resolve his anger until he'd had it out with Conroy. Conclusion drawn, he turned away from the patch of new flooring and left Fort Severn. With quick, resolute strides, he went in search of his adversary.

Trace headed toward the seawall, where midshipmen and faculty otherwise unoccupied gathered to watch the exercises on the bay. The beauty of a strong breeze, brilliant blue sky, and brisk autumn air contrasted sharply with the acrid smell of gunpowder and the earth-shaking blasts that signified military might.

Miss Partridge had expressed an interest in watching these exercises close at hand, but Trace discouraged the petite governess. Misfortune followed her. If she should venture anywhere near live ammunition, he feared for her life.

But he admired her accomplishments. In just a short matter of time, Susannah had won the hearts of his daughters, she'd domesticated the wild, shaggy beast known as Fred, kept Bilge in his cage, and cooked a mouth-watering meal with only a few hours' notice. She'd even managed to put Aunt Cellie's fears about her suitability to rest.

Susannah Partridge, as unpredictable as the weather, had become as necessary to his household as the honey in his aunt's tea. But what had led his thoughts to Miss Partridge? The firing of a cannon? She increasingly plagued his thoughts.

*Kaboom.* The ground shook beneath Trace as he leaned against the seawall. While the smoke cleared, he looked for the man who had been dodging him. He found Elliot Conroy only about twenty feet away. The seaman propped himself against the wall on his elbows, measuring the impact of the last barrage on the *Santee*. His attention focused entirely on the action in the bay.

Trace strolled up to the broad, bearded figure. "Enjoying the firepower, Seaman?"

Caught by surprise, Conroy jerked and spun to confront Trace. It was the movement of a man who'd learned to watch his back. The seaman's dark olive eyes grew murky. Surrounded by a mustache and a full, brown beard encrusted with forgotten meals, his lips paled, then drew tight and narrow. What little skin showed on his face resembled dark, gnarled rope.

"So Johnny Reb has left his playground," he hissed in a soft, threatening tone. "What business do you have with real men, Reardon?"

"I know you started that fire, Conroy. I just don't know why. Why did you want to punish the midshipmen when you really wish to take revenge on me?"

"Well, I'm thinkin' you're too southern dumb to know enough to leave the academy on your own. I'm helping you out."

Trace drew himself up, squaring his shoulders, narrowing his eyes. "I'm not leaving. As I told you once before, I'm not responsible for what the entire Confederate Army and Navy did during the war. I'm an officer of the United States Navy. This is where I belong and where I'm going to stay."

"Yeah?" Conroy pushed his face within inches of Trace's. "What are you gonna do when that playground is open officially?"

Trace had never backed down from a bully. Suppressing the urge to deliver another blow to the bristly chin so close to him, he folded his arms across his chest. "I'll do whatever I'm assigned to do."

"Yer a pansy."

"Those are fighting words." The blood ran hot in Trace's veins. He dropped his arms. His hands balled into fists.

Conroy stepped back, but sneered. "You think you can take me in the ring?"

"I know it."

A movement over the glowering seaman's shoulder distracted Trace. Midshipman Rand Noble had raised his hand in a lazy salute as he sauntered toward the seawall.

"Midshipman Noble. A word." Trace had a message for Rand Noble. He took the moment to diffuse the escalating anger between Conroy and himself. Nothing would be gained by engaging in a brawl by the seawall in front of a hundred onlookers. They must settle their differences like gentlemen, and settle them soon, once and for all.

Trace was aware that Conroy's contorted expression had relaxed, but the instructor's body remained rigid with tension. His gaze shifted from Trace to the midshipman.

"Lieutenant." An unsmiling, properly respectful midshipman greeted Trace with a sharp salute before dipping his head in acknowledgment of the snarling seaman.

"Noble, this is Seaman Conroy."

Conroy grunted.

"Have I interrupted?"

"The seaman and I have just about finished our business. We have agreed to meet in the ring for a battle of fists."

Frowning, the instructor shook his head, slowly and firmly. "Nah. I didn't agree to meet you in the ring. I'll wrestle you in your new playground; two out of three takes it."

"A wrestling match between instructors?" Noble asked rhetorically. His eyes widened with evident delight. "Grand!"

It was not grand. Trace shot him a frown. "Did I give you permission to speak, Noble?"

"No sir."

Elliot Conroy moved closer to Trace until they stood jaw to jaw. "Are you still willin' to meet me on the mat, Reardon?"

"Two weeks from today." He took up the challenge without thinking. He simply reacted to his clenched fists, his tension-filled body, muscles aching from restraint.

Trace had no talent for wrestling. He knew little about the sport. But he possessed enough arrogance to believe that with two weeks to learn, he could win. He would best and silence the blackheart once and for all.

"I'll be countin' the days." With a sneer that

might have struck fear in the heart of an untested warrior, Conroy limped off.

Trace drew a deep breath. If he didn't learn quickly, he'd be mincemeat. But with another matter to resolve, he turned his attention to Rand Noble. The midshipman stood at attention. His tall figure brought him almost to eye level with Trace.

"At ease, Midshipman."

"Yes sir."

"I'm afraid that I have bad news for you."

"Sir?"

"Miss Partridge asked me to convey her . . . regrets. She will not be home tomorrow when you had asked permission to call."

The handsome midshipman appeared crestfallen. "That is bad news. I'd been looking forward to taking her sailing on the bay."

More than likely, Susannah would enjoy a sail about the bay, Trace thought. He'd been meaning to take his family sailing. Perhaps they'd do it when Miss Partridge returned. "You might try again at another time."

"It's not a family emergency that has called her out of town, is it?" Noble asked, and continued before Trace could reply, "Because I stand ready to be of service to Miss Partridge if she should require any help at all."

Trace hadn't thought to ask what business took Susannah away. He hesitated to pry into his governess's affairs.

"I'm certain that Miss Partridge does not require your help, but I shall inquire." If he arrived home in time to see her before she left.

Trace knew that Susannah planned to leave on the afternoon stage, earlier than he would like. Originally, she had asked for only Sunday and

Monday. Now she would be gone Saturday afternoon, Sunday, and Monday. The girls were sure to miss her.

"Thank you, sir. Your governess is the prettiest woman in Annapolis."

"Dismissed, Noble."

"Yes sir."


Susannah couldn't be certain what she felt swirling in the pit of her stomach. Trepidation, excitement, and more. She had arrived in Baltimore too late last evening to do anything but find a room at the Baltimore Eagle Hotel. After indulging in a hot bath to soak away the dust and grime from her coach travel, she prepared and practiced what she would say to her long lost husband.

But this morning as she stood at the door of the Kirkwood Boarding House, her mind had gone completely blank. Unable to move—to raise her hand to knock or to open the door—she waffled. A thousand questions raced through her mind. Had Patterson been damaged during the war? If so, would he know her, remember her? Would he be happy to see her, or had he purposefully neglected to see her?

She rubbed her hand over her racing heart.

What should she do if it appeared he'd lost his memory? Should she stay at his side and nurse the stranger he'd become for the rest of her life? Must she give up her dream of having children, a family of her own? After marrying Patterson, Susannah had dreamed a dozen variations of the family and life they would share together. Only lately had the dreams faded.

She'd searched for him too long to turn back

now. Lifting her chin and straightening her shoulders, she knocked lightly on the door. No answer. Hoping not to be mistaken for an adventuress prowling for clients, Susannah opened the door and walked into the foyer. One glance told her that this was an exclusive boarding house. Pink cabbage-rose wallpaper, heavy mahogany furniture, and Currier and Ives prints decorated the vestibule.

"Hello!" she called. "Is anyone at home?"

Of course there must be.

Within seconds, a large, stoutly built lady descended the staircase. She had a lovely smile. "Good morning, I'm Adelaide Kirkwood."

"And I am Susannah Partridge."

"Are you looking for a room?"

"No. I am looking for . . . for a man. We became separated during the war."

Adelaide Kirkwood's pleasant expression gave way to a compassionate frown. "Oh, my dear. I shall try to help you."

"Thank you. I understand that a Mr. Harling Patterson resides here."

"Yes, he does. But Harling is at church. The Methodist church on the corner."

Church? Patterson had not been a churchgoing man during their brief time together. But the war had changed many a man's heart.

Mrs. Kirkwood took advantage of Susannah's pause. "But I find it curious that Harling is the man you seek. He has never mentioned having family."

"Perhaps he is not the same Harling I am searching for," Susannah conceded. "But I shall stop by the Methodist church to make certain. Thank you for your help, Mrs. Kirkwood."

Her heart thudded against her chest as Susannah hurried down the street toward the small church constructed of white clapboard and redbrick. A symbol of hope, its steeple rose high against the blue sky. Within the church walls, Susannah's future awaited.

Just as she reached the bottom step, the door opened and the church bells began to chime. Stepping to the side, she waited, searching faces as the worshipers left the building. She recognized no one.

"May I help you, young lady?"

The elderly gentleman had been about to pass Susannah.

"Perhaps. I . . . I am looking for Harling Patterson."

"This must be Harling's lucky day," the kindly old gentleman said with a chuckle. He looked back for a moment and reached out to a man talking with another parishioner. His back was to Susannah, but his height was as she remembered Patterson's. "Harling. Harling," the old man called. "This young lady is here to see you."

Susannah's heart fluttered wildly. Harling turned.

Her insides wilted like a day-old daisy. This craggy-faced man, tall and gangly, must be fifty years of age, if not more. Harling Patterson was not Patterson Harling.

She thought she had prepared herself for disappointment. Susannah knew the odds of finding her husband with the solicitor's first reference were slim. Still, she had hoped to finally resolve the uncertainty that dogged her. The letdown she experienced cast her into the doldrums.

Smiling, Harling Patterson stepped forward, extending his hand. "How do you do?"

"I . . . I'm fine, sir. But . . . I, it seems I have the wrong man," she stammered apologetically.

"I hate to disappoint such a pretty young woman," he said, with a gap-toothed smile. "Who is it that you wish to find? Perhaps I can be of help."

She didn't think so. "I'm looking for Patterson Harling."

"Ah, yes. Several others have been before you."

His reply took her by surprise. "Several others?"

"One was a young man and the other a naval officer. I understand that Mr. Harling is a deserter. Deserted the navy, he did."

Susannah stiffened with shock. An icy numbness swept over her. "No."

"I'm afraid so. The young man, can't recall his name, figured that Mr. Harling might have hightailed it out west to the gold fields. The navy officer mentioned going to look him up in Washington."

"Washington," she murmured. "How long ago has it been since the navy officer was here?"

"A few weeks." He rubbed the gray stubble on his chin. "My memory's not as good as it was."

"Thank you, Mr. Patterson. You've been very helpful."

"Would you join me for lunch?"

Susannah forced a smile. Harling Patterson had earned her respect in just a few moments. He was more the gentleman than the brash young Patterson Harling had ever been. Why *had* she married him? "No, thank you, Mr. Patterson. I must catch the next stage. But I appreciate your kindness."

With one more free day to search for her husband, she prepared to leave on the next coach for Washington. If the navy believed him to be a deserter, Susannah might find Patterson in the brink. An icy shiver, unrelated to the early November frost, swept through her. For the briefest moment she considered abandoning the search and proclaiming herself a widow. But she could not live with a lie. She must know the truth, for she'd taken a vow of fidelity until death.

Susannah's sense of disappointment was relieved a bit by knowing that at the end of this journey, Emily, Alice, Amelia, and Grace awaited her. And their father.

Lieutenant Reardon. Honorable. Staunch. Solid as granite. He'd become a doting father, and around the house he whistled cheerful tunes, albeit off-key. And his tentative, lopsided smile Susannah found quite seductive. Combined with his charming southern drawl, he could sweep an unsuspecting woman off her feet.

For exactly that reason, she renewed her resolve to distance herself from Reardon when she returned home.

"Fred misses Miss Partridge," Grace solemnly told Trace as he tucked her into bed Monday evening. Fred lay at the side of her bed.

The big shaggy dog had taken to sleeping at the foot of Grace's bed. He jumped up on the down comforter as soon as any adult in the house was out of sight. For a reason he could not explain, Trace pretended ignorance of the dog's misbehavior.

"I'm sure that he does," Trace replied. "And Bilge, too."

"When will she be home?"

"Soon, Grace. Miss Partridge will be home when you wake up tomorrow."

After kissing his youngest, most vulnerable daughter on her forehead, he stood and turned down the gaslight. "Good night, girls."

"Good night, Father." The unison of voices brought a smile to his lips. As Susannah had told him, he'd been blessed with good girls. They were obedient and bright. They studied hard and, most importantly, none appeared to have inherited their mother's penchant for deception.

As Trace ambled down the stairs headed for his study, the house seemed unusually quiet. It lacked the spark he'd become accustomed to, a sense of vitality. In some mysterious way, Susannah's absence during the past two and a half days had created a pall over everything.

Understanding the anxiety of his daughter who talked with fairies, he had assured Grace that her governess would return. Grace had only been two years old when her mother had gone away "for a few days." And never came back.

Until Trace saw Susannah's face, even he could not feel confident. He had no idea where she had gone nor what she meant to do. And now Louise's betrayal niggled at the back of his mind. His wife had told his father, the housekeeper, and Emily that she was going into town to visit the doctor. She'd been trained to be an excellent actress. When Louise got to town, she never stopped. She kept on going until she reached New Orleans, where she boarded a ship. One day later, she was gone forever, lost at sea.

Swiping a hand through his hair, Trace sank into his desk chair. Where was Susannah? It was getting late. She should be home by now.

"Are the girls settled?" Aunt Cellie asked, bustling into his study without so much as a knock.

"Yes. But they are asking about Miss Partridge. Grace misses her."

"Susannah does well with the girls," his aunt allowed, nodding her approval.

"Your opinion of Miss Partridge has changed?"

His aunt absentmindedly pulled at the extra, wrinkled flesh at her neck. "The Millbanks are still raving over the dinner she prepared."

"Are you willing now to relinquish your nieces' care to Susannah and make your return to Uncle Edgar?"

Aunt Cellie flashed him a broad, scarlet-mouthed smile. She'd overdone the rouge on her lips. "As soon as you have settled on a bride. Mary is a comely young woman. She played the piano like an angel. Why have you not seen her again?"

"Yes," he agreed. "She plays the piano well."

"Did you get on with her?"

"She laughed too much."

"Nerves, my dear. The poor girl felt nervous. You can be intimidating, Trace."

"Her laugh was strange. I fear it might prove trying over any length of time." Mary Millbanks laughed like a horse. And now, Trace was missing Susannah's low, soft, girlish laughter.

"You must spend time with Mary when she's more relaxed," Aunt Cellie stated with a nod of her head as if she was agreeing with herself. "I'll arrange it."

"No. Please, Aunt Cellie. I don't feel that I would be a good husband for Mary."

"Why not?"

"She leaves me cold. I could not persuade her to converse about anything other than her needle-point. She never smiled or looked me in the eye." Trace had spoken the truth and prepared himself for a tongue-lashing from his aunt.

"I had hoped she would be a little more lively," Cellie agreed ruefully.

"Aunt Cellie, it's time for you to go back to

Uncle Edgar. I can get along without a wife for quite some time now that we have Susannah."

"But what if she leaves?"

"Why would she do that? I pay her well. She has her own attic chamber and the devotion of four wonderful children."

"She may wish to have a family of her own. Although she is getting on in years, Miss Partridge is still quite attractive. She may charm some fellow into being her husband."

"Rand."

"What?"

"Nothing."

"Are you certain you would not like another meeting with the widow Witherspoon, then? There's a rumor that Admiral Porter might hold a military ball at the academy. She would be an excellent dance partner."

"A ball?" he repeated, and then shook his head. "I don't know how these rumors start."

"It may be more than a rumor, Trace. You must admit, the admiral seems afire with innovations. Just look what you are doing: building a gymnasium."

"I suppose we cannot discount anything where the admiral is concerned. But promise me, Aunt, to put any thoughts out of your head of finding me a dance partner."

"Trace, I cannot promise. You are my only nephew, and I cannot bear to see you unhappy."

"But I am not unhappy," he protested, realizing it was true. He was happier than he'd been in months.

And he could not bear any more of the awkward matchmaking. He had other things to worry about—like his wrestling match with Elliot Conroy.

"You require a wife to be truly happy."

"Good night, Aunt Cellie."

"Good night."

Trace watched his aunt leave his study before standing and crossing to close the door behind her. He wanted no further conversation about securing a wife. Besides, with Susannah as the girls' governess he did not have to worry about marrying as quickly as he'd once thought.

Susannah was attractive and intelligent. He suspected she might understand that marriage did not guarantee happiness. She may have even chosen spinsterhood.

But what if she hadn't? How could he keep her from marrying? How could he coax the golden-eyed governess to remain with his family?

Agitated, Trace looked up at the clock. He paced to one end of his study and then the other. Where was she? She had been gone far too long.

How to keep her? The first answer to come to mind was amazingly simple. Marry her himself!

The thought struck him with such force that he stopped in his tracks. Of course. He and Miss Partridge got along well enough together. Not to mention that he had thoroughly enjoyed holding her in his arms on those rare occasions. She had sparked his desire more than once.

But a marriage in name only would be acceptable. It would satisfy her need to have a husband—if she indeed had such a need—and his desire to obtain a mother for his girls. It was not a giant leap from governess to mother, and the girls adored Susannah. Of course, it would pose a problem if Susannah wanted babies of her own. But how absurd. Why would she want more children when she already had a ready-made family?

Trace couldn't remember feeling this excited

about an idea in a long time. He glanced at the clock. The hands hadn't moved since the last time he looked. If only she would come home. A small noise outside his study made him pause.

Was it the front door? Had she come home at last?

# CHAPTER 11

Susannah slipped into the house unnoticed. From the hall she could see a light shining from the lieutenant's office. He was either working late or had waited up for her. The latter thought both charmed and appalled her. On tiptoe, she made her way past the parlor to his door.

He'd fallen asleep in his chair. Susannah's heart gave a curious lurch at the sight of him. His head had fallen forward with his chin resting on his chest. Even slouched in sleep the lieutenant's massive figure was mesmerizing. She felt like a Serengeti explorer who had stumbled across a sleeping lion in his den, as she quietly observed the strong, splendid beast at his most vulnerable.

In the firelight, his disheveled ebony hair had a glossy sheen. A dark stubble of beard shadowed his jaw. Oddly enough, Reardon's slightly unkempt appearance made the lieutenant even more appealing. And in sleep, he did not seem nearly so fearsome, nor arrogant, nor proud. If she did not wake him, however, he might suffer from a stiff neck and a kink or two in the morning.

Softly glowing embers were all that remained of the fire. The study had grown cold. Susannah approached slowly and gently brushed a few stray strands from Lieutenant Reardon's forehead. He stirred, shifted, growled deep in his throat, but did not wake.

Susannah whispered his name. "Trace."

She'd always wanted to call him by his first name, but from the hired help such boldness would be grounds for dismissal. Since he couldn't hear her, though, it did not matter. Wondering what had kept him up, she glanced at the papers on his desk.

The lieutenant had compiled a list that began with her name. And her name was underlined. Susannah stiffened. She should never have asked for the extra free day. She had gone too far. With her penchant for accidents, bringing a stray dog into the home, not to mention Bilge, the lieutenant might have decided to dismiss her. With Aunt Cellie's help, more than likely he and the girls had gotten along just fine without her. They didn't need her.

If he planned to let her go, she would not wake him. Her gaze drifted down the list: *Learn body throws.*

That sounded violent.

Good lord! Did he mean to remove her with physical force if necessary? Perhaps she should just slip away now and leave him to experience the pain of a stiff neck in the morning. It was all extremely puzzling since the lieutenant had never given evidence of being a violent man. The next item on his list was to send a message to Uncle Edgar. Susannah did not know what to make of the list. Uncertain of his intentions, she took mercy on her employer.

Leaning down low, she whispered into his ear, "Lieutenant."

He smelled manly. Leather and soap and spice filled her senses like the most tantalizing perfume.

She spoke a little louder, "Lieutenant."

His head moved from side to side.

"If you do not wake up, Lieutenant, you shall regret it in the morning."

He uttered a deep, guttural sound; his body jerked and his head snapped up. "What? What?"

"It is I, Susannah." She moved to Reardon's side where he could see her clearly. "I regret the hour, but the stage broke down, and we were all delayed while the wheel was fixed. I did not mean to be late," she added, in hopes of staving off any thoughts he might have of dismissing her.

He squeezed his eyes shut as if clearing his vision and mind from the cobwebs of sleep. He looked up at her. "Miss Partridge?"

"Yes sir," she said softly, with a smile. Certainly, he could not have mistaken her for an apparition.

Shaking off the last vestiges of sleep, the lieutenant repositioned himself in his chair, assuming the heads-up, spine-stiff posture of an officer. "I've been worried. Where have you been?"

"I . . . I have been in Washington."

She'd spent the entire day pouring over the records of those lost at sea, fatally wounded in battle, or known to have died in Confederate prison camps during the war. Patterson's name never appeared in her search. She'd reached another dead-end in the search for her husband. Downcast, Susannah had returned to the lieutenant's home, the heavy weight of another failure on her shoulders, burdening her as if she wore epaulets of iron.

"Washington?" Reardon repeated as if he'd never heard of the city. Obviously, she had stirred his curiosity. He wanted to know why she had traveled to Washington but refused to pry.

"Yes, Washington." And she would have to return. The officer in charge of tracking down deserters had been away for the day.

The lieutenant's eyes narrowed on her. "Why?"

His need to know what her business had been about apparently overcame any reluctance to appear meddlesome. Caught off guard, Susannah hesitated. What would he think of her if she told him the truth? *Because I've lost my husband.*

She could not bring herself to make such a confession. Her handsome employer would believe her a dimwit and dismiss her on the spot. Worse, he might believe she'd made a shrewish wife and her husband had abandoned her at the first opportunity. Even more mortifying, he might think, as she did every now and again, that Patterson had never loved her.

Unwilling to confess her predicament, she improvised a nebulous answer. "It's a . . . a family matter."

"Your sister?"

"Oh. No. I . . . I may be close to finding my lost relative, the one who disappeared during the war."

"An uncle, I assume."

What made him assume it was an uncle she sought? And then Susannah remembered. Lieutenant Reardon considered her well on the way to the lonely town of spinsterhood. Unable to suppress her annoyance, she frowned.

Apparently mistaking the cause of her frown, her employer shifted his weight, swiped a hand through his inky hair, smoothing the tousled strands, and attempted to take command of the situation. "Many men and women disappeared during the war. If I can help you in any way, I would be happy to do so. An officer has many more means at his disposal for such a search."

"Oh. Ah. No. No," she replied, forcing a smile. "Thank you, but that won't be necessary."

"Very well, then. But I shall leave my offer open in the event you change your mind."

"You're very kind." And he was. He had meant no disrespect. Beneath Trace Reardon's hard-shell military exterior, there beat the heart of a sensitive soul. There was even more to him than what the eye could see: a tall, striking man of honor.

She released a small rueful sigh, generated by the forbidden pleasure she took in gazing at the lieutenant's physical attributes. He had a magnetism that created a warming ache within her. She could not deny it. She was a hopeless sinner. A married woman had no business admiring any man but her husband.

The clock struck midnight, jolting Susannah from her wicked musings. "I shall say good night now."

She quickly made for the door. The wisest thing she could do was to put distance between Reardon and herself at once. From this moment until the time she found Patterson, Susannah meant to avoid the lieutenant like a meadowlark avoided a hawk.

"Wait," he ordered sharply.

She stopped in her tracks. *What now?*

Reardon stood, straightening to his full, towering height.

Susannah's heart beat a warning tattoo.

His smoky gaze met hers. "A question before you go."

"Yes?"

The lieutenant approached her, hands clasped behind his back. "This may strike you as sudden.

But during your absence, I believe I have come up with the perfect solution for my dilemma and yours."

"My dilemma?" Her knees went to paste. Did he know about Patterson, then? How had he discovered the truth?

"You are an unmarried woman of advancing age, and I am an unmarried man who requires a wife and mother for his children."

*He did not know.* Susannah's relief was so great she clamped down on her lip to prevent a gale of nervous laughter. But what was that he said? *Advancing age?*

Indignation fired through her veins. Inhaling deeply, mustering her pride, Susannah raised her chin. "Advancing age, sir?"

The honesty ingrained in her as the daughter of a preacher prevented her from agreeing that she was an unmarried woman.

Lieutenant Reardon stood no more than a foot away from her, smiling. Smiling!

His voice, soft, soothing and persuasive in tone, wrapped around Susannah like a warm silken robe. "Although you might think this a shocking idea," he admitted, "I think that once you consider my proposal, you will be pleased."

Transfixed by Reardon's heart-swelling smile, her pulse pounded with apprehension. "Wha . . . what proposal?"

"I should like you to marry me, Miss Partridge."

Susannah felt as if she had been struck by lightning. She rocked back on her heels, blinking in astonishment. "I beg your pardon?"

His piercing silver-gray gaze pinned her to the spot. "Will you be my wife, Miss Partridge?"

For a moment Susannah thought her heart had stopped. Had Reardon taken leave of his senses?

Perhaps he was still sleeping. She'd heard of people who walked and talked in their sleep. Still stunned, she could almost feel the blood draining from her face, from her limbs, but she remained speechless.

"I do not expect an answer immediately," he said, quickly withdrawing behind a cool mask of indifference. "But if you will think upon my proposal for a few days, you will likely come to see things my way. By marrying me, Miss Partridge, you shall live a life of comfort and be very well taken care of in all matters. All I shall ask in return is that you continue to care for my daughters, attend certain functions with me, and provide . . . comfort . . . from time to time."

That was all he asked? Everything! But there could be no mistaking his thoughtful expression. The lieutenant was serious. And what did he mean by *comfort?* Why had her body tingled at the word? Because her body knew.

"You may retire now," he said softly.

She nodded dumbly. "Good night, Lieutenant Reardon."

Marry him! Did the lieutenant seriously think she would consider marrying a man who did not love her, no matter what the circumstances? What sort of woman did he take her for?

Not a woman already wed, that was for certain. She turned to flee.

"One more thing."

Would she never make her escape? Reluctantly, Susannah turned back, only to be caught in the lieutenant's arms. Before she understood what was happening, he pulled her against his broad, muscular chest. His mouth came down on hers, bruising, intense, passionate.

Her head spun, her knees trembled, and—oh,

dear God, forgive her—but Susannah did not want him to stop kissing her. She did not want the moment to end. Ever.

The lusty lieutenant kissed her deeply, hungrily. He kissed her as if he'd been longing for her and her alone. He tasted minty and male-delicious. Her entire body tingled, alive and willing. Oh, so willing.

Oh no! Abruptly coming to her senses, Susannah pushed against his chest. At the first sign she wished to be free, Reardon released her. Stepping back, he cleared his throat, and hiked one dark brow as if in surprise. "Well, I . . . I thought we should have some idea of what might be."

Susannah had never been kissed so completely. She would have remembered if Patterson had ever kissed her with such passion. She would still be reeling.

Swallowing hard, she struggled to find her voice. Her throat felt as dry as a dirt road and twice as gritty. "I believe . . . I believe I have quite a remarkable grasp of the concept. Th-thank you."

The lieutenant's steady gaze burned into hers. Silver fire danced in the depths of his eyes. His breathing seemed to come in ragged gulps as his lips curved into a seductive smile.

"Now you shall have something else to consider while pondering my proposal," he drawled.

As did he! The arrogance of the man! Susannah could not feel that Reardon had been entirely indifferent to her kiss, either. But it was her body she felt burning, she who craved more of him. She dared not linger. "Good night, Lieutenant."

Despite feeling fall-down light-headed, Susannah spun on her heel, lifted her chin, and sailed toward the staircase. Dare she hope to make it up the stairs without taking a tumble?

* * *

Trace tasted Susannah for days. He savored the surprise of a kiss sweeter than pure sugarcane. Once more, he'd given way to impulse, but he was glad for the unintended weakness. Right beneath his roof, he'd discovered a delicate morsel of a woman. A woman who had melted in his arms and answered his desire with eagerness—at first. He thought it likely that the natural inhibition of a preacher's daughter, combined with common propriety, had claimed her in the nick of time. She had simply lost reason for a moment. Trace had as well.

But he could still feel her lips, soft and moist beneath his. It had been months since he'd held a woman in his arms. The fires that burned within him demanded to be quenched. He did not require nor want to love again, but making love was another matter.

Taking Susannah as a wife would answer his needs nicely as long as she did not insist on words of love or desire children. His daughters thought the world of her and would readily accept their governess as his wife.

Marriage to Miss Partridge would be just the thing.

Once she had time to digest his proposal and recover from her obvious shock, she would see the benefits of his proposal. Trace planned to list the conditions and details of what would be a suitable marriage of convenience. In the end they would sign a contract agreeable to both. He intended to assist Susannah in finding her missing uncle so that she might concentrate on his home and family—and him. Trace prided himself on his planning.

The planning for the official opening of the ten-pin lanes and gymnasium came to an end several days later. He'd been working since just after dawn preparing for the ceremony that would take place within the hour. Although chairs lined the cavernous second-floor space, he expected there would be standing room only.

At midafternoon his student assistant reported to him. "Sir. Everything is ready, sir."

"Midshipman Maloney, you've done an outstanding job."

"Thank you, sir."

"Lieutenant Reardon!"

The call came from across the gymnasium floor, and Trace recognized the voice as belonging to Rand Noble, the academy's oldest midshipman.

"Dismissed, Maloney."

After Maloney executed a sharp salute and strode off, Trace turned to see the tall figure of First Classman Noble approaching him. Noble seemed never to be far from Trace these days.

Trace hadn't time for delays. He expected Admiral Porter to arrive soon. The superintendent was scheduled to make a brief speech and cut the official ribbon. It had been decided to hold the ceremony here rather than on the first floor. The ten-pin lanes were for recreation, and the shooting gallery had been operational for several weeks. But the gymnasium and the revolutionary concept of building physical strength and stamina utilizing its equipment were new. The academy community had been curious about this strange addition to the curriculum. Trace expected a large crowd of officers, wives, and children as well as midshipmen to attend this afternoon's ceremony.

The guests had begun to arrive. To a person,

they looked about them as if they were in a museum. Engaged in hushed conversation, they pointed to outfitting they'd never seen before.

"I'm busy, Rand."

Noble nodded in smiling acknowledgment. "Yes sir, I understand. One question."

"What's that?"

"Has Miss Partridge returned?"

The man had a one-track mind. If he would study instead of chasing the ladies, he might make a suitable officer one day. "Yes," Trace snapped, "she's back."

"Excellent! May I ask her to accompany me on a sail this Sunday?"

Noble's perseverance rankled Trace more than he could say. He longed to inform the genial midshipman that Miss Partridge had been spoken for, but he could not. Trace hadn't had the time in the last few days to seek out her answer to his proposal. Instead, he bit out, "Do you mistake me for Miss Partridge's father, Noble?"

"No sir. I shall ask the charming governess to sail with me, and not bother you again seeking permission." He flashed a cocky grin. "And congratulations, sir. This is a big day for you, the opening of the gymnasium."

"Yes, it is."

"What sort of demonstrations will be presented?"

"The use of the striking bag and a round of boxing, followed by an exhibition on the vaulting horse. Midshipman Maloney will demonstrate what can be accomplished on the bouncing board."

"No wrestling?"

"No."

Noble grinned. "I had hoped to see your match with Seaman Conroy this afternoon."

"That is quite another matter."

"I could demonstrate several wrestling holds if you like."

"Do you wrestle?" Trace asked, his interest in Noble suddenly increased.

The midshipman's blue eyes twinkled mischievously. "I'm an excellent wrestler, if I do say so myself."

"By all means, a brief demonstration would be appreciated."

"Glad to help. Sir."

Although it went against his grain to accept Rand Noble's help, Trace knew he needed it. "Would you be interested in sharing your wrestling expertise with . . . your fellow midshipmen, until an instructor can be hired?"

"It would be my privilege to assist the academy. For extra credit, of course," he added quickly.

Trace shook his head. It wasn't every student who bargained. Only the cheeky ones. "Be here every evening at seven."

"My apologies, but I can only make it three times a week. Contrary to popular opinion, I do study."

A midshipman negotiating with an officer. Noble's extreme arrogance irked Trace. But it came with the territory. Officers were trained to have utmost confidence in themselves and their decisions. In other words, the academy training fostered arrogance. Trace hadn't thought about it, but he allowed that he might have a touch of that quality himself. It was what made him believe that in a matter of weeks he could learn to wrestle as if he'd been doing it all his life.

"You have a deal, Midshipman Noble. I plan to be among your students."

Noble's brows shot up. "Oh?"

"So that in the future, if called upon, I will stand ready to pass on whatever knowledge I can glean from you."

Rand grinned. He was no fool. "It will be my pleasure to teach you everything I know, sir." Stepping closer to Trace, he lowered his voice. "Can't think of anything I'd like better than to see you pin Elliot Conroy to the mat."

Trace slapped a hand on the conspiring midshipman's shoulder. There might be hope for Noble yet. "I appreciate that."

"Oh, there's Miss Partridge now!"

Trace followed Rand's gaze to the door.

Wearing a blue silk gown the color of hyacinths, Susannah strolled into the gymnasium with his daughters in tow. Appearing enthralled with the trapezes, she moved slowly, holding Grace with one hand and Amelia with the other. Emily and Alice followed, with Aunt Cellie bringing up the rear.

Viewing them across the hall, Trace felt an overwhelming sense of pride. He'd been blessed with a fine and beautiful family.

"Permission to be excused, sir."

"Dismissed, Noble."

In growing irritation, he followed Midshipman Noble as he made a beeline for Susannah. Her face lit up with a welcoming smile. Helpless to do anything but observe, he watched the indefatigable, and immensely likeable, midshipman take Trace's family in hand, making certain they were seated comfortably.

Alice caught sight of Trace first and waved as she nudged the other girls. Soon Aunt Cellie and all of his smiling daughters were waving. Susannah's gaze rested on his for a fleeting moment. He'd hoped that she would feel some pride in his accomplishment today, but the faint smile she gave him appeared more wistful than one elated with his success.

Trace's decision to take a moment with his family was derailed by the arrival of Admiral Porter. The ceremony was about to begin. He would have a word with Miss Partridge this evening. Patience not being his strong suite, he was eager to have the answer to his proposal. Once she accepted, they had much to discuss.

As he stepped forward to greet the superintendent, he saw Elliot Conroy. The surly seaman leaned against the door frame, arms folded, narrowed eyes on Trace.

Susannah's attic chamber felt chilly. Even wearing a wool shawl, she could feel the cold seeping to her marrow. While she suspected fire burned in every fireplace in the house, tonight the heat didn't seem to be rising to her space.

"Blow the man down. Bail, mate!"

"Hush now, Bilge. I know you are cold, so I will put two covers over your cage. I promise that you shall be as warm as Fred with his big heavy coat this evening."

As she looked for another covering, Susannah heard the telltale squeak of someone climbing the ladder to her attic chamber.

"Miss Partridge?"

Lieutenant Reardon.

"Permission to come aboard?"

Oh, good gracious.

# CHAPTER 12

Susannah's pulse thumped hard against her wrist. She had no doubt as to the reason for Lieutenant Reardon's surprise visit tonight. He sought the answer to his astonishing proposal. Feeling a bit like a cottontail cornered by a coyote, she sucked in a trembling breath. She could not give her employer the reply he wished to hear. Neither could she deny him entrance into his own attic.

"Yes, of course, Lieutenant. Come in."

Reardon's head and broad shoulders emerged first through the square opening. Susannah's heart fluttered wildly. Dressed in a full-sleeved white linen shirt and dark trousers, he wore a disarming grin. He was too tall to stand completely upright under the rafters in the attic. The problem in no way diminished his presence.

"Has something happened downstairs that requires my attention? When the girls fell asleep I thought it safe to retire."

"No one has stirred, nor made the slightest peep," he said. His eyes locked on hers. "I came up to see you."

*Just as she feared.*

Susannah gestured to the rocking chair. "Please, make yourself comfortable."

A crackling tension, an uncertain energy chased the chill from the attic air. Inexplicable warmth infused Susannah's body, as if she stood by a roaring fire.

The lieutenant nodded. "Thank you."

He folded his long frame carefully down into the rocking chair. Although he appeared uncomfortable, it was the only chair that would withstand the weight of his splendid figure. He planted his feet firmly on the floor—in order not to rock, she supposed.

Her nerves stretched taut, Susannah perched on the delicate French elbow chair, its faded blue damask covering worn bare. The two chairs were separated by a round rosewood table.

She smiled.

He smiled.

Attempting to forestall the dreaded marriage conversation, Susannah smiled even more brightly, and said, "Congratulations on your great success this afternoon. Admiral Porter and the midshipmen seemed delighted with the gymnasium and ten-pin lanes. You are surely the most popular officer at the academy tonight."

"Not the most popular, but I may have gained new friends. Antoine Corbesier, the sword master, and several other officers congratulated me on the achievement."

"As well they should!" Susannah exclaimed, hopeful that the lieutenant at last had overcome the burden of being looked upon as the pariah from the South.

"I have not been accepted by my fellow officers as readily as I'd hoped," he confessed with a wry grin. "Except for Julian, the librarian. He fought for the Confederate Navy as well, but I believe he is thinking of leaving the military. He rather dislikes being a librarian."

"There is little adventure in being a librarian, except between the pages of books. I don't wonder that a man who has been in the line of fire must find the library tedious and unfriendly. But I feel certain that the gymnasium will win you many friends, Lieutenant," Susannah assured her pensive employer.

To avoid what promised to be a trying conversation about a marriage of convenience, she intended to discuss the gymnasium until dawn if necessary.

Reardon cast her a small, speculative smile. "We shall see. I meet with the superintendent tomorrow to receive my next assignment."

"Do you have any thought to what that will be?"

"No, but I am hoping it's not in the library."

Trace Reardon completed his jest with a lopsided smile that caused a strange reaction. Lost in the teasing curve of his mouth, Susannah's heart trembled and skipped like that of a moonstruck girl. *Oh no.*

What was happening to her that she could no longer control her emotions? Emotions that she should not be having! Even now the devil was probably making a place for her in his fiery home. Her parents, waiting for Susannah in heaven, would spend eternity wondering what had happened to her. She would never take her place among the angels.

She managed a chuckle, adding in truth, "I can't imagine you among the book stacks."

"Nor can I. I should like to teach more classes. We learned many valuable lessons during the war."

"About torpedoes and submersibles?"

"Yes. You have an excellent memory." He looked around, his gaze settling on her wrap. "Miss Partridge, are you not cold up here?"

"Cold? Is it cold? I hadn't noticed."

"Your bird may be bottom-up."

"Oh no, I just covered his cage with two layers of fabric. Bilge is fine."

"The weather grows increasingly colder. I believe it would be wise to move into the spare chamber that Aunt Cellie uses for sewing and such. It has a fireplace and is much closer to my daughters in case there should be an emergency."

She'd stayed in that spare chamber her first night in the Reardon residence. Located directly across the corridor from the lieutenant's chamber, it now seemed too close for comfort.

"Thank you. I shall think on it."

"If forced, I will order you to make the move," he said in a teasing banter. "I am used to giving orders and being obeyed."

"But I am not a midshipman," she balked.

"For which I am grateful. You are far more attractive than any midshipman I have ever known," he quipped, with an appealing twist of his lips.

Caught off guard by the lieutenant's compliment, Susannah's heart swelled to an uncommon size, squeezing against her chest. Did he truly believe she was attractive, or did he simply want her to agree to marry him?

"Speaking of midshipmen," he said, not waiting for her reply. "I happened to see Rand Noble approach you this afternoon. He seems to have developed a . . . a fondness for you."

Susannah smiled. Midshipman Noble, with his good looks and swaggering charm, amused her. But she could not lead him on any more than she could Lieutenant Reardon.

"Miss Partridge?"

"Oh, yes. Midshipman Noble asked me to go sailing with him on Sunday but I had to decline."

The lieutenant's eyes darkened. He hiked a brow. "Oh?"

"My personal business requires another personal day. I was hoping that if I stayed with the girls on Sunday that you might see your way to allowing me to make one more journey on Monday," she explained in a rush. "I must return to Washington."

"You are determined to find your lost relative."

"Very determined."

"I shall accompany you."

Susannah's stomach somersaulted. She bounced to her feet. "No, no. That won't be necessary," she assured him, hurriedly. "You have much to occupy you, and I feel this is something I must do on my own."

The lieutenant nodded gravely before standing. "Miss Partridge?"

"Yes?"

His silver-edged eyes locked on hers. "Have you given any more thought to my proposal?"

Susannah clasped her hands at her waist and took a deep breath. Her lips quivered as she smiled up at him. "Lieutenant Reardon, I am extremely flattered, and I do appreciate your offer, but I have never, not for one minute, ever entertained entering a marriage of convenience. Love is the only reason I can think of to marry."

His brows dove into a fierce frown. "Love?"

"Love."

Clenching his jaw, the lieutenant lowered his gaze to the floor. He spoke softly, tersely. "Miss Partridge, I married once for love. While I was away at war, my wife proceeded to betray me. She gave herself to another man. Louise died running off to be with him."

"I . . . I am so sorry."

"A marriage of convenience is more practical and is far less likely to lead to a broken heart."

"Betrayal is a terrible thing. But—"

"I do not require your pity," he interrupted sharply.

Susannah raised her eyes to his. "I am not dispensing pity, only suggesting that you do not judge all women by Louise. I believe in lasting love. It's there for everyone. Sometimes it takes longer to find than we would like."

"Most likely you also believe in Twinkle, Grace's imaginary friend," he said drolly.

The proud lieutenant's stubborn refusal to accept the possibility of true love grated on Susannah. "You are not the only man to ever be wounded by a dishonest woman. And though this thought may come as a shock, men have been known to betray the women who love them as well."

He rolled his eyes to the ceiling before replying in a tone that suggested he was calling upon the last reserve of patience. "I respect you, Miss Partridge. I admire your intelligence and spirit. Why is that not enough when I can offer you security and a ready-made family?"

"Lieutenant, I adore your daughters. Each one of them is unique in her own way. Emily, so studious; Amelia, curious about everything; Alice, who approaches the world carefully; and Grace, who is extremely imaginative. But I want to have children of my own."

"At your age?"

"At my age?" she repeated, incensed. Balling her hands on her hips, she took on the towering oak of a man. "I am well able to bear a child, Lieutenant Reardon. Perhaps two or . . . or twelve!"

Folding his arms across his wide chest, he cocked his head. "Twelve?"

"It could happen."

Releasing a sigh of surrender, Reardon's arms dropped to his sides. "Miss Partridge, you drive a hard bargain, but knowing the value of compromise, I shall concede. I will agree to fathering one more child."

"I am not bargaining!"

But the lieutenant continued to argue in a rising, incredulous tone. "If anything should happen to me at sea or in the ordinary course of our lives, you will inherit a substantial independence."

"I appreciate your offer," Susannah replied quietly. "You are a good and honorable man. But I am not interested in acquiring tangible items. I do not live for silk gowns and crystal chandeliers. When I marry, it will be for the greatest intangible of all— love."

"You are a most obstinate woman, and you are making a grave mistake," he warned with a shake of his head. "When you come to your senses, I shall be waiting."

His arrogance astonished her. She had all she could do to contain her anger. "Do not refuse any meals while you wait," she lashed out, blood at the boil. "You shall become—"

Reardon's icy glower prevented her from finishing. She slapped her hand over her mouth. What had she done?

"Impatient, perhaps?" he finished for her.

She'd had "skeletal" in mind.

"I have long needed to learn patience, Miss Partridge."

Susannah lowered her head. She felt trapped,

ashamed, angry with herself for losing her temper. "I did not mean to snap, but . . . but there are others to consider. Aunt Cellie would not be happy with me as your bride."

"My aunt has come around to liking you as well as she would any woman."

Somehow Susannah could not feel that was a rousing endorsement. "Your aunt appeared to favor both Miss Millbanks and Mrs. Witherspoon."

"My aunt is not choosing my wife."

"Of course not."

He slanted her one last long look. He was plainly baffled by her refusal. At least he had not dismissed her. "Good night, Miss Partridge."

"Goodnight, Lieutenant."

Her unhappy employer stopped at the ladder. "Do not be fooled into thinking Midshipman Noble will offer for your hand in marriage."

"I had not given it a moment's thought."

"In the morning I shall have Adam and Jane move you downstairs to the spare chamber."

"But—"

"You shall be warmer downstairs."

Susannah had no doubt. Lying in her bed, across from the lieutenant's chamber, she feared there would be nights when she would be more than warm. She might find it impossible to ignore her sinful thoughts of him, thoughts that crept into her mind more and more of late.

Reardon had given her no choice, however. Like it or not, in the morning she would be trading her attic sanctuary for a chamber that was ordinary in every way but one: it was located a heartbeat away from his.

Unwilling to argue the move, after turning down his proposal, she acquiesced quietly. "I shall help Adam and Jane."

With a curt nod of his head to seal the agreement, the tight-lipped lieutenant stalked to the stairs and descended without another word.

If she were not already married, Susannah wondered if she would entertain the idea of a marriage of convenience with Reardon. He had already made one concession. He'd agreed to father an additional child. She assumed it possible that a marriage of convenience might lead to more children and possibly love. It was possible, but nevertheless a risk, and one she would never take.

She must search for her husband until she found him. Even if she should discover she'd been widowed, she knew she would never settle for a marriage without love.

Trace had never met a woman as mulish as Susannah Partridge. When by all rights the accident-prone governess should be giddy with the prospect of marrying him, even thanking her stars that he had proposed, she'd refused him. For love! What woman in her right mind would behave in such a manner? Did she not know that men of his age and wealth were few? Any number of women, especially the southern belles, would jump at the opportunity to marry him.

Perhaps Susannah Partridge was daft and until now had managed to conceal her madness behind a pretty face and lithe figure.

Trace had never expected the governess to turn him down. His wounded pride looked for reasons outside himself for Miss Partridge's firm rejection and melodramatic excuse. Love. She had not seen his battle scars, so therefore she could not have been physically repulsed by him. He found it difficult to believe her a mawkish, overly sentimental woman who trusted in love to conquer all, but he did not know what else to think.

He looked inside himself. Had he become too rigid, too wary of suffering another broken heart? Louise's perfidy had been as painful as the burns on his back, and as difficult to overcome. Since then, Trace had taken life more seriously than he ever had before. Except for his work and his daughters, he'd closed out the world. His joy of living had been lost in a dark tunnel of intensity.

Susannah was right. Mrs. Witherspoon and Miss Millbanks seemed to like him well enough. He just did not feel the same about them. In comparison to the cookie-baking, dog-washing, bird-owning, skirts-ablaze governess, they seemed so ordinary.

But Susannah was wrong about a marriage of convenience.

She was right. She was wrong. Trace hadn't been this confused about another human being since Aunt Cellie had dealt him his first hand of faro with the skill of a charlatan.

The diminutive governess with the strong will had not heard the last from him. He would hone his old, abandoned powers of persuasion and change her way of thinking. He would win Susannah Partridge.

Pushing his personal concerns to the back of his mind, he made his way to the academy headquarters and strode into Admiral Porter's office. He'd been called to receive his new orders. This was no time to be thinking of a woman.

The admiral slapped him on the back. "Well done, Lieutenant Reardon. My congratulations again on a job well done."

"Thank you, sir."

"At ease."

Trace couldn't feel at ease. Though he assumed the stance, the prickly edge of anticipation darted through him.

"The gymnasium will build competitive young men, Reardon. Our graduates will possess physical strength and stamina as well as having the finest education and military training. A new breed of naval officer will leave Annapolis, in part thanks to the work you've done."

"Yes sir."

Although the admiral stood only five foot seven inches, his commanding presence intimidated many an officer. "The gymnasium has already raised academy morale," he said. "You may not receive thanks, or the regard that is befitting your achievement. But know that you have laid the foundation for a program that will last generations."

"Thank you, sir." Trace would like less suspense. He silently urged his barrel-chested superior to get on with it.

"You have done an outstanding job, and I feel that I can trust you with another, equally as important."

"Yes sir." At last. The swift beat of his pulse belied the mask of stoicism he wore.

"You will plan the first Naval Ball." Once more, the admiral slapped him on the back.

Trace could not have heard Porter correctly. "Sir?"

"The weekend hops are a pleasant diversion for the midshipmen and the young ladies of Annapolis. But we must enlarge upon that effort to provide an elegant evening. An evening to thank the people and politicians of Annapolis for their hospitality. We'll invite every politician in Washington worth his salt to our ball. It will be the event of the year!"

"A dance, sir? Are you suggesting a dance?"

"Yes, but bigger than a dance, Reardon. A ball, held in the name of the graduating class. You may call upon any of the first-class midshipmen to assist you." The admiral's eyes glittered with pleasure as he paced the office, dreaming out loud. "I want to reward those who have been kind to the academy with a splendid evening, an evening they shan't forget. We shall also invite those who we hope will be kind to the academy in the future."

A ball at the academy. Trace could not wrap his mind around the idea. The Naval Academy and anyone who had a part in the dance would be ridiculed across America. He quickly made his excuses.

"Admiral Porter, I know nothing about planning and executing a ball. My field is torpedoes and submersibles."

"You knew nothing about building a gymnasium before you started, either, Lieutenant Reardon. I have the utmost confidence in you. You have demonstrated that you can turn a controversial undertaking into a richly successful enterprise."

"I appreciate that, sir."

"It shall be a grand affair attended by cabinet members, members of Congress, even foreign dignitaries. They will come from Washington, Virginia, Boston, and New York to attend the First Class Navy Ball."

The admiral was admired for the many plans he'd made for the academy's future. This plan, Trace felt, was doomed to failure. The admiral's dreaming had gone too far.

"When would you like to hold this . . . ball, sir?"

"January. January is a bleak winter month," Porter said, giving a thoughtful tug to his bristling black beard. "You will have sufficient time to prepare, and we shall all feel cheered with a midwinter ball."

"Very good, sir."

*It couldn't be worse.*

"I know that you are a widower without the benefit of a woman's guidance. If you require a knowledgeable female's advice, Mrs. Porter will be at your disposal."

"Thank you, sir."

"Following the ball, if all goes well, I should like you to take command of our *David*, the Confederate torpedo boat we've recently acquired. Perhaps with selected students you might outfit and make it usable. As you are aware, the South far exceeded us in the development of submersibles."

"Yes sir." The wily admiral had dangled a carrot. There was hope for Trace. After the ball.

"That will be all, Lieutenant Reardon."

"Yes sir."

Trace had no doubt this new social event would prove popular with the students, but he feared the rest of the navy would not feel the same about it.

At the risk of seeming less than eager, and losing an important day of training for the wrestling match with Elliot Conroy, Trace requested twenty-four hours of leisure before immersing himself in this new and improbable task.

Despite her objections, he meant to accompany Miss Partridge to Washington. She would never know. During the war he'd learned how to be a ghost.

\* \* \*

The following day Trace rode his chestnut gelding into Washington and arrived before the stagecoach Susannah had taken from Annapolis. He'd waited in the shadows of the depot until the coach pulled up.

The cool November day gave warning of a bitter winter. Although he wore a heavy cloak over his civilian clothes, a chill swept through him that shook his body from his shoulders to his ankles.

When he spotted Miss Partridge descend from the coach, his heart gave a strange hop, as if it wished to fly to her. She wore a troubled expression and worried her bottom lip, plump and rose-petal pink. Her petite figure cried out for protection, Trace's protection. He likened her to a jolly boat—the smallest boat carried aboard ship. The one that a sailor in trouble ran to.

She was dressed in a dark moss-green traveling dress and cloak, a bonnet of the same green shade perched atop her head. Her usual severe bun with its net had given way to a cache of buttermilk curls drawn to the back of her head, bouncing below her bonnet with each step she took. Miss Partridge walked with her head held high, with a sense of purpose and a spring to her step. Watching her made him smile.

Trace admired the governess's dedication. Although he wished Susannah had allowed him to be of help, her resolve to find her uncle must surely be rewarded. If it weren't, he would step in.

Employing old methods of avoiding detection, and staying at a discreet distance, Trace followed the seemingly fearless woman to what he recognized immediately as the naval complex. Most of the official business of the navy was conducted in these four brick buildings located near the Potomac.

The three-storied structures housed records, archives, admirals, and a plethora of paperwork. The future of the navy would be decided here, even as the past was chronicled for history. Trace knew the headquarters well, having been here before, not long after the war started with the firing on Fort Sumter.

As he suspected, Susannah's business took her to the records office. Trace slipped into the shadows of the stable across the road to wait, pacing impatiently, waiting for her to reappear.

# CHAPTER 13

After waiting for over an hour, shivering on a hard bench in a chilly corridor of the Navy Bureau of Records, Susannah was paged.

"Next!"

The gruff voice belonged to Master-at-Arms Gilbert.

Susannah jumped up and hurried into his office. Knowing the end of her search might be moments away produced a queasiness in her stomach that threatened to undo her. She clasped her trembling hands together as she came to an abrupt stop just inside the cubicle of an office.

A young man sat behind a badly marred desk, making notes on the paper before him. "Shut the door," he barked without looking up.

A sole, dirt-streaked window prevented Susannah from feeling as if she were being locked in a closet. Still, she hesitated before closing the door and taking a seat. She kept her eyes on the gray outdoor scenery. Bare-branched trees reached up to a slate sky.

Ignoring her presence, the master-at-arms continued his work. He appeared to be in his late twenties. His curly copper hair sorely needed a trim. While his chin was clean-shaven, he sported a mustache and muttonchops that descended beneath his jaw on either side. Susannah thought the style peculiar, but a great many men favored it. She was glad that Lieutenant Reardon did not. She wondered if Patterson did.

"My name is Susannah . . ." she paused, uncertain whether to use her maiden name or the married name she had never used. As it happened, neither was required.

"Master-at-Arms Gilbert. What can I do for you?"

She addressed the top of his head. "I . . . I have come to inquire about my husband."

"What's his name?"

She took a deep breath. "Patterson Harling."

At last the master-at-arms looked up. A large hooked nose dominated his face. His muddy brown eyes narrowed on her.

Susannah's pulse leapt to a swift and slightly irregular beat beneath the master's probing gaze. He knew something. She could feel it. Goose bumps feathered the downy hairs on her arms.

"Seem to recall the name. Patterson Harling. It's different."

"Yes, it is." Susannah shifted nervously to the edge of the chair, while her inner voice urged the officer to get on with it.

*Tell me what you know.*

"Something came across my desk recently."

"He's alive, then?"

Gilbert rocked back in his chair. "Not sure that's it. Let me see."

The master-at-arms rose and took half a step to

the stack of boxes piled behind him to the right of the window.

Though Susannah's eyes were on the cantankerous young officer as he rummaged through the contents of the topmost box, in her mind she was seeing a hazy image of Patterson as he had been the first time she'd met him. The young man with the mocking smile and cocksure swagger had come to her rescue on the floor of the Newport Assembly Dance Hall. When she found herself in the arms of an overzealous traveling peddler, Patterson cut in, asking for the remainder of the dance. Before the peddler could refuse, the handsome midshipmen took Susannah into his arms and swept her away. He whirled her across the dance floor until, dizzy, she fell against his chest, laughing.

At the time, Susannah worked as a cook at the Newport Hotel. The navy housed as many midshipmen as possible there at the start of the war. The rest lived aboard the *Constitution,* where they all studied. She had never seen such a peculiar sight as the midshipmen's desks lined up on the gun deck of the great ship.

Much to her discomfort, Susannah lived with her married sister, who had already begun giving birth to babies. The small cottage was crowded and uncomfortable, but Mabel insisted. She felt that since Susannah had raised her after their parents died, providing a home was the least she could do.

By this time quite independent, Susannah would have preferred a room in a boarding house, but she would not hurt her sister's feelings for the world. Besides, now that she was freed from her obligation to take care of Mabel, the time had come to find a husband. Every Saturday evening she attended the dances at the Newport Assembly Dance Hall in search of love. She thought she'd found her dream with Patterson Harling.

He courted her every evening, and after ten days broke the sad news. "I'm leaving the academy to fight for the Union, Susie."

"No!"

"I'm leaving in three days' time."

"No, please don't go," she begged.

Patterson was three years younger than Susannah, and there were moments when she thought him young and foolish, but she figured that was something the responsibilities of having a wife and children would fix.

"Will you marry me before I go?"

"We've only known each other for a short while, Patterson—"

"Long enough to know that I want you for my wife." Holding her hand tightly, his gaze locked on hers, he pled. "In the heat of battle, I shall be strong knowing there is someone waiting for me, someone to live for."

How could she resist? They were married the next day. There had been no time nor money for a wedding dress or ring or family gathering. Patterson and Susannah dashed off to a justice of the peace whose office he'd seen camped at the edge of town. After the hasty ceremony, Susannah spent that evening and the entire next day in her husband's arms saying good-bye. Patterson made love to her like a wild man, roughly taking her virginity and quickly satisfying himself over and over again.

Weary and sore, lying beside her snoring groom in the bed of a small room at the Atlantic hotel, she experienced her first doubts. Was she doomed to regret this hasty marriage for the rest of her life? Or did all brides feel this way after their wedding night? At the very least, Susannah hoped that it was not all for naught. She silently prayed that he would leave her with child.

He hadn't.

Before Patterson left, she'd pressed the only article of any value that she owned into his hand. "I shall always be with you as long as you carry this."

"A cameo?"

"It belonged to my mother."

A crash of boxes brought Susannah back to the present with a start. The master-at-arms had overturned one of the boxes, and its contents spilled across the floor behind his desk.

"I think I've found something," he said as he went down on his knees. When Gilbert reappeared, he held a large leather pouch in his hands as he came around.

"These are Patterson Harling's effects," he said, peering into the pouch. "Tobacco, a few coins, half-drunk bottle of whiskey, hardtack, and a woman's cameo."

"My mother's cameo!" She never thought to see it again.

Gilbert fished it out of the pouch and handed it to her. Her eyes misted with tears. The cameo became a blur that she tightly enclosed in her palm.

"Would you like the pouch?"

Susannah shook her head as she stared at the worn article. "Does . . . does this mean Patterson is dead?"

"I reckon. Though we never can be sure," he added quickly. "A lot of men died; a lot of men deserted. Things get all mixed up during war."

"I'm . . . I'm a widow?" she asked aloud, attempting to get used to the idea. What Susannah had long suspected seemed to be a reality now.

Curiously, the reality neither relieved her nor greatly saddened her.

"Sorry, ma'am."

She nodded. "Thank you for your help."

"If I hear anything else, I'll let you know."

Susannah left the records building in a daze. She was a widow. A widow. A half-full bottle of whiskey, hardtack, and tobacco were all Harling left behind.

She hoped his end had come swiftly and without pain. She wondered how long he had been gone. Had he even been alive while she searched for him?

Recovering her mother's cameo had come as an unexpected boon. Before she'd given the carved ivory jewelry to her husband, Susannah had always worn it close to her heart.

Needing time alone, she walked toward a small park. Susannah had much to think about. She must reconstruct her dreams. The future seemed bleak and her choices few. Her chances of finding a new love and having the babies she'd always wanted seemed dim. She was no longer a young woman, and the number of young men available was disproportionate to the number of eligible young women. Too many men had died during the war. Many women would live their lives without husbands to love them. Apparently she would be one of those women, a fact that made her melancholy and angry at the same time.

Lieutenant Reardon had offered her a marriage of convenience. Susannah kicked a pebble in her path. She would rather return to Newport and live her life as a spinster than settle for a man who could not give her his heart. Just thinking of his outrageous proposal vexed her.

\* \* \*

Trace watched Susannah walk from the records building across the cobblestone street to the park. With downcast eyes, she made her way slowly, as if in a daze.

Poor Miss Partridge. Evidently she'd received bad news. She would need Trace's steading hand and comforting shoulder now. He was glad he had come.

Another hard, cold chill seized him. He should have dressed more warmly. Chastising himself for being caught unprepared, he hurried from the stable and chased Susannah to the park.

"Miss Partridge?"

She whirled around. She looked quite pale. Her amber eyes grew round, as if she could not believe her eyes. "Lieutenant Reardon?"

"At your service." He smiled broadly, anticipating a smile in return. In light of the situation, he expected her to appreciate his presence and respond with an exclamation of delight.

Instead, she glared at him. "What are you doing here?"

"I thought you might need help."

"You followed me!"

"Yes—"

"Are you attempting to rob me of what little pride I have left?"

Taken back by Susannah's unexpected vehement reaction, Trace spoke softly, hoping to soothe the anger he did not understand. Whatever had happened inside the records office had disturbed the usually agreeable governess.

"No, not at all," he said, wishing to show her his sensitive and understanding nature. Trace was not unaware of a woman's capricious emotions. Ofttimes, a man could be hard-pressed to strike a delicate balance when dealing with the opposite sex.

"I am not a child, Lieutenant Reardon."

"Of course not, but I have connections here in Washington and thought that if you should need them to find your uncle—"

"And I do not need your connections. Nor your help. I thought I made that quite clear."

Cold fury flashed in her eyes. He chose his words carefully. "Not knowing if you would face—"

But not nearly carefully enough.

"One free day a week," she interrupted again, lashing out. "One free day and you do not permit me the dignity to use it as I see fit."

He held up two fingers. "Two days this time. But I did not mean to anger you."

"Well, you have. You followed me!"

He could hardly deny it. "Did you receive bad news, then?"

"That is none of your concern." She spun on her heel and stalked away from him.

"Quite right."

"I wish to be by myself, Lieutenant," she called over her shoulder in an unmistakably frosty tone.

"Yes, but alone in a strange city?"

Trace continued to dog her steps despite the chill that took hold of him. He'd begun to feel feverish as well.

She came to an abrupt halt. Trace could almost see the steam rising from her shoulders. Clasping his arms to his body, he rubbed them for warmth as Susannah turned slowly to face him.

"Being a woman of 'advanced age', " Miss Partridge threw his words back at Trace with steely emphasis—"I have been in strange cities alone before."

"But you are prone to accidents and in need of

protection. From yourself," he added with an uncertain smile.

Susannah was not amused. Her arched brows knit together in an irritated frown. "I have not had an accident since my skirts caught fire."

"You are due. That's what worries me."

"I did not ask you to worry about me."

Confound the woman! What had he done to deserve her wrath? He'd meant no harm, only to help. Miss Partridge had reached a new plateau of unreasonable and ungrateful behavior. "Very well," he said, enunciating softly and distinctly. "I shall not spend another moment worrying about you. I have other things to worry about."

His upcoming wrestling match with Elliot Conroy for one, a grand ball for another.

The inexplicably furious governess threw up her hands. "One free day a week, that's all I asked."

"Take two, Miss Partridge. Take another full day. Spend tomorrow in Washington if you wish. I'll be returning to Annapolis at once."

"Fine."

"If my daughters did not admire you as much as they do, I would dismiss you on the spot for your, your . . . insolence."

She balled her small hands against her hips. "Dismiss me?"

Susannah's angry defiance startled him. Trace would give his father's cutlass to know what had happened within the walls of the records office. What had happened to turn this sweet woman into a veritable shrew?

"Think it over," he said.

"I shall."

But as another series of body-rocking chills swept down his spine, Trace knew he was too sick to make inquiries or continue arguing with Susannah. He also recognized the signs. His chills weren't the result of a cold day. He must return to Annapolis as soon as possible.

"Good day, Miss Partridge."

"Good day, Lieutenant Reardon."

Susannah turned on her heel and once more stormed away from the lieutenant. She'd only learned moments ago that she was a widow. Faced with an uncertain future and assaulted by myriad conflicting emotions, it hadn't been a good time to discover that her employer had followed her to Washington. The audacity of the man! Did he think she'd traveled all this way for a tryst? The injustice of that awful suspicion was enough to put any woman in a dither.

Finding it too cold to linger in the park, Susannah made her way to the small hotel that also served as the stagecoach depot. Sitting at a small window table, she ordered tea in the belief that a soothing pot of the brew would warm and calm her. Like a sailor floundering at sea, she must decide upon a course.

Her husband was dead, and yet there was no body. She'd become a widow but had no proof she was ever married. A thick black fog of frustration curled through Susannah's mind. She might never know the truth. She had no choice but to accept her lot in life and go on as a widow.

Although she and her meddling employer were at odds, Susannah's position in Reardon's household provided a reasonable income and a comfortable life. She could only speculate how it would feel to see Trace Reardon marry another while she cared for his children. But that would be the way of it, for returning to Newport to live with her sister again would not do.

By the time the stagecoach for Annapolis stood ready to leave, Susannah had regained her composure. She would return to the Reardon residence, explain her behavior, and fall on the lieutenant's mercy. He was a reasonable man. Surely, he would commiserate with her distraught state. Certainly, he would understand that a woman who has just discovered she's a widow cannot be held accountable for anything she might say.

That would definitely be her defense.

Snowflakes fell through the dark night, slowing the stagecoach's progress. It was late, and Susannah was weary when she finally arrived at the Reardon residence. The house was quiet; no light burned in the lieutenant's office.

As she started up the steps, she saw Grace sitting on the top step. "I was waiting for you," she said in a small voice.

Susannah dashed up to the little girl's side. The child's eyes were wet with tears. "What is it, Grace? What's wrong?"

"Papa is sick."

"Oh no." Susannah's heart leapt into a swift, shallow rhythm.

"Twinkle says you can fix him."

"I shall do my best," she said softly, lifting the girl, who was much too heavy to carry, into her arms. "Come now, back to bed with you. No more worrying."

As soon as she'd tucked Grace back into bed, Susannah hurried next door to the lieutenant's chamber.

Aunt Cellie met her in the doorway. "Thank goodness you're back, Miss Partridge."

The simple presence of Reardon's aunt alarmed Susannah. Cellie Stuyvestant went out to play faro most evenings.

"What's happened?"

"My nephew went off for the day, gracious knows where. The fever must have been upon Trace when he left. He arrived home weak from fever and racked with chills. The malaria has returned with a vengeance."

Although bone-weary from her own ordeal that day, Susannah nursed the lieutenant through the night. Several times during the course of each hour, she wiped his brow and face with a cool, wet cloth. Still, he remained feverish. Chills convulsed his body with alarming regularity.

Aunt Cellie had been to the apothecary for the only known remedy. She'd brewed the quinine tea from the bark of the cinchona and left Susannah with strict instructions to make certain her nephew drank the tea at least once every hour through the night. With a good deal of effort, Susannah had managed to force a few drops of the healing tea into him.

When the lieutenant mumbled incoherently, she held his hand and soothed him. When he tossed and turned and threw off the covers, she pulled the blankets back over his chest. Troubled more than hired help should be over the lieutenant's condition, Susannah left his side only to tend the fire. The doctor had given orders to keep Reardon's chamber warm on the theory that the illness would exit the lieutenant's body through his perspiration.

To prevent herself from falling asleep, Susannah sat in a hard, wooden rail-back chair close to her employer's bedside. She feared that she might have had a part to play in his illness. The lieutenant had not appeared to be ill when he waylaid her on the streets of Washington, but she could not be certain. Any malaise he felt would have been simple enough to hide from her.

Mired in her own misery at the time of their unhappy encounter, Susannah had not been thinking clearly and certainly had not been interested in Reardon's appearance. The strong, handsome man she knew had been rendered pale, weak, and vulnerable. A sad sight indeed, a sight that wrenched her heart.

In those quiet moments when the only sounds were the clicking of the hands on the clock, the hiss of the fire, and Reardon's labored breathing, Susannah realized she had set the lieutenant apart from the beginning. In her mind, she'd always regarded him as a warrior bigger than life, stronger than a battalion of fighting men, and wiser than Socrates. A man who never fell ill or suffered the life consequences of mortal men.

Determined to nurse him to health, she renewed her efforts to cool his feverish body. Dipping the soft cloth into the basin of cold water, Susannah tenderly dabbed at beads of sweat on his broad forehead; she pressed the cloth softly against his lips . . . sensuous lips, lips that had made her heart dance when they'd touched hers. Once, only once had the lieutenant kissed her, but Susannah would remember the moment for her lifetime.

Even though she had believed herself a married woman at the time, she had delighted beyond all measure at the deep, body-tingling touch of Trace Reardon's lips. Patterson had never kissed her that way.

Many men had contracted malaria during the Civil War and never been permanently cured. This would be the lieutenant's fate. He could count on the disease returning when least expected, causing fever and chills for days at a time.

Reardon's white linen nightshirt had become damp with perspiration. If she had been strong enough to lift him by herself, Susannah would have removed the garment and replaced it with a clean, dry one. But she could not do it alone. She could only watch, wait, and keep him cool.

In the wee hours of the morning, the lieutenant's incoherent mumblings became more distinct. Susannah leaned in closer.

"Union Navy. Reardon reporting." Obviously in the throes of a nightmare, he spoke in short, agitated gasps. "Union Navy."

"No, no, Lieutenant Reardon."

Perhaps it was more than a nightmare, perhaps the fever had caused delirium. He thought he fought for the Union Navy.

"Union. Got to . . . believe . . ."

"Hush, now. Hush," Susannah soothed. Perching on the edge of his bed, she brushed back the damp raven locks that had fallen on his forehead.

But his exasperation only increased. His voice grew louder, more insistent. "Sketches. Submersible. Brought them back. Brought them back. Got to go; can't be missed."

"There, there," she replied, attempting to humor him. "You're safe now. You can stay."

Lieutenant Reardon bolted upright in the bed, "Got to go back!"

The sudden strength of his movement dislodged Susannah. Taken by surprise, she bounced from the bed to the floor. On the way down, her arm struck the bedside table holding the basin of water. Half of the water splashed out, spilling onto her head.

After wiping the water from her eyes, she pushed herself up, and, wrapping one arm around her wild-eyed patient, eased him back on the pile of pillows. "After you rest. First you must rest."

Fortunately, the glass of water on the bedside

table was still standing. She brought it to his mouth. Dazed ashen gray eyes met hers. The lieutenant regarded her with an expression of profound confusion, as if he did not know who she was.

"It's Susannah. I'm home."

Home. The officer's residence was indeed the only home she had at the moment.

"Su . . . Susannah," he murmured.

Smiling, she nodded, wondering if he could see her clearly in the dim light, wondering if he knew who she was.

His frown deepened and he groaned. He knew. He hadn't really wanted her to come back, but he was too ill to banish her from his chamber. His restless thrashing and muttering began anew.

Since he could not tell her to leave, she would make herself useful. In a bold move, Susannah made space for herself on Reardon's bed. Wrapping her arms around his broad shoulders, she began to croon softly. She sung the love ballad "Lorena," a song favored by the Confederate soldiers and sailors. Fortunately, it did not seem to matter that she sang off-key: ". . . linked my soul to thee . . ."

Soon her patient quieted. His dark lashes fluttered and his eyes closed as he fell into a less active slumber. And Susannah slept with him.

# CHAPTER 14

Two hours later, needles and pins prickled sharp paths along Susannah's arms, forcing her awake. She'd sung herself to sleep holding the lieutenant in her arms.

*A sailor would be sent to the brig—or worse—for falling asleep on duty.* Susannah fixed her gaze on the lieutenant's chest to make certain he was still breathing. That wide expanse promised pleasure to a woman with the daring to explore. But how could she be entertaining such thoughts? The man was ill!

Slipping from the bed, she resumed her nursing duties. She bathed Reardon's forehead and jaw with a cool cloth, gently pressing along his neck to the hollow of his throat. An enticing crop of dark chest curls peeked above the vee neckline of his nightshirt. Susannah watched with rapt fascination as several drops of water trickled downward to disappear into the captivating mat. If she possessed the magical powers of Grace's fairy Twinkle, she would be small enough to ride those crystal drops of water, to a place where a preacher's daughter dared not go.

Wearily chastising herself for the shameless woman she'd become since moving into the Reardon residence, Susannah took a vow. She vowed to concentrate solely on her patient's recovery.

When Aunt Cellie marched into the room shortly after dawn, the lieutenant's fever had abated somewhat and he slept soundly. After setting a fresh pot of tea down on the bedside table, the round, full-bosomed woman held the back of her hand to the lieutenant's forehead and then pressed her ear to his chest. Assured that her nephew had indeed survived the night, she turned to Susannah.

"He seems no worse."

"I did my best to keep him cool through the night."

"Thank you, Miss Partridge. You have nursed him well," she said quietly. "I shall stay with my nephew now."

"I, I hope the lieutenant regains consciousness soon."

The older woman gave her a grateful smile. "As do I, but we have no control over nature. After you take the children to school, I would advise you to get some rest. You may be needed again tonight."

"Of course. I shall help in any way that I can." Susannah started for the door.

"Before you go, there is one more thing."

"Yes?"

Baggy, coffee-colored eyes met Susannah's. "Will you help me change his nightshirt? I know you are a maiden, but—"

"I should be glad to help. The nightshirt that he's wearing is quite damp." Under the guise of lifesaving duty, she would be afforded the opportunity to see the lusty form of the lieutenant unclothed. Buck naked. She could only think that he promised to be a splendid sight—one she would not like to miss.

"If you can brace him up a bit," Cellie directed, "I shall pull until the shirt lifts over his head."

If Susannah held Reardon as she had done before, Aunt Cellie should be able to remove the shirt with the covers still tactfully in place upon his lower body. Stationing herself close to the bed, but not on it this time, she used all her remaining strength to wedge an arm behind the lieutenant's back.

"That's good," Aunt Cellie said. "Now, close your eyes."

"Close my eyes?"

"For your own good and sense of propriety. You are a maiden and not a nurse by trade."

Susannah obediently closed her eyes. But she could feel the yanking, the brush of Cellie Stuyvestant's body against hers as Reardon's aunt drew the shirt up to his waist. She heard him groan. Had he wakened? She opened one eye. No. He was still sleeping—or unconscious.

*But oh my!* Susannah's one open eye fixed on Reardon's sculpted torso.

"My nephew is a strapping boy."

*An understatement, to be sure.* "Mrs. Stuyvestant, would you rather hold him while I—"

"No. No. I have done this many times for my husband, Edgar."

When she was a younger, stronger woman perhaps. They were attempting to undress one hundred and ninety-five pounds of steel muscle. Susannah doubted Aunt Cellie's husband could match the lieutenant's remarkable physique even in his best year.

There was much grunting, shifting, and weight exchange as Susannah did her best to help Cellie while keeping her one eye open for forbidden glimpses of Reardon's chest.

"Perhaps I should ask Adam to help us, Mrs. Stuyvestant."

But Reardon's aunt demurred. "With one good tug, I think I shall have this wet old shirt off," Aunt Cellie announced with a note of triumph.

Susannah felt the tug and opened her other eye. *Aaaah.*

The lieutenant's bare chest proved to be more than splendid. It was an extraordinary example of the male anatomy from waist to neck. Thick, bronze, corded muscles sprinkled with the virile dark mat that had tantalized her earlier. She followed the curls as they narrowed to a teasing trail leading down to the manly region hidden beneath the covers.

"That will be all, Miss Partridge."

*No, not now. Don't dismiss me now!*

"But our task is only half finished," she objected, adding a plucky smile. "I don't mind staying for a moment more. I shall hold the lieutenant upright while you put on a clean nightshirt."

Cellie pursed her lips as she regarded the figure of her nephew resting upright against the pillows. "If Trace were to discover . . . no, on second thought, I think you should send Adam to help me."

Adam—butler and carpenter, and the man who did whatever Trace had not time for and the ladies could not do around the house. He could not appreciate the task as . . .

Susannah's thoughts came to a sudden halt as her gaze shifted to Reardon's right shoulder. A molted crimson patch of dense, puckered scarring spread from the flesh on his shoulder down the entire length of his back. She judged the scarred area to be more than six inches in width. The lieutenant had been badly burned, disfigured. The beauty of his muscular symmetry existed on one side of his body only.

A chilling wave ricocheted along Susannah's spine. She could not imagine the agony Trace must have endured, might still endure. "What . . . what happened to Lieutenant Reardon?"

Cellie heaved a sigh. "My nephew was traveling aboard the *Sultana* when the steamship exploded." Her sparse brows gathered in a frown as she hurried to Susannah's side. "You must never let Trace know that you saw his scars."

"The wounds appear fresh."

"The accident happened in April. The poor dear was hospitalized for four months afterward, and he's still healing, as you can readily see. He was just released in August, three months ago."

"Is he in pain?"

"I don't think so, not that he would say if he were. It's not his way. I wish he'd taken my advice and rested for a year. But he insisted on taking this position at the academy before he had healed."

A giant fist pressed against Susannah's chest, forcing the air from her lungs. "The lieutenant has known a great deal of suffering."

"More than his share," Cellie agreed with a sympathetic cluck. But her mood quickly took a turn. "And this, this malaria, he contracted in a Union prison camp. A Union camp, our own army," she reiterated in a huff, as if the source of his illness was beyond belief.

"Both sides suffered," Susannah murmured. But her heart cried for the pain heaped upon Trace Reardon during the war years. By Louise, by the enemy, by fate. She longed to hold him and comfort him.

"Trace was one of the Union prisoners, just released and heading north on the *Sultana* when the ship exploded. He was on his way to Lowell to be with his girls again."

"I remember reading of the explosion."

The older woman clucked again. "It was a dark day in history. Sixteen hundred people were killed, mostly Union soldiers. There would have been more if it wasn't for Trace. He received those horrid burns saving lives, you know."

Of course she knew. She had known instinctively. He was Trace Reardon. It was what he would do—think of others, save them before he saved himself.

"Your nephew is a brave man," Susannah whispered, feeling a near reverence for the lieutenant, lying so quietly in his bed.

"Braver than anyone knows." Aunt Cellie inhaled deeply, swelling her breasts to amazing proportions before lowering her voice in a surreptitious manner. "But you must keep this our little secret. Trace would be angry with me if he knew you had seen his wounds and I'd told you what he'd done. He's a private man, a proud man."

Susannah nodded. "You have my promise, Mrs. Stuyvestant."

"Call me Cellie, dear."

"Cellie."

She would keep her promise to Cellie Stuyvestant. She would tell no one, especially not the lieutenant, that she knew about the torment he'd endured.

He relapsed during that first day. But as she sat at his bedside during the long evenings to follow, Susannah would think of Trace Reardon's heroism often.

* * *

Trace had vague memories of drifting in and out of consciousness to visions of the sweet, smiling face of Susannah Partridge. He'd even heard her soft murmurings. But based on his experience with previous bouts of malaria, he figured he owed these memories to hallucinations.

When he opened his eyes, he raised them to the familiar ceiling of his chamber while he made a mental checklist of his feelings: no fever, no chills; slight weakness and a parched throat.

A sound similar to a page turning caused him to turn his head. Miss Partridge sat by his bed reading. So, the governess *had* been with him. She'd nursed him through the long shadowy nights.

Trace took advantage of her absorption in the pages to study Susannah. The low gaslight cast ribbons of gold through her hair, especially the fine tendrils that fell to frame her face. The delicate contrast of her peach-pink cheeks against the rest of her paler porcelain complexion took his breath away. His gaze fell to Susannah's lips, moist, plump and inviting. He must be well on the road to recovery if he was admiring a woman this way. And not just any woman. What the hell was he thinking? He closed his eyes, shutting her out.

This woman didn't want him. She'd rebuffed him. Trace had made her a generous offer, a marriage of convenience that would satisfy the most particular woman. But she wanted love. What did she know of love and the heartbreak it brought?

He opened his eyes. "Miss Partridge."

"Lieutenant!" She jumped from her chair, dropping the book.

"I'm sorry. I didn't mean to frighten you."

"Are you . . . are you well?" She regarded Trace with eyes as large as a ship's chain-plates.

"I believe the fever has vanished," he said, forcing a smile. "But I am in need of water if you have some."

"Certainly." She acted as if he had returned from the dead, as if she would leap to fulfill his smallest command. Suppressing a chuckle, Trace watched as she poured a glass of water for him. She would have brought it to his lips if he hadn't stayed her hand.

He couldn't help grinning. "I'm capable of holding my glass, Nurse Partridge."

"Yes, yes, I know that." She beamed at him as proudly as if he'd declared he'd been named superintendent of the academy. But she watched him closely.

The water cooled and soothed his throat, but the room seemed overly warm, and Trace felt drained. Oddly enough, his main feeling was relief that Susannah had returned from Washington.

"What time is it?" he asked, handing her the empty glass.

"Just after midnight."

"How long have I been ill?"

"Four days. This is the fourth night that I have sat with you."

"Four nights by my side," he mused.

"I volunteered after the first night."

"Why?"

"I . . . I thought you would rather have me than a stranger, a nurse hired from the outside. I'm practically a member of the family."

"Yes, you are." A warmth, unrelated to the fever, spilled through him. She'd chosen to nurse him, and to Trace that meant she cared for him.

Perhaps there was hope Miss Partridge might yet agree to his proposal. But then another, disturbing thought struck. "Did I say . . . say anything strange that could not be explained?"

The golden wheat–colored curls drawn to the back of her head bounced when she shook her head. "No, you were simply confused about which side you fought for during the war."

He *had* relived his worst nightmare. It returned again and again, sometimes when he was out of his head with the fever, sometimes in the course of a normal night.

Susannah perched on the edge of the chair. She inclined her head with a sense of anticipation. The hint of a sweet smile played on her lips as she waited for him to speak. Unwilling to have her think him an idiot, Trace weighed the consequences of telling her the truth. Were there any? Did it matter anymore? It might, sometime in the unknowable future.

The bigger question was, could he trust this diminutive woman with his heart? But, then, who could be trusted if not this preacher's daughter? His own children plainly adored and trusted her. Evidently, Aunt Cellie trusted Susannah as well. She'd demonstrated enough faith in the governess to allow her to nurse him.

"No, Miss Partridge, I was not confused. Can I trust you to keep a confidence?"

"Yes, Lieutenant Reardon." Miss Partridge's gaze locked on his, but she blinked nervously. Her long, dark lashes brushed her cheeks. "Any secret will be safe with me."

With a dip of his head and a deep breath, Trace took a leap of faith. "My father wished me to join the Confederate Navy. I did so only after having conferred with my Union officers."

Susannah's remarkable eyes widened as her mouth formed a silent "O." "You were a spy?"

"I worked with the Confederates on the submersibles. I copied the plans of the Hunley and brought them to the North. When I made my way back behind Union lines, I was mistaken for the enemy before I could make my true identity known." Trace paused, the natural rhythm of his heart suspended as he recalled the moment he thought he was about to die.

"You wore a Confederate uniform?"

"Yes, but I had code words and a contact. Still, I knew the risks, and, as it happened, I was wounded before I could make myself known. While I was unconscious the plans for the Hunley were ripped from me and I ended up a prisoner in Fort Monroe in Virginia. None of the Union officers believed me, believed that I was one of them. They thought I was just some Confederate coward. And I had no way of making contact with the officers who could set me free. Though, God knows, I tried."

"You were a prisoner of war of your own side?" she asked in a soft, incredulous tone.

"At least I wasn't killed."

His story obviously left Susannah speechless. Her stunned expression brought a smile to his lips.

"That is the irony of my life. While you have a history of accidents, Miss Partridge, my history is of double-edged dilemmas."

Susannah's brows gathered in a puzzled frown. "Why do you keep your role during the war a secret? Would you not gain more friends among the faculty by explaining?"

"The fewer people who know, the better. I might have to resume my spying activities in the future. Besides, I wish to earn their respect for what I do today, not for what I did yesterday. Why do you think I have a position at all at the academy?"

"Because you are an excellent officer."

He shook his head. "The officers who served in the Confederate Navy saw their careers come to an end. I'm only here because I was an officer in the Union Navy spying on the Confederate Navy. I was rewarded with the assignment I wanted."

The governess raised her chin and straightened her shoulders. "You . . . you make me feel privileged to work for you."

"I didn't share this information with you to gain your esteem."

But even as Trace denied that intention, he knew it had been the only reason to reveal what he had been, what he might be again if called by his country. He trusted her. But more than anything, he wished to win Susannah's admiration.

"All the same, I am honored," she said.

"How are my daughters? These bouts of malaria scare them."

"Although I explained the illness, the girls required much attention, much comforting. When you are sick, they worry they might lose their father and be orphaned."

He lifted his head from the pillow. "What do you know about malaria?"

"I know enough," she replied. "It was not having any understanding of the disease, of being in the dark that frightened the girls. Your daughters are all old enough to hear the truth. I explained malaria as a reoccurring illness much like ague. And with fine nursing care the patient always recovers."

Trace pressed his lips together. Once more Miss Partridge had done the right thing. "I appreciate your putting their minds at rest. And giving me fine nursing care."

She smiled and blushed at his compliment. "They will be happy to see you today."

His heart swelled as his gaze settled on hers. "As I will be to see them."

An uneasy silence fell. She lowered her eyes demurely. Trace wondered if he dared risk telling Susannah how inexplicably comforted he had felt when he woke to find her by his side. Would she lash into him as she did in Washington when she discovered he'd followed her?

"Would you like something to eat?" she asked.

"No, but as I must regain my strength as soon as possible, I will have whatever you can find in the pantry."

"Now that the gymnasium is completed, surely you can take a few days to rest?"

"No. I must be at the gymnasium to receive wrestling instruction from Midshipman Noble."

"Wrestling!" she exclaimed, her delicious mouth forming another "O" of astonishment. "Why on earth do you wish to wrestle?"

"Because Elliot Conroy has challenged me to a match."

As she stood, Miss Partridge slanted Trace a look that suggested the fever had left him addled. Heaving a deep sigh, she sailed from the room. "I shall fetch some broth, bread, and cheese."


Susannah's nursing days ended abruptly. By week's end, the lieutenant was up and about and rapidly gaining strength. Life returned to normal—except for the fact that she was a widow, her chamber was just steps away from his, and her admiration for the lieutenant had soared.

The following week, while Susannah was putting

the children to bed, Emily asked her a question she did not wish to answer. The girl's mournful gray eyes met Susannah's as she said, "Why is my father at the gymnasium almost every night?"

Emily's sad expression tore at Susannah's heart. "He is learning how to wrestle," Susannah replied.

"What is wrestle?"

"It's a sport devised by ancient Egyptians that men find amusing. I know very little about it, but the object, I believe is to throw the opponent to a mat and hold him there."

Amelia, who squinted continuously of late, frowned. "Why would Father want to wrestle?"

Susannah had asked herself the same question without coming up with a satisfactory answer. She could think of no intelligent reason for the lieutenant to bother with a man like Elliot Conroy. The surly seaman must have challenged Trace. But Susannah had no wish to share her speculation with the girls.

"I am not certain, Amelia, but men enjoy many sports. It helps them feel . . . more manly."

"I want Father to be home with us."

"Me too," Alice piped in. "Would you have a talk with him, Miss Partridge?"

Susannah would rather swim the Severn. "I can't promise my talking will do any good at all."

"Twinkle would be happy if you try," Grace pleaded, her large eyes moist with gathering tears. "Please try."

If Grace asked for the moon, Susannah would attempt to fetch it for her. "Very well. I shall try."

After the children were in bed and with Aunt Cellie home, tatting in the parlor, Susannah donned her cloak and set out for the gymnasium. What better time to talk with the lieutenant than when the melancholy expressions of his children were fresh on her mind?

Blurry streams of gaslight and a golden harvest moon lit the "Yard" as Susannah hurried through the cold, windy night to the gymnasium. The truth was that even though she carried news that might dismay him, she looked forward to seeing the lieutenant. These past few days she'd worried that he had been pressing himself too hard and too soon after his illness. But overriding Susannah's practical concerns was the impractical and undeniable fact that she missed him.

She missed the new spark in his eyes and the endearing, lopsided smile he'd been casting about more frequently since being bedridden. She missed his looming presence at the dinner table, missed hearing his booming voice as he called for the girls when he came home each night. She lay awake each night waiting to hear his steps in the corridor, the sound of the door to his chamber, across the hall from hers, open and close. Susannah missed her compelling employer more than she cared to admit.

The girls had given her an opportunity to seek him out. She was on a mission. Increasing her pace, Susannah rushed toward the gymnasium . . . and the lieutenant. No doubt he would be surprised to see her.

# CHAPTER 15

Cold and shivering, Susannah marched into the gymnasium as if she belonged there. Ribbons of moonlight streamed through the high widows, slashing rays of golden light across the polished wood floor. While most of the lights in the gymnasium had been turned off, several gaslights remained on to provide a flickering work light for the tall figure dragging a mat to the far corner of the hall.

The lieutenant had removed his uniform and wore only an undershirt above loose, dark trousers. Susannah's gaze fixed on his muscular chest, straining against the fabric of his shirt. The long white sleeves had been rolled back to his elbows, and the top three buttons of the collarless knit undershirt were open, offering enticing avenues for a woman's imagination.

Susannah envisioned Reardon enfolding her hands in his, and lifting them up, pressing her palms against his bare chest. Her fingertips tingled as she fancied them sliding slowly through his mat of tight, dark chest curls, lingering on the flesh beneath, solid and strong, hewn of granite. Sucking in a tremulous breath, Susannah stared in breathless admiration, knee-deep in sinful thoughts. And then he must have sensed someone watching. He looked up.

Susannah smiled. "Lieutenant!"

"Miss Partridge." He dropped the mat.

Taking advantage of the fact that she'd caught him off guard, Susannah hurried to his side before the lieutenant could say nay.

"Good evening," she said, greeting him with a quick, fanciful curtsy.

"Good evening," he said, with a wry twist of his lips.

Susannah's gaze fell from his eyes to his lips— lips that had aroused her, lips that she yearned to taste again. But this time without guilt.

She was no longer a married woman. With a magical, single, terse pronouncement and the gift of an old worn pouch, she'd become a widow. A widow could not be faulted for feeling—no, for *enjoying*—the titillating heat that signaled the stirring of desire.

A dark stubble of a beard shadowed Reardon's jaw. Susannah experienced a mysterious urge to lift her hand to his cheek and feel the coarse texture of the lieutenant's beard, his leathered skin, beneath her palm. If she were a harlot who gave in to strange temptations, Susannah knew what she would do next. With kisses as light as a feather, she would brush her lips from his ear, down along his neck, to the hollow of his throat and then to his unbuttoned shirt. And if she tore the shirt as she slipped her fingers beneath it to the crisp dark mat nestled atop steely muscle, she didn't think he would mind.

Realizing with a start that she had never been

alone with the lieutenant when feeling quite this way, she raised her gaze again to his eyes. Indeed they were alone. There were no children clamoring for attention here, no fussing aunt, nor cursing bird nor rude shaggy dog.

Susannah and Trace Reardon were utterly alone. Just the two of them, standing inches apart in a cold, empty hall. There was nothing between them but the air they breathed. Air scented with the faint fragrance of spicy bay rum and blended with that of a rare and powerful male virility. It was a dangerous, dizzying combination for a woman who had come to believe this particular male had no equal.

He hiked a dark, sardonic brow. "Have you come to observe my wrestling skills?"

"Yes. I have come to witness your wrestling expertise firsthand. And, and to have . . . a word with you."

"You are too late to witness my death-defying wrestling holds, I'm afraid," he said, lowering his voice to avoid an echoing conversation in the vast, empty gymnasium. "My partner, Midshipman Noble, has left."

"We are alone?"

"Quite alone."

"I shall be your partner," she declared brazenly.

The lusty lieutenant shook his head. "No, I shan't risk hurting you."

But Susannah persevered. "Can you not demonstrate any of the moves you've learned without Noble's assistance?"

Cocking his head, he regarded her silently for a moment. "Perhaps there is one. You will not hold me responsible for any complications that might arise, will you?"

A good and proper preacher's daughter would never have responded the way Susannah did. But, then, other good and proper preacher's daughters might not feel the same bubbling excitement rushing through their veins, as she did.

"I shall hold only myself responsible. You have my promise, Lieutenant."

He grinned. "You are fearless, Miss Partridge."

"No, but I am curious." She unbuttoned her cloak and let it fall to the floor in a thick woolen pool.

Reardon did not appear to notice. His soft, morning-mist gray gaze locked on hers. "The match is won by whoever pins their opponent's shoulders to the mat."

"But this is a demonstration, not a match."

"Back in fifty-four when I was a midshipman, my competitive nature was nurtured to the point of no return. I may push to a victory."

His steady, piercing gaze ignited a simmering fire deep within Susannah; its smoke curled between them like a curtain separating mind from emotion. She could not catch a full breath. "Very well."

"For safety's sake, I suggest you remove your shoes."

Susannah obliged the lieutenant.

"Bonnets are not allowed on the mat, either."

She removed her bonnet and attempted to tuck back the strands that had been blown free from her tidy bun on the way to the gymnasium.

"Perhaps you should unbutton those at the throat of your gown. I would not want you to choke during the demonstration."

Like the most accommodating tart, Susannah unbuttoned three of the six buttons keeping her tight bodice together. In a matter of minutes she would be completely undressed. The flames of hell licked at her heels.

Reardon bowed at the waist and gestured toward the mat. "I believe we are ready to begin."

Susannah took small, careful steps on the polished floor, but to no avail. Just as she reached the mat her cotton stockings slid on the slick surface, and her feet went out from under her. The lieutenant reached out for her, but the next she knew—and it all happened very quickly—she went up in the air, and over her employer's knee before being lowered to the mat and gently deposited there.

She lay flat on her back, a bit dazed but marveling over the swift moves that landed her in this near spread-eagle position. Looking up, Susannah discovered Lieutenant Reardon standing over her. An enigmatic smile played at the corners of his mouth. Her heart beat wildly.

Dropping to his knees, Trace Reardon straddled Susannah. He braced himself with one hand on either side of her head. But he did not touch her. His eyes danced with silver mischief. His crooked smile spread to a wide, warming grin. If Susannah hadn't already been lying down, her knees would have buckled beneath her, causing her to fall down.

"Is this . . . is this your best move, Lieutenant?" she managed to ask in a raspy voice quite unlike her natural tone.

"You haven't seen my best . . . yet."

"Show me."

He gulped.

"Is there a rule that says a man and a woman should not wrestle?" she asked.

"I haven't heard of such a rule," he replied faintly, like a man mesmerized. "Still . . ."

"Do not worry about me," she whispered. She gave him a calm, flirtatious smile even though her pulse raced wildly. "I have moves of my own."

He spiked one brow in question, but his mouth curved up into a delicious crooked smile. He regarded Susannah as a man torn with indecision might, a man who desired a sweet and yet feared devouring the tempting chocolate.

*Devour me!* the devil within her cried.

Moonbeams streamed through the high windows, bathing them in golden light. She held her breath, waiting.

At last, he responded. "You are a lovely woman, Miss Partridge," he said in a voice thick with desire.

And tonight she would be the lieutenant's woman. Susannah's body ached with sweet arousal, tingling anticipation. He could warm her with words alone.

His large hands tenderly pressed Susannah's shoulders to the mat. Her breath caught in her throat. Closing her eyes, she arched her back, feeling her shoulders press against the rubber mat. Her breasts rose toward him. The lieutenant had barely touched her, but her body came alive as if his hands were everywhere, exploring her bare flesh.

Susannah opened her eyes. Reardon's face was only inches away. She felt the warmth of his breath, was held imobilized in the smoldering gray light of his eyes.

"I . . . I think you have won this match." she stammered

He moved his hands from her shoulders to rest flatly on either side of her head.

"A kiss for the victor, Miss Partridge?" he asked.

*Oh, yes. Yes, yes. A kiss.*

But the lieutenant did not wait for Susannah's permission. He did not pause for her to put her wicked thoughts into words.

His mouth came down on hers. And with his touch, Susannah's body burst into flame. A need as deep and wide as the Severn River exploded from within Susannah as Reardon's lips took hers with a fierce urgency. It was an urgency to which she responded wantonly.

He refused to love again, so this was the closest she would ever be to the lieutenant. She could not marry a man who did not love her, but she would savor this one night in his arms—a night in which she would pretend that he returned her love, a love she hadn't planned. Surely a young widow could be forgiven for one night of surrender to a man who had come to mean everything to her.

He lifted his head. His eyes burned with desire so raw, his gaze scorched her. "Oh, God, Susannah, I want you," his ragged voice stirred goose bumps. "If you don't leave now, I can't promise that I . . ." his voice trailed off. Sighing, he rumbled miserably, "Go, before I lose complete control."

A moment of decision. A moment when her heart beat so loudly its echo seemed to fill the gymnasium.

She raised her hand, rested her palm tenderly along his cheek.

"Susannah, do you understand what I'm saying to you?"

"Have we reached a point of no return in this match?"

Closing his eyes, his chin fell to his chest and he nodded.

In answer, Susannah slipped her hand to the

nape of the lieutenant's neck and lowered his head. He did not fight her, but instead groaned in exquisite surrender when his lips met hers again.

Awash in new and thrumming sensations, Susannah lost the ability to reason. She could only feel. She felt Reardon's tongue slide into her mouth, probing, exploring. She felt her body warm and moist; she felt her breasts swelling.

Too soon, he dragged his lips from hers, hauled himself away to lie beside her on the mat. "Are you certain?"

"I have never been so certain."

Reardon breathed hard, like a man who had raced for miles, as he helped Susannah to her feet. His eyes were glazed with desire as he reached toward her bodice. Searching for buttons, their fingers entangled, burned to the touch. Soon she tossed her bodice aside and stepped out of her skirt. Susannah heard the lieutenant's ragged intake of breath as her petticoat fell to her feet.

Keeping her gaze steadfast on his, Susannah stripped away her chemise and stood naked before him. With her body ablaze she no longer felt the cold chill of the gymnasium. Anticipation overcame her inhibition.

Trace Reardon swallowed hard. In a slow, blistering appraisal, his gaze raked Susannah from her full breasts to the curve of her waist and hips, along her legs and down to her ankles. "You are more beautiful than I ever imagined," he said at last.

The hoarse timbre of his voice sent a flood of warm, silken waves through her. She smiled. Thankful. Elated. But she wanted more than words. The needling, aching need within her intensified with each passing moment.

His gaze never wavered from hers as Reardon

removed his trousers. Susannah did not comment but watched in rapt, heart-pounding attention. At the sight of his magnificent manhood, she sucked in her breath. His erection left no doubt the lieutenant desired her. Liquid fire flowed between her thighs.

He mistook her open-mouth gawking. "I promise not to hurt you, Susannah. I never will hurt you."

Unable to speak, she nodded her head. Understanding. Wanting him. Aching for his touch. Reardon closed the gap between them as if he had read her mind. Her breasts brushed against his warm body as he snatched the pins from her hair. Soon her thick curls tumbled to her shoulders. Framing her face between his hands, the lieutenant kissed her with knee-buckling passion. With a sigh of pure ecstasy, Susannah melted into him.

As Reardon tenderly lowered her to the mat, she whispered, "Take me, take me now."

But he proved more patient that she. With each brush of his lips, stroke of his fingertips; with each breath he took, Reardon created an unforgettable moment. He whispered about her beauty, about the many ways in which he would make love to her. He whispered in his soft, deep southern drawl. She trembled with white hot excitement.

Caressing Susannah with kisses, the lieutenant skimmed his palms along the curves of her body, stoking the fires within to a torrid blaze. His thumbs gently brushed her nipples, nipples taut with desire. And when he suckled her breasts, she whimpered with delight. Susannah had never known this bliss. She had never loved like this, nor been as thoroughly loved as this.

The truth flashed as pure and simple as the sparkle of diamonds, as startling as a sudden burst of thunder. She felt more than admiration for this proud man, more than a liking for his keen mind and droll sense of humor. She loved Trace Reardon. The truth acted like a miracle tonic. She felt alive again, flying, soaring, singing like a nightingale. Joy rang in her heart as well as in her body.

Arching her hips in bold invitation, she held her breath. Within seconds, the lieutenant accepted, jettisoning his self-control.

Reardon entered Susannah reverently, tenderly. Her arms circled his neck. At the instant he became one with her, he groaned softly, as if every dream he'd ever dreamed had been answered. She shivered with delight, filled with his steely strength, eager to please him.

Soon they danced to a frenetic rhythm. Each thrust grew stronger, brought him deeper, closer to her core. Her head spun and her body was afire, melting into itself like a burning candle. Just when Susannah thought she would pass out from the fervor of unrestrained passion, her world exploded in a glorious burst of dazzling sun and stars.

Her body trembled and shuddered with the most exciting sensations any woman, anywhere had ever felt. She did not know what magic the lieutenant had spun, but her heart hummed. Her body smoldered, tingled, purred. All at once.

Tears streamed down her cheeks as Susannah whispered his name. "Trace . . . oh, Trace."

With a final thrust, the lieutenant shuddered and filled Susannah with his seed.

Oh, dear God. His seed! As much as she wished to have a child, this was not the time.

Trace fell away from her, but quickly gathered her into his arms. "Susannah. Are you all right?"

"No," she murmured. A blissful peace, unlike

any she'd ever experienced, flowed through her body, washing away her fear of having just been given an illegitimate child. "I shall never be the same."

Laughing, he proceeded to sprinkle her face, her neck, and the sweet hollow of her throat with kisses until her giggles echoed around them and vibrated off the walls of the gymnasium.

And later, much later, when they arrived at the house, he walked Susannah to her chamber door.

"If you should need me, for anything, remember that I am close at hand."

She smiled. A silly smile. She knew it, felt her silly smile.

Once inside his chamber, Trace undressed very quietly, listening for any sound that might signal Susannah at the door. He could make love to her all night long, *would* if only she'd asked.

Fortunately, because of her inexperience, she had not asked why he didn't remove his shirt while he made love to her. There had been enough light in the gymnasium for her to see his back if he'd removed his undershirt.

Trace had certainly seen every inch of Susannah. And he liked everything he saw, from her lush, melon breasts and deep rose nipples, to the delicate waist he could easily circle with his hands. He grew hot again just envisioning her full hips and the sweetly curved calves of her legs.

To his relief, Susannah's lack of experience had not dampened her enthusiasm. She'd quickly cast off any inhibitions and given full reign to passion. She was delicious. Trace could not get enough of her.

Perhaps now the spirited governess would come

around to his way of thinking. She might be more than satisfied with the benefits of a marriage of convenience. He meant to press his proposal.

Trace fell into bed with a smile. He felt energized in a way that he hadn't felt in months, maybe years. And he felt hope. An emotion he never thought to feel again.

In the following days Trace made more time for his girls, and was encouraged to find that Grace talked less about her fairy friend Twinkle. But Susannah became elusive. He'd been convinced that she'd enjoyed their night in the gymnasium as much as he, but ever since, it seemed as if she avoided him purposefully. She made poor excuses to absent herself from his company when he was at home. She claimed to be teaching Bilge a new vocabulary, or having to walk the dog. Whereas they should have been with each other more, he saw less of her.

Caught up in last-minute preparations for his wrestling match, Trace decided to wait until he'd dispensed once and for all with the annoying Elliot Conroy before confronting Susannah.

He would ask her once again to marry him.

# CHAPTER 16

In the days following Susannah's wrestling match with the lieutenant, she avoided him, torn by the pleasure she'd found in his arms and bittersweet wonder. She watched for signs that she might be carrying his child. What would she do? The lieutenant had already made it clear he intended to have no more children. And she longed for a child. His child.

She wondered if in time she might win the lieutenant's love. If he might come to love a child of theirs as dearly as he loved his daughters. She even wondered if in turning down his offer of a marriage of convenience she'd been too rash and began to give serious thought to it.

Until her wondering came to an end, until her questions were resolved, she meant to keep her distance from the lieutenant. With one look he could dissolve her willpower. He was a dangerous man to her. And, dogged by the recurring realization that she had no proof Patterson Harling was indeed dead, Susannah dared not lose herself in pipe dreams. A body, even a headstone, would make all the difference.

On the day of the lieutenant's wrestling match with Elliot Conroy, Susannah stationed herself at the front door in order to speak with him before he left the house. He looked surprised to see her there, but of course she had to wish him luck.

"Good morning, Lieutenant."

Bowing his head slightly, he smiled. "Susannah."

She read genuine pleasure in his smile, a smile that took her breath away and ignited a flood of memories. She would never be able to regard the gymnasium mat in the same way as before.

Lowering her voice, she said, "Good luck this afternoon."

He slanted her a devastating smile, a wry twist of his lips that turned her heart to soft taffy. "Thank you. You were of invaluable help in my training, Miss Partridge."

Her cheeks flamed. She lowered her eyes. "The pleasure was all mine."

Reardon started out the door, then turned back. "Ladies are not invited to wrestling matches, you know."

"Oh, of course not. I understand." She gave him a reassuring smile. Susannah did not add that she'd never let dumb rules stand in her way before. Giving him no hint that she meant to sneak into the gymnasium and watch the match, she stood at the door and waved good-bye like a dutiful, loving . . . lover.

If he thought she could wait idly by, not knowing if Conroy was hurting him, well, Reardon was terribly mistaken.

Her morning routine did not vary. She walked the girls to school, bringing along Fred. Quite domesticated now, the shaggy dog looked forward to his daily exercise. Today, instead of heading home after leaving the older girls at school, Susannah took Grace and Fred with her for an extended walk on the academy campus. In fact, she searched for Midshipman Maloney, the young midshipman Trace had taken under his wing. She found Maloney in study hall and beckoned him with a crook of her finger and a smile.

Later, when Fred, Grace, and Susannah returned home, she carried a small package to her chamber. Mission accomplished. Lulu, her friend who owned the sweet shop, had agreed to watch Grace and meet the girls at the end of the school day. Reardon's daughters would eat ice cream until Susannah could return for them. She hardly thought they would complain.

As soon as Aunt Cellie departed for her afternoon faro, Susannah put her plan in action. The dark blue uniform provided by Midshipman Maloney proved large, but acceptable. Pinning her hair beneath the cap, she ventured forth with what she hoped appeared to be a masculine swagger. Fortunately, Susannah went unnoticed in the crowd. She was only another body in the rowdy gathering of midshipmen jamming the gymnasium. She found a spot in front to watch. Her gaze darted immediately to the mat. Images of love tumbled through her mind. Her heart pressed against her chest, making her prepared to fly once more.

Unwilling to tease her poor heart, she shifted her gaze. On one side of the mat, Lieutenant Reardon practiced slow-motion moves with Midshipman Noble. Elliot Conroy did nothing but gloat at Reardon from the opposite side of the mat. The seaman was saving his strength, she supposed. But his supreme air of confidence grated on her nerves. Both men wore knee breeches and undershirts. Their feet were bare.

She hated to think that the same mat Reardon had made love to her on would now be used for combat. On the other hand, anointed by love, the mat might bring Reardon good fortune.

Susannah steeled herself as the match began, held her breath as the referee signaled the start.

Within seconds, Conroy flipped the lieutenant to the mat. The crowd moaned. But Trace rolled to his left and jumped to his feet before the burly seaman landed in a body flop. The crowd cheered.

Susannah shuddered. The lieutenant would have been crushed if the hulking instructor had fallen on top of him. Conroy possessed a massive body, but a great deal of it was fat and the lieutenant appeared quicker, more agile. Moreover, despite his recent illness, he seemed equal in strength to the seaman.

The lieutenant crouched in a waiting stance, concentrating on Conroy, patiently awaiting an opening. As Conroy pushed himself to his knees, Reardon managed to hook his arm around his colleague's neck. Heaving his body toward Trace, Conroy fell to the mat, bringing the lieutenant down with him.

Trace leapt to his feet, hunkering low for attack. The crowd cheered, Susannah among them, pitching her voice as deep as it would go. "Yahoo!"

Still, fearing for Trace, her body buzzed with tension. Her heart skipped every other beat.

Conroy slowly pushed himself up once again and, then, in a sudden move, kicked the lieutenant. The crowd of midshipmen booed. Forcing the pitch of her voice to its lowest octave, Susannah joined the boys. "Booooo! Booooo!"

She could not help but overhear pieces of the conversations around her. To her surprise, while the midshipmen preferred Trace to Conroy, they'd bet their money on a Conroy win. And wouldn't she be the smug one when they lost their allowances? The lieutenant had overcome the odds before, and Susannah firmly believed he would do so again.

The referee issued a warning to the burly instructor. Kicking was not permitted, although tripping was, which Susannah found odd. But she'd never understood the rules men played by.

For thirty minutes Susannah watched the match with her heart lodged in her throat and her fingers crossed. She did not blink, could not move. She'd hoped for a speedy end to the match, but the two men tortured each other until they were panting and dripping with perspiration.

Elliot Conroy made grunting noises. He sounded like a grizzly bear about to have the lieutenant for dinner. In fact, Susannah thought the seaman *did* rather resemble a bear due to an inordinate amount of facial and body hair, some of which poked out from beneath his undershirt.

Unfazed by the menacing sounds of his opponent, Trace retained an inscrutable expression as he sprang on the big man or, in turn, dodged him.

Conroy's steps faltered. He lunged at Trace and missed him. Gasping for breath, he narrowed his eyes at Reardon. Even from where she stood, Susannah could see the gleam of hostility in those eyes. He wanted to kill Trace. A shudder ran through her. If he hurt the lieutenant, she would find a way to make him pay.

In a move so swift Conroy appeared stunned by it, Reardon twisted the big fellow's arm behind his back and brought him to his knees. The instructor had been worn down. Too big, too heavy to continue, he fell forward. Pulling him over, the lieutenant pinned Elliot Conroy's shoulders to the mat.

The crowd went wild, throwing caps in the air. Some of the smaller fourth classmen were hoisted to the shoulders of the larger, older students. It did not seem to matter to them that most of their money had been on Conroy. Susannah held her cap on her head, fearing one of the midshipmen might yank it off to toss in the air and reveal her masquerade. A tumble of curls would give her away. She didn't imagine that the lieutenant would be happy to discover that she'd disobeyed another of his orders.

She longed to run to him, to hold his battered—and more than likely aching—body. Although bruised and breathing heavily, he flashed a great grin of happiness as Rand Noble held his arm in the air, signaling victory. He then leaned down to help Conroy up, but the angry instructor batted Reardon's arms away.

Susannah had seen enough. She ran to collect the lieutenant's daughters. She hoped to arrive home before Reardon did. But as she started from the hall, two hefty midshipmen seized her. One hoisted her to his shoulders and as he did, the other grabbed her cap and tossed it. Sitting gingerly upon the midshipman's shoulder, Susannah sat wide-eyed and as still as the Herndon Monument. Half the gymnasium, the half that saw her, quieted. The midshipman who carried her did celebratory circles as he made his way toward the victor.

"Miss Partridge," Midshipman Noble exclaimed, "Thank you for accepting my invitation. So glad you could join us."

He flashed a devilish grin as he looked up at

her, acting as if her method of transport were not at all unusual. Rand Noble, of the unsavory reputation, thus saved her from complete humiliation—but not Reardon from complete shock. Seeing the stunned expression on Reardon's face, (stunned, but not angry, Susannah noted), the midshipman realized he'd unwittingly participated in a grand faux pas and swiftly swung Susannah down. She stood wavering before Noble and Reardon.

Dizzy from all the circling, she nonetheless took the offensive, speaking before Reardon had the opportunity. "Thank you, Midshipman. I *do* think women should be able to attend wrestling matches. I saw nothing to offend me, and women are allowed at the horse races, after all."

With that, she turned on her heel and sailed from the gymnasium. Taking one last look over her shoulder, she caught a glimpse of the lieutenant surrounded by well-wishers. She had been quickly forgotten. Trace Reardon had become the most popular officer at the academy. Except with Conroy—she could almost see the steam rising from that man's shoulders as he stalked away in his uneven gait.

For the next few hours, Susannah waited for the lieutenant's return and the scolding she would certainly receive. But he did not return for dinner. Aunt Cellie, looking forward to another evening of faro, appeared unconcerned.

As Susannah tucked Reardon's daughters into bed, she explained that their father had won the wrestling match that day and most likely had gone to town with friends to celebrate his victory.

"Is that where you were this afternoon?" Emily asked. "Did you attend Father's wrestling match?"

"Yes, I did. But I would not recommend that any female of sensibility do such a thing."

"You are wonderful!" Alice exclaimed.

Amelia agreed. "Miss Partridge, I have never known anyone as daring and bold as you."

"I want to be just like you when I grow up," Grace said.

"One day," Emily predicted, "no one shall say nay to us. Ladies will do whatever we wish, and go wherever we please. Just like you."

"Perhaps," Susannah replied vaguely, not wishing to dash their hopes, and bid them good night.

Retiring to her chamber, she listened for the lieutenant's return. She did not know that he was celebrating his win as she'd told the girls. But as he was with Rand Noble when last she saw him, it seemed a certainty.

Trace sat on the steps and removed his boots at the bottom of the stairs. Feeling a bit light-headed, he did not wish to risk waking his family. At one o'clock in the morning, everyone in the house would be asleep, including Aunt Cellie. She always returned from her evenings of faro by eleven.

He stopped at the door to his chamber and glanced over at Susannah's. Ah, but he would enjoy a visit.

As if she had read his thoughts, her door opened.

"Lieutenant."

In two lurching strides he crossed the corridor to her open door. "Susannah."

"Are you all right?"

"Very well, thank you." In fact, he felt quite inebriated.

"I could not sleep."

She worried about him. He grinned.

"Come." A small, warm hand slipped into his and tugged. "I need a better look at you."

Chuckling softly, he gladly gave in to her tug. She wanted him. She wanted him now.

Feeling quite full of himself, despite being a bit unsteady on his feet, Trace followed Susannah into her chamber. He'd known all along that she'd come around to his way of thinking.

A small fire burned in the fireplace. One gaslight and a single candle provided the only other light. Keeping to the shadows, she led him to a velvet chaise near the fire. She had made the spare chamber as cozy as her attic hideaway.

"I believe you need to sit down," she said, peering at him as if he'd grown a horn from his forehead.

"I do. It's true." Clearly, she meant to seduce him slowly.

Her hair, drawn back and tied with a white ribbon, fell to her shoulders in shimmering butterscotch waves. He itched to collect a handful of her silky curls in his palm.

Clasping a cotton paisley shawl around the shoulders of her long white dressing gown, Susannah regarded Trace with a puzzled expression. "Are you feeling well?" she asked.

"Never better," he replied.

Although Trace strained for a better look, he could see only a hint of her generous breasts outlined beneath the thin fabric of the nightgown, but it was enough to warm and cause a tightening of his loins. He took a deep, steadying breath and looked away from temptation.

"Congratulations on your victory," she said, studying his face.

"Thank you. Midshipman Noble took me to Reynold's Tavern for a celebration."

"Did you enjoy yourself?"

"Yes," he replied without hesitation. "I drank

several glasses of ale, sang a few rowdy songs, and won two out of three games of darts."

"Men enjoy themselves differently from women," she murmured.

"I am certain. But I haven't had such a good time in years," he admitted, wondering how long a conversation they must have before Susannah would invite him into her bed.

"Midshipman Noble has proved himself a good friend to you," she said.

"I believe so. Noble seems not to care what color uniform I wore during the war."

And now if she would just get to it. His body was hot, his need evident, if Susannah would but notice.

But she turned her back to him to warm her hands at the fire.

"Don't stand too close," Trace warned, remembering the night not long ago when her skirts caught flame. To staunch the fire, he'd gathered her in his arms and rolled on the floor . . . entwined in paradise.

"I shall not catch fire again."

Probably so. Susannah never had the same accident twice.

She turned to him then with a wistful expression. She reached out.

His heart hammered in anticipation. The time had arrived at last. She would soon be in his arms again, pressed against him, smothered with his kisses.

Her fingertips were inches away from Trace's jaw. He could almost feel her touch. And then, in an apparent change of heart, she dropped her hand. His heart sank.

"The left side of your face is black and blue," she said.

"That must be why it's sore," he replied, with a grin."

"You'll be aching in the morning," she said as once again she took his hand. "Come."

Evidently, the play on her sympathy had produced the desired results. His pulse pounded with excitement.

"Where are you taking me?" he asked in mock ignorance. Rising, he stood by the chaise, waiting, waiting like a lamb about to be led astray. Susannah was taking him to her bed, at last.

"To the door," she said, bestowing a brilliant smile upon him. "It's time to say good night."

"Goodnight?" He couldn't believe it.

Could she really be casting him out? Trace stopped in his tracks. He could not leave without holding her sweet little body in his arms again.

"Yes, Lieutenant. Good night."

"But I thought we would—"

"Would what?" Her hand clutched the door knob.

"Discuss the ball."

Susannah's hand fell from the knob. "What ball?" she asked, inclining her head.

"The superintendent has charged me with putting on a grand ball as a farewell for the first classmen. I'd like you to help."

She smiled for the first time, a smile that lit up the shadows of the chamber and struck Trace's heart, warming it like a shower of sunshine. "How wonderful!"

"I thought you would approve. Women like balls."

"Yes, a Naval Academy ball is a splendid idea," she declared. Her golden eyes glistened with excitement. "We'll discuss it tomorrow."

Trace stood firm, shaking his head. "Susannah,

you have been avoiding me since . . . since that night in the gymnasium."

"I . . . I've been very busy. Thanksgiving is only days away."

Her excuse did not appease him. Trace's gaze settled on Susannah's lips, if he could have one honeyed kiss he would leave a happy man. "Have you given any more thought to my proposal?"

"A marriage of convenience?"

"Yes. More than ever, I believe we shall suit one another well."

"My answer remains the same."

"Love." He huffed. "You are a demanding woman, Susannah."

She appeared to suppress a smile before briskly leading him to the door. "Lieutenant, you must leave my chamber now, else I shall sic Bilge on you."

To prove she meant what she said, Susannah yanked the drape from the cockatiel's cage.

"Blow the man down," the bird squawked. "Blow the man down."

"A kiss before I go."

Closing her eyes, she stood on tiptoe and pursed her lips as if expecting a chaste buss on the lips. But that's not what Trace had in mind. He pulled her into his arms, crushing her against him. His heart slammed against his chest and he kissed her fiercely, as if his lips would never taste hers again.

At first tentative, Susannah returned his kiss with a sweet compliance that threatened to undo him. Purring softly, she parted her lips. As his tongue plunged into the delicious recesses of her mouth, his exhausted body came alive. His blood drummed through his veins. He wanted her, longed to cradle her breasts and brush his lips against the dainty, circular indentation in her flat satin belly.

Susannah pulled away on a shaky sigh.

"You must go," she whispered.

"But oh, my beauty, I would rather stay."

"Go."

"No." His voice broke on the word. Her body stiffened. His ale-addled brain warned him that this was a battle he must lose. Brushing his lips against her forehead, he murmured softly, "Good night, Susannah."

"Blow the man down!"

Damn bird.

Everyone helped prepare Thanksgiving dinner. Susannah baked apple and pumpkin pies. Aunt Cellie supervised the roasting of the wild turkey. The girls broke bread for the stuffing, and Babette prepared a tasty plethora of vegetables.

It was a true labor of love, and Susannah could not remember ever feeling as happy. She gave thanks every day for this wonderful family that she'd stumbled upon—and for the rugged, good-looking lieutenant who had come to her rescue and stolen her heart. He appeared to enjoy—no, more than that, to look forward to the time they spent together making plans for the ball. For the sake of the academy and the success of the ball, Susannah had relented. She no longer completely avoided Trace.

She had invited Lulu, and the lieutenant had invited Rand Noble and Midshipman Maloney to share their Thanksgiving feast.

"I asked Elliot Conroy, too," Trace told Susannah as he picked up the silver tray holding the turkey. "But he declined."

"You invited the man who lives to torment you?"

"If we could find common ground, perhaps the seaman might overcome his dislike."

She nodded but didn't believe it. People like Elliot Conroy *needed* to blame, to dislike. It made them feel better about themselves. "Come, the company awaits that beautiful bird you're carrying."

"Too bad Bilge wasn't big enough to take its place," Reardon muttered before slanting a playful grin Susannah's way.

After Emily said a prayer, family and friends dug into the dinner as if no one had eaten anything for days.

Edgar Stuyvestant, who had traveled from Lowell to spend Thanksgiving with his wife, was the first to pause for conversation. "I'm going to take Cellie back home with me, if you don't mind, Trace. You've got a good woman here to take care of the girls. You don't need my Cellie any longer."

"The girls and I shall miss Aunt Cellie, Uncle Edgar, but it's true. Susannah is quite capable."

Capable? Is that what he thought of her? She wanted to be indispensable to him, to his heart. Perhaps he required a gentle reminder.

"Miss Partridge is going to stay forever," Grace announced.

Susannah laughed, then colored as Trace's gaze locked on hers.

"No one can stay forever," Emily objected. "Miss Partridge is quite old."

"Emily," Aunt Cellie corrected primly, "We never hint at, let alone discuss a woman's age."

Susannah laughed. She'd found true acceptance if Aunt Cellie defended her.

After dinner the party retired to the parlor for a game of charades. A fire roared in the fireplace, and light snow drifted by the window. Charades were followed by a family musical as Emily played the piano and her sisters entertained with song.

Susannah nestled into the love and the warmth surrounding her. If the lieutenant would declare his love, her happiness would be close to complete.

Later, in the girls' chamber, Susannah helped prepare Reardon's weary daughters for bed. But her mind was on other matters. She planned a midnight seduction of the magnificent lieutenant, a gentle reminder of what she was really capable of.

For a moment she thought he'd read her thoughts when he unexpectedly appeared at the door of the girls' room. But his grim expression rid her of such musings immediately.

He held an envelope. "A message has come for you, Susannah."

"For me, on Thanksgiving Day?"

He frowned as he handed the envelope to her. "It must be urgent. I hope that it's not bad news."

With trembling hands, Susannah tore open the envelope and quickly read the message. It came from Master-at-Arms Gilbert. *Come quickly. Patterson Harling is alive.*

# CHAPTER 17

There would be no midnight seduction. Susannah's mind reeled in disbelief. Her hands trembled so severely, the paper she held rustled.

"What is it, Susannah?" Trace's dark brows gathered in an anxious frown.

"A . . . a family matter of extreme urgency," she stammered.

"What can I do to help you?"

*Nothing. All is lost. I am lost.*

Just when she'd allowed herself to nurture hopes and dreams of a new future, fate had intervened. Badly.

"I must leave first thing in the morning," she said, averting her eyes from his penetrating gaze. "Would you ask Aunt Cellie if she might stay a bit longer?"

"Aunt Cellie will be delighted not to give up her favorite faro partners quite as soon as she expected," he assured her. "And I shall escort you wherever you—"

"No, no," she interrupted quickly. "That won't be necessary."

Reardon's worried frown tore at Susannah. If he knew why she must leave he would not be concerned about her, he would be furious with her. She had not been completely truthful with him.

"We have a ball to plan," he pointed out. "Will you be away for long?"

*Forever.* She would never return, but she had not the courage or heart to tell him.

"Aunt Cellie will plan the ball with you in my stead. She is far more familiar with social protocol than I."

But Trace would not be dismissed. He hovered over her like a besotted suitor. "Do you have enough funds for your journey?"

Forcing a quavering smile, Susannah shook her head. "Yes . . . yes, I do. You are most kind, the kindest man I have ever known. I shall never forget you."

*Heaven have mercy.* She'd made a dreadful slip of the tongue. A mixture of shock and suspicion darkened the lieutenant's eyes. An unspoken demand to know the reason for her sudden leave-taking lay behind his steadfast gaze. The piercing, silent search for answers in those eyes caused Susannah's stomach to churn.

"I only meant that your many kindnesses are unforgettable," she hastened to add, holding her nervous stomach. "When Clara Devonshire dismissed me, you were there. You immediately invited me into your home."

"No man would do less."

"No one else came to my rescue but you."

The last thing in the world Susannah ever meant to do was hurt Trace Reardon. He'd suffered enough physical and emotional pain. She refused to bring him more grief.

He clasped both of her hands in his, forcing her

to look up into his troubled eyes. "You are coming back, aren't you? As soon as your business is done, you shall return?"

"Yes, I shall return when my business is over." She might be old and bent, but no matter how long it took, no matter how far she had to travel, someday Susannah would return to Trace.

He nodded, appearing appeased. "We shall care for Bilge while you are gone."

Did he mean to keep the cockatiel as hostage to ensure her return? No, of course not. Her mind was mush, and she could not think straight. Patterson might be angry that she left his bird behind, but at this point she would rather face her husband's wrath than the lieutenant's disappointment in her.

"I would appreciate that, Lieutenant. Grace is teaching Bilge new words. And you won't forget to walk Fred?"

"Both Bilge and Fred will be well taken care of during your absence, I promise."

Susannah's heart weighed heavily within her. She pulled her hands from his. "I must go and pack now."

"Please don't be away any longer than necessary, Susannah. I . . . the girls will miss you."

"If matters were up to me, alone, I would never leave. Never leave at all," she said, her voice thick with building tears. Before embarrassing both the lieutenant and herself by dissolving into a waterspout, she hurried along the corridor to take refuge in her chamber.

Trace paced within his bedchamber. He could find no warmth from the fire and did not feel the least sleepy. Susannah was leaving. Her reluctance to discuss the reason for her sudden departure made him wary. Her refusal of his help only strengthened his suspicion that all was not what it seemed to be with the artless beauty.

The prospect of being duped by another woman bedeviled him. Despite the safeguards he'd taken to guard his heart, Susannah had slipped beneath his skin and scaled the walls protecting his heart. Without even realizing it, he'd come to care for her. He'd become accustomed to hearing her laughter, her lively steps on the stairs, the sweet spring-flower scent of her.

He took comfort from the admiration that shined for him in her jeweled amber eyes. Trace also took an ordinate amount of pleasure in matching wits with Susannah. He likened their conversations to chess with words. Most of all, she'd given him back the dreams he'd once held. She'd given him hope.

And now she would leave without a word about why, or about where she was going or how long she would be.

Weary of pacing, he stood at the window and held back the lace curtain to view the campus below: a beautiful expanse blanketed with snow. Staring into the pristine snowbanks glistening beneath the gaslights, Trace asked himself how he would deal with the changes Susannah's absence would bring.

For the last few months he'd looked forward to coming home, especially on those afternoons when she'd taken to cooking with the girls. The fresh-baked scent of sugar cookies wafted through the house in a most comforting manner. His daughters adored her, obeyed their petite governess without question. Much to his astonishment, Trace had even come to tolerate the animals acquired by the household since her arrival.

Susannah's accidents no longer alarmed him— when he was there to protect her from herself. But he would not be there to protect her if Susannah's sudden journey took her into harm's way. If she was hurt in any way, Trace would never forgive himself. Clearly, there was only one thing to do. He must follow her once more to make certain of her safety. He trusted her. It was fate he did not trust.

Susannah set off before dawn the next morning. When the coach for Washington arrived, she was waiting, huddled against the cold. Unable to sleep, she felt weary and sick to the core of her soul. She would miss the girls beyond all telling. Her love for them was almost as great as the love she felt for their father.

For a few brief weeks she'd had all she ever wanted in life and hadn't realized it. One question tormented her: had she ever really loved Patterson Harling at all? Or had she been fooled into thinking a girlish infatuation was love?

She arrived in Washington feeling as if she inhabited a stranger's body. Shrouded in a pall of lethargy and pain, she walked slowly from the coach stop to the office of the master-at-arms.

The door was open, Gilbert read a newspaper as he slurped from a mug of steaming coffee. The fragrance of the strong brew filled his cubicle.

"Good morning, Master-at-Arms Gilbert."

His head snapped up. "Mrs. Harling?"

They had only met once, briefly. She could forgive his uncertainty.

"Yes, I received your message and came at once."

*Though I much rather would have pretended I never received the disheartening communiqué.*

Gilbert rocked back in his chair, his expression stern. "Your husband's alive."

"Where is he?"

"In jail. I hate to be the one to tell you, but Harling's been charged and convicted as a deserter."

Susannah lowered her head as if the shame were hers.

"He never said anything about having a wife or you would have been notified when he was captured down in North Carolina."

"I see."

It was as she had suspected all along. Patterson had forgotten her. He'd sustained a war injury so great that he had deserted the navy he loved and his wife, too.

"Would you like to see him?"

She lifted her head, met the master's hard eyes. "Yes, of course. How long will he be held in Washington?"

"For another week." Gilbert shuffled through his papers until finding what he had been looking for. He read it silently for a moment before telling her the rest. "Harling's been sentenced to serve his term in the Fort Jefferson prison off Key West."

"So far away." She would never be able to visit him.

"He's lucky he ain't going to be shot."

"May I see Patterson?"

The master-at-arms pushed himself away from his desk. "Come with me. He's in the next building."

"Thank you." Susannah stood on legs that felt as if they might buckle with the first step.

She feared that meeting her husband again would be like greeting a stranger. That he had been convicted of being a deserter only complicated matters.

"If I were married to a pretty woman like you, it isn't likely that I'd forget her," Gilbert muttered as he lumbered ahead of her. The passel of keys on his belt jangled with each step.

In just a few minutes, after three long years, Susannah would be reunited with her husband. Her heart beat so rapidly she feared she might swoon. Quite unlike what she'd once imagined, trepidation spawned the racing beat, not happiness.

Susannah followed Gilbert down into the damp, roughly hewn cellar that served as a holding facility. With barely concealed walls of rock and hard dirt floors, the land-hugging brig resembled a medieval dungeon holding only a few prisoners captive. Those she passed lay on narrow cots.

"Wait here," Gilbert barked.

Unable to draw in a deep breath, Susannah waited nervously as Gilbert approached a guard who paced the long, dank corridor. Orders apparently dispatched, the curt master-at-arms returned to where Susannah waited while the guard placed a small stool in front of a barred cell ten feet away. The stool was stationed close enough to conduct a conversation but far enough to prevent the inmate from seizing her.

"Go on," the surly desk sailor told her. "You've got ten minutes to say your good-byes."

*Ten minutes. Not nearly enough time!* Susannah's feet felt shackled to the ground beneath her. She could not move. She could barely breathe.

"Go on, now," Gilbert urged in his brusque manner.

She must go on. She could hardly turn back. The moment she'd long awaited and now desperately feared had arrived. The pounding of her heart shook Susannah's body as she moved slowly forward. When she reached the stool, she looked into the cell.

Patterson Harling, the inmate, sat hunched on the edge of his crude cot. His eyes narrowed on her before he unfolded his long, thin frame and ambled up to the barred door of his small cell. Despite the terrible nature of his crime, her heart went out to him. If Susannah were ever incarcerated in such a dark, pantry-sized, windowless place, she would keel over and die as soon as the cell locked behind her.

She stared frankly at the man behind bars, whose lips were drawn in a sardonic smile. Her scrutiny revealed no resemblance to the boyish young man she remembered.

Matted waves of dark copper hair fell to Patterson's shoulders. A scruffy beard covered the strong jaw and the cleft in his chin that she'd once thought so appealing. The prisoner's homespun shirt and dark gray trousers were grimy with dirt, and he smelled as if he hadn't bathed in weeks. She wouldn't at all mind sitting a distance from him.

Susannah sank to the stool.

She could not accept this man as her husband, and Patterson did not appear to recognize her. They might have crossed paths hundreds of times and never recognized each other.

The reunion she'd once imagined had Patterson's blue eyes shining with happiness. Elated, he would take Susannah in his arms and thank her for not giving up her search for him. Instead, this man peered at her from behind iron bars in squinty-eyed fashion, as if he were trying to place her.

She gazed at him, a stranger. Susannah felt nothing for this man. A numbness settled over her. No matter how estranged she felt, she was bound to the deserter until death "do they part." Patterson had been sentenced to life in prison, not death.

She knew she must say something, but words refused to form. Her breath came in shallow gulps, blocked by the knot lodged in her throat.

"Well, well," he said, by way of a greeting. "I have a visitor."

"Hello, Patterson." With all the dignity she could muster, Susannah looked to the guard. "May we have privacy?"

"Yes, ma'am. I'll be within calling distance, ma'am."

Patterson's gaze remained fixed upon her. He spoke in a deep whisky voice. "Well, darlin', to what do I owe this pleasure?"

Thunderstruck, Susannah gawked in quite an unladylike fashion. He still did not recognize her. He did not know why she was here. There was only one explanation. Patterson indeed had lost his memory.

Susannah found that odd, because he did not seem to be without his full faculties. His eyes gleamed in rakish appraisal as his gaze drifted from her face to her breasts, to her waist, and back to her breasts.

Grateful that she'd dressed modestly in a dark green traveling dress, she primly smoothed her skirts. Eerily enough, she felt as if Patterson could see straight through the wool fabric of her dress. As a result of his intense scrutiny, Susannah's cheeks burned.

"Do you not remember who I am, Patterson?"

His gaze drifted back to hers as he stroked his beard. "I think I do, as a matter of fact."

"We met in Newport when you were a midshipman." She tilted her chin proudly. "I am your wife, Susannah Partridge."

Patterson threw back his head and howled.

Susannah jumped to her feet. Like dry tinder struck by lightning, her anger burst into flame. "How dare you laugh? Do you find it amusing that after searching for years, your wife finds you in jail?"

Stepping back, her good-for-naught husband raised his hands as if she held a rifle on him. But he continued to smile as if he found her fury entertaining. "Forgive me, no. No, Susannah. I've often wondered whatever happened to you."

"What do you think happened? You told me to wait for you. You promised you'd return to Newport for me."

"But that was before I knew we weren't married."

"Weren't married?" Once again, she sank to the stool, stunned. "You . . . you and I are not married?"

"Nope." His eyes narrowed on her again as he stepped forward again, clutching the bars. "You didn't go and have a babe, did you?"

"No." But, oh, how many nights had she wished she'd become with child during her short time with Patterson. She'd wanted a baby so desperately. Susannah realized now how fortunate she had been. How unfair for a child to have a father like this man. He hadn't an ounce of the character possessed by Trace Reardon.

Harling wiped his brow in a mocking display of relief. "That's a relief."

Confused, and disliking this man more with each passing moment, Susannah attempted to make sense of what he was saying. "I . . . I don't understand. We were married."

"By a traveling justice of the peace."

"Yes."

"Do you recall that I didn't have enough to pay him?"

Susannah nodded. "Yes."

"After I borrowed the rest of the money, I went back to the wagon to pay up. When I got there, I discovered another justice of the peace."

"Another? What do you mean?"

"Turns out when we showed up to get ourselves married as speedily as possible, the real justice was passed out drunk in the wagon. Since his brother didn't want to pass up a fee, he married us. But he had no right. He wasn't a justice of the peace."

"We were married by a man who wasn't authorized to marry us?" Susannah repeated stonily.

"What a joke, heh? Being a red-blooded young man, I didn't want to spoil the fun we were about to have. Didn't know when I'd have the opportunity to be with another lady, one as pretty as you. So I paid the imposter and kept the secret."

"You took advantage of me!" Susannah jumped up so quickly, she knocked over the stool. "How could you do such a thing?"

"Felt I was entitled to a little womanly comfort, goin' off to war and all."

"And you never wrote to tell me that it was all a hoax. For the past three years I've been worrying over you, searching for you, and fearing the worst."

Patterson shrugged. "Knew you weren't stupid. Figured that you'd realize sooner or later that I wasn't coming back."

"That's why you urged me to use my maiden name until you returned."

"You see. I gave you a clue."

"You're despicable!"

"So I'm told."

"You stole my heart, took my virginity, robbed me of my innocence and . . . and ruined my life!"

"No." Shaking his head slowly, his leering gaze flitted from her neck to her toes. "I don't think I ruined your life. You're looking finer than I remember, all dressed up in your fancy clothes."

"Once you left Newport, you never looked back. Never gave me, and what might be happening to me, another thought, did you?"

"There wasn't a lot of time to think, darlin'. Those of us who left went straight to war. We thought we were men and ready for the fight. Took me some time to figure out that I wasn't ready at all."

"You left the academy, and then you deserted. Do you expect me to feel any sympathy for you?"

"I did give you some thought on quiet evenings when I could crawl into my hammock. You're a good-looking little woman, Susie. You stay sweet on a man's mind."

"You are no man. You're a, a . . . snake!"

"Have to admit, I've heard that before."

Faced with Patterson's smirking smile and swaggering posture, Susannah understood nothing she could say would pierce the man's thick hide. He thought their illegitimate marriage quite a joke. She guessed some people just enjoyed being wicked. Patterson Harling could give lessons in evil to the devil. He was kin to Elliot Conroy.

"They told me you were dead. They gave me your effects."

"Yeah. I found a body and planted those things.

Figured they wouldn't go looking for me if they thought I was already dead. Nearly made my getaway, too. Was waiting on the gangplank, almost aboard the ship and bound for the gold fields."

"May you roast in Hades!" she hissed.

Patterson's mouth curled up in a caustic smile.

Susannah stiffened, waiting to be struck dead by a bolt of lightning from above. When the bolt didn't strike, she turned on her heel and stormed from the dungeon.

Distraught to the point of stumbling, she could feel the screams building within her. If only she could make her way to a mountaintop and howl to release the pain and fury.

The master-at-arms called after her when she brushed by him.

"Mrs. Harling! Miss Partridge!"

Silently cursing Patterson Harling, she did not turn. Tears of anger and humiliation blinded her. Susannah felt more angry with herself than with the traitor Harling. This is what came of succumbing to hooded blue eyes, a silver tongue, and the excitement of a whirlwind courtship. She had no one but herself to blame.

Awash in self-reproach, she made her way from the building, her gaze firmly fastened on the cobblestones at her feet. She moved in a cloak of darkness, lined with pain. Mortified, Susannah feared she might drown in this sea of shame. She could barely breathe for the tightening of her chest, the ragged gulps of air that seemed to settle in her stomach like the lieutenant's torpedoes.

How could she have been so dull-witted as to believe each word that dripped from Patterson's mouth? He'd said the loving things that every woman yearns to hear, when she needed to hear them. She'd been in love with love, not with

Patterson Harling. With war in the wind, she'd jumped headlong into quicksand. She'd made the mistake of a lifetime by marrying someone she hardly knew.

Susannah choked on the one truth she could be certain of: she would never regain what she'd lost—the wasted years, the wasted tears.

But she could return to Trace Reardon and his daughters. They would never have to know what a fool she had been. No—she could not live with herself if she did not tell Trace the truth. There could be no lies or half-truths between them. After all he'd been through, he deserved honesty, no matter what the cost.

Trace raced his horse toward Annapolis. He'd learned more than he wanted to know. Susannah Partridge had deceived him.

Only to make certain of her safety, he'd followed her to Washington. He'd watched as once again she'd entered the records department, watched as she followed the master-at-arms into the adjoining building that he believed housed a jail. Worried that her uncle had landed in jail and she would need his support. He'd hurried to the master-at-arms's office. A young one-armed sailor manned the small space.

"Lieutenant Reardon to see the master-at-arms."

"He'll be back directly, sir. He's escorting Mrs. Harling to the jail to visit her husband."

"Her husband?"

"Yes sir. Patterson Harling—"

"You mean her uncle, don't you?"

"No sir. Her husband, sir."

Trace didn't wait to hear more. Livid with rage he could barely contain, he'd stalked from the office. Once again, he tasted the bitterness of betrayal, but this time far worse than before. His teeth ached from clamping his jaw so tightly. Mounting his sleek gelding, he spurred the horse into the wind, away from Susannah. The pain triggered by her treacherousness shot through him. His blood throbbed red-hot through his veins.

No wonder she'd refused to marry him. But she had made love with him. The vixen had allowed him to believe that the joy she'd brought to his home and his heart might be everlasting.

As he sped recklessly toward Annapolis, his heart felt as heavy as an ironclad, as battered and torn as an old frigate's sail. Never again would he allow another woman close to him. He would hire a new governess and remain a widower until the end of his life. Perhaps on his deathbed he might forgive Susannah Partridge. But the way he felt now, Trace never wanted to see her again.

# CHAPTER 18

Susannah felt as dumb as a doorpost. She'd been naive and trusting—and royally duped.

Wishing to be alone in her misery, she decided to remain in Washington, staying overnight in the first small inn she came to. She needed time to compose herself and lick her wounds. The man she'd believed to be her husband for the past three years had played her for a featherhead. Patterson Harling had taken advantage of her youth and innocence. Well, she was not so innocent anymore.

The following morning Susannah returned to Annapolis on the first coach leaving Washington. It was just past midday when she arrived home. Aunt Cellie's apparent delight to see her did little to lighten her somber mood.

Reardon's aunt clasped her hands in front of her bountiful bosom and smiled with genuine pleasure. Or was it relief?

"Oh, Susannah, I am so happy that your business did not take long. Is everything all right?"

"Yes. Thank you for asking," she replied softly as she removed her cloak.

"Grace has been beside herself. You must see to her at once. I haven't been able to do a thing with her. Obviously, it is time for me to return to Lowell with Edgar. I've lost my touch."

"You haven't lost your touch," Susannah assured her. "Do not doubt it for a moment. Sometimes Grace is difficult to understand."

"Yes. I have known no other children who talk to fairies."

Susannah started up the stairs but stopped. She looked over her shoulder. "If you don't mind me saying so, I think that you and Mr. Stuyvestant should stay until after Christmas. The girls will be disappointed if you don't celebrate the holiday with them."

Aunt Cellie inclined her head, obviously considering Susannah's request. "It has been years since we've all been able to be together for Christmas."

"Then you must stay." Once more she started up the stairs and stopped. "Is the lieutenant at home?"

"No. He is at the gymnasium this afternoon."

Susannah nodded. After she soothed Grace, she would go to the gymnasium.

A blend of pungent fragrances spilled though the big old house. Susannah inhaled the homey, comforting scents of lemon polish and cinnamon potpourri blended with a dash of dog. The aroma from the constantly simmering soup pot in the kitchen made her mouth water and reminded her she hadn't had anything to eat for quite a while. Just breathing in the scents of the sprawling old house provided Susannah with a sense of solace.

She dashed up the stairs to the girls' chamber in

search of the small raven-haired angel whom she so shamelessly spoiled. Although a book lay open on her bed, Grace was nowhere in sight. "Grace? Grace!"

"Miss Partridge?"

The small, questioning voice came from Susannah's chamber. She hurried across the corridor. The door to her chamber was open. Grace stood by Bilge's cage, Fred at her side. She clutched one of Susannah's pillows to her small body.

Her puzzled expression turned to one of joy when Susannah rushed into the room. The little girl ran to her, flinging her arms about Susannah's knees. "You're back!"

Susannah could not have imagined a better welcome home. Her heart swelled with love, and her eyes filled with tears of happiness. Fred barked and pranced. Bilge squawked, "Blow the man down."

Susannah fell to her knees beside Grace, enfolding the child's fragile body in her arms. "I missed you while I was gone. Did you miss me?"

"Yes." With her head resting on Susannah's shoulder, Grace's voice jerked, between ragged gulps of air, as if she was trying not to cry. "I was afraid. I was afraid you weren't coming back, like . . ."

"Like your mother?" Susannah asked gently.

Grace nodded her head. Tears splashed on the back of Susannah's neck.

"Grace, I promise you that I will stay as long as you need me. As long as your father allows." She added the last, fearing that when she told Reardon the truth of what she'd been through, he might dismiss her. The lieutenant might not think so highly of a preacher's daughter who had been used, a victim of a heartless ruse. She had been no virginal spinster as Reardon had supposed. He might find that he no longer required her services as governess to his daughters.

But if they were to have any future together, she must maintain his trust by being honest and explaining what had happened to her. Though the story was unlikely to surface later, if it did, he might feel betrayed that she hadn't told him about it.

"I'm teaching Bilge new words," Grace said, stepping back.

"That is an excellent idea. What are you teaching him to say?"

"Love you."

"That's very sweet." Susannah's heart swelled to double its size, overflowing with love, pressing against her chest. And in that moment she learned something important about herself: the more love she found, the more love her heart could hold.

Taking Grace's chin between her thumb and forefinger, she looked into her sweet face and said the words slowly and softly, "I love you, Grace."

A silver light shot through the little girl's eyes. "You do?"

"And your sisters, too."

What she had known for some time, she should have shared with the girls. During their young lives, their father had been at war much of the time and their mother had abandoned them. They had been left with an aunt who knew more about faro and fashion than child rearing.

Emily, Alice, Amelia, and Grace deserved unconditional love in copious doses. And Susannah intended to give it to them. They required hugs, and they needed to hear they were loved, just as someday Susannah hoped to hear she was loved. Patterson Harling may have stolen her innocence, but he had not destroyed her hope.

This family was her family, and no matter what

Trace Reardon's reaction was to her experience, she would fight to be with them forever. The first step was swallowing her pride and confessing her past mistakes.

*Wham.*

Trace hit the striking bag again and again. The midshipmen were in classes. Alone in the gymnasium, he worked off the anger that burned within him. The sweet, beguiling, accident-prone governess had seduced him when she already had a husband. And she'd claimed to be a preacher's daughter. What other lies had she told him?

*Wham.*

His daughters adored her; he never wanted to see her again. Stymied, he sought a solution in case she returned to Annapolis believing she still held a position in his household.

With her husband in jail, Susannah must earn her own keep. He looked for a way to dismiss her without breaking his daughters' hearts. His had already been shattered.

*Wham.*

"You've got a good arm, Reardon."

Engrossed in his predicament and distracted by the noisy thump and vibration of the striking bag, Trace hadn't realized he wasn't alone.

Elliot Conroy had sidled into the gymnasium without him hearing. The seaman's surly presence took him off guard. Ever since the wrestling match, Conroy had steered clear of Trace

In the event the civilian instructor finally had come round to make peace, Trace forced a smile. "Conroy. Haven't seen you in a while."

Conroy cocked his head. "Been thinkin' about your good luck."

"Good luck?"

"That's how you won the wrestling match. Luck."

"No, it wasn't luck. Midshipman Noble taught me the moves that I needed to know. It took his help and hard work to win that match. You're a fine wrestler, Conroy. You were a worthy opponent."

The big man folded his arms across his barrel chest. "Don't go thinkin' you won by skill. And don't go thinkin' your luck is gonna hold out. You're going to run out of luck, and soon."

"I thought we'd settled this . . . this grudge you hold against me. I understand your loss. Losing a brother is difficult, But I'm not to blame."

"You didn't lose any of yer family. You've got a lot of gals and a pretty little governess looking over them. Tried to make me think she was your wife, but I found out different."

"I didn't tell you I had a wife."

"Maybe you'd like her to be." The civilian instructor paused, slanting a knowing smirk before continuing. "You've got a rich old aunt and uncle and a big house on officer's row. You ain't lost no one. You've got it all now, Reardon. But I'm warnin' you, your luck's going to run out soon."

Trace regarded his bitter colleague through narrowed eyes but kept his voice calm and steady. "Get out of my sight, Conroy. Take your threats elsewhere."

Conroy's chapped lips parted in a biting smile. "I'm goin'. Just remember, you've been warned."

Watching the knots-and-shrouds instructor limp away, Trace had visions of making a knot himself— of Elliot's throat.

*Wham. Wham. Wham.*

The striking bag became Elliot Conroy's jaw.

Trace struck the bag with all his strength three times in succession. He could report the instructor's threats, but such a move would raise eyebrows and damage Trace's reputation. The navy expected an officer to solve his own problems. Besides, Conroy's angry bluster might be an empty threat. Yet, Trace couldn't take a chance. *Wham.*

"Papa!"

Grace's high-pitched voice echoed in the gymnasium. He turned to see his youngest daughter running toward him at full sail. Behind her, Susannah Partridge strolled as if she were in a park. She held Fred by his leash. He hadn't expected her back this soon. What did she want from him? What was she doing here?

And dammit, didn't she know dogs were not allowed in gymnasiums!

He stepped away from the striking bag. Ignoring Susannah, he scooped Grace up into his arms.

"You're all wet," she complained. But she smiled as she ran a soft little finger across his brow.

"Men perspire in gymnasiums, and that is why little girls do not visit here." He aimed a steady, meaningful gaze at Susannah. "Governesses do not bring their children to gymnasiums."

Ignoring his disparaging remark, the governess with a mind and style of her own flashed him a bright smile. "We are on our way to school to meet Emily, Amelia, and Alice."

"Isn't this a bit out of the way?" he asked icily.

"Yes, it is." Her extraordinary harvest-moon eyes met his. "But I wished to speak with you."

Unaccountably his heart skipped a beat, serving to further disgruntle him. He would have to dismiss her immediately. Tonight. "You couldn't wait until this evening?"

"No. Otherwise, I would not have brought Grace here."

"I like being here," the child piped up, oblivious to the tension sparking between Susannah and her father. "Do girls have gymna . . . gymasi . . . gyms?"

"No," Susannah replied quickly. "But someday they will."

"I would not be so certain, Miss Partridge."

Susannah held the dog's leash out to Grace. "Would you mind taking Fred and waiting for me by the door while I have a word with your father?"

Trace kissed his daughter on the cheek and set her down. "I'll see you at dinner."

"I'm a big girl now, aren't I?" Grace asked as she took the leash from Susannah.

"Yes, you are," Susannah declared with a wink.

It always astonished Trace to see how well mannered the big dog was with the children. Always gentle with Grace, the shaggy canine seemed to know she was no match for his strength.

"What is it you wished to see me so urgently about, Miss Partridge?"

She took a deep breath as if bracing herself. But Trace, unwillingly captivated by her delicate beauty, had lost interest in words. Her long black wool cloak and fur-trimmed bonnet contrasted against the smooth, translucent ivory of her complexion. Just in from the cold, Susannah's crimson cheeks and deep berry mouth beckoned to him. At the moment he could not fathom how one so beautiful could have betrayed him. But she had, and he could not forget it.

"As you know, I traveled to Washington yesterday on a delicate matter."

"You are not obligated to divulge your private affairs."

"Lieutenant, I can see that you are . . . disturbed. All I ask is that you hear me out and I shall not bother you again with my private affairs."

Steeling himself for whatever was to come, he drew in a deep breath. "Go on, then."

"Three years ago I married a midshipman in Newport. He swept me off my feet. He had no money for a wedding ring, and no time for the wedding with friends and family that I'd always dreamed of having. He advised me to retain my maiden name and pretense of being an unmarried woman until the war was over and he returned for me."

Trace felt as if he'd been run through the heart with his own blade. Gritting his teeth, keeping his voice low and even, he asked, "When you made love with me here, in this gymnasium, did you forget you were a married woman?"

Closing her eyes, she shook her head. "No. I believed I was a widow. I thought that my husband was dead. After years of searching, I finally learned from Master-at-Arms Gilbert that he'd been killed in the war."

"But Master-at-Arms Gilbert was mistaken?"

Susannah looked him directly in the eyes as she answered, "Yes."

"I suppose it happens," he allowed, quickly lowering his eyes.

"To the best of my ability, I followed proper procedures. I came to Annapolis in search of Patterson. When I could not find him here, I hired a solicitor, and then I went to the records department in Washington."

"You told me you were searching for your uncle."

"No, you suggested that I was searching for my uncle, and at the time, it seemed better to leave it at that until I had answers."

"Did you find your answers?" he asked coolly.

"Yesterday in Washington I discovered that Patterson Harling deserted from the Union Navy. I found him in jail."

Running a hand through his hair, Trace could only shake his head.

"Patterson confessed to me that we were never married. The man who married us was not a justice of the peace as he'd claimed. He was the brother of the justice of the peace. Patterson knew, but neglected to tell me."

Trace ran both hands through his hair. "You weave an imaginative tale."

"Don't you believe me?"

She appeared contrite and sounded convincing. He wanted to believe her, but he'd been fooled by a woman's wiles before. "It matters not whether I believe you."

Her forehead wrinkled as her finely arched brows dove into a deep frown. "Yes it does matter," she insisted stubbornly. "I was betrayed by a man I trusted, just as you were betrayed by a woman you trusted. I'm . . . I'm mortified, and I need you to believe me. Better than anyone, you should understand how I feel."

"Did you marry for love, Miss Partridge? You once told me that you would marry only for love."

"Patterson pressured me to marry him. He was going off to war, and I felt sorry for him. I admit that I married for the wrong reason. When I understood what I'd done, I vowed that if I ever found myself in the position of marrying again, it would only be, could only be, for love."

Duly chastened and struggling with warring emotions of grave doubt and the overwhelming desire to believe her, Trace weakened. "I . . . I am sorry for your experience."

Her astonishing amber eyes locked on his. "Were you in love with Louise?"

"Louise dazzled me," he confessed quietly.

Now he'd done it. He'd revealed his most terrible secret to this tiny, tenacious woman who had the power to make him feel like a king one moment and a pauper the next. He jammed his hands into his pockets. "Not that I should be discussing my personal history with you," he added, in a defensive tone. Damn. He hadn't wanted to sound defensive.

"Your history is safe with me, Lieutenant," Susannah said, raising a hand toward him as if she would touch his cheek. But with an apparent change of mind, she stayed it in midair, withdrawing it to rest against her throat. "Can't you see, we were both young and bewitched? You can understand my feelings and my actions if you but will. Please do not dismiss me for not being completely forthcoming from the start. I didn't know the truth then."

"My daughters would leave me and go with you if I should even consider dismissing you," he admitted, with the start of a smile. "Do not worry yourself on that account."

"I'm asking for more than that. I'm asking for your trust. I should like another opportunity to prove my . . . my loyalty and devotion to . . . to your family."

At the moment Trace would have given Susannah the moon. He could not resist the appeal of her forthrightness combined with her beauty. Before he could form a wise answer, or fall on his knees and beg Susannah's forgiveness for assuming the worst, Grace called for her governess.

"Miss Partridge!"

Dragging his gaze from Susannah's luminous face, Trace looked to the far end of the hall.

Eyeing the big dog uneasily, Grace called once more. "Fred has to go, Miss Partridge."

"Oh dear."

Trace knew what Grace meant. "If Fred has an accident in this gymnasium, I shall have your hide, Miss Partridge," he promptly warned. "We'll continue our discussion this evening."

With downcast eyes, Susannah nodded and turned from him. Evidently believing she had not in the least persuaded him, she headed toward his waiting daughter and whining Fred.

Trace watched with fascination the gentle sway of her hips as she walked away. Even the wispy silk strands that had escaped from beneath her bonnet enchanted him. The scent of lilac she left in her wake aroused a deep need in him, and it wasn't for her precious body alone.

Releasing a soft groan, he realized he had much to think about before he returned home.

*Wham.*

Holding Fred's leash in one hand and Grace's hand in the other, Susannah and her entourage made their way from the academy grounds. When walking Fred they avoided Main Street in favor of the less traveled Duke of Gloucester Street. The homely dog pulled Susannah along, sniffing at the cobblestones ahead of him.

Grace's mittened hand squeezed Susannah's tightly. She leaned down and pulled Grace's muffler up to the little girl's nose and then lowered her own head against the cold. Still, the frigid air stung her face like a shower of icy pinpricks.

Returning the child to the warmth of home was out of the question. Grace refused to leave Susannah's side.

Her mind returned to her conversation with the lieutenant. She knew that he valued honesty and trust above all and that she seemingly had failed him. But by telling him all, she'd hoped to redeem herself in his eyes. He had seemed coldly indifferent at first. Tense and rigid, his tall, imposing form reminded her of the rocky cliffs of Newport, impossible to scale. At first, he'd avoided eye contact and challenged her every explanation. Despite his stubbornness, she'd persisted. She could be as stubborn as he.

Susannah noticed with encouraging relief that as she explained what had happened, the stiffness had eased from Reardon's shoulders, and his smoky eyes grew warmer. She realized that her sudden departure for Washington must have alarmed him. He'd assumed the worst of her.

Absorbed in thoughts of how she might convince Reardon that nothing had changed except her marital status, Susannah was barely aware of the deserted streets. Most people stayed inside their homes and shops on a day like this, warming themselves by their fireplaces. Beside her, Grace chatted merrily, but nothing she said could be understood. Her wool scarf muffled her words to the point where they became a stream of gibberish.

The man who slipped out of the shadows of the dark alley startled Susannah. She drew back, yanking on Fred's leash and Grace's hand. The dog sat down on the icy cobblestones. She noticed the large seaman wore a navy pea jacket. Susannah recognized the jacket, made from pilot cloth, as a cold-weather version of the first authorized navy uniform, one this man was not authorized to wear.

His black knit cap, pulled down to fit snugly on his head, only intensified the ominousness of his appearance. He planted himself in front of Susannah and Grace.

She knew him immediately. She'd seen the grisly man wrestle and lose to Reardon.

"Miss Partridge," he greeted her with a dip of his head. "Fancy meetin' you here."

"Mr. Conroy."

Elliot Conroy's lips parted in a smug smile. Surrounded by his coarse, dark mustache and beard, they were chapped pink as a tea rose. "You've heard of me."

"Yes." *But nothing good.*

"Then you will know that I'm not a man to be argued with on any matter. So, if you and the girl come with me quietly, I won't be usin' the weapon I'm carryin'." The menacing seaman held out his giant, calloused hand to Grace.

Grace regarded him with a puzzled gaze and made no move to take his hand. "Who are you?"

Conroy snatched her hand. "I'm a friend of your father, girlie, and he says for you to come with me."

"Let go of her," Susannah demanded, incensed.

"Why would I do that?" he asked, looking down at Grace. "You're a fetching little girl."

Needles and pins prickled beneath Susannah's skin; fear knotted her stomach. Lifting her chin in a haughty imitation of Clara Devonshire and hoping to call the villain's bluff, she said, "Mr. Conroy, Grace and I are on our way to meet her sisters as we do every afternoon. If we are not there on time, we shall be missed immediately."

Leaning toward her, he lowered his voice to a conspiratorial rasp. "You may be missed, but you won't be found. What will it be, Miss Partridge?

Will you come quietly, or will you watch me take little Gracie alone?"

Chills shot down Susannah's spine. "I'll come with you, but you must let Grace go."

"I'm not here to bargain, Miss Partridge." Before she could respond, Conroy seized her hand roughly. "Come, yer carriage awaits."

Jerking her to his side, the seaman pulled Grace and Susannah into the alley. As he pulled at her, she let go of Fred's leash. She had no idea what the dog would do. She hoped he would head for home.

Conroy locked them into a small, closed carriage, similar to a phaeton. "I'll be yer driver."

The carriage lurched forward.

"Are we having an adventure, Miss Partridge?" Grace asked, her voice small in the darkness.

"We certainly are."

# CHAPTER 19

The moment Elliot Conroy slammed the door, darkness enveloped the small carriage. Small bubbles of air lodged in Susannah's throat. For Grace's sake, she must suppress her old fear of confinement. The lieutenant's daughter remained blissfully unaware of their dire predicament.

"Emily, Amelia, and Alice will be sorry they missed this adventure," the child crowed. Her silver-blue eyes sparkled with delight.

Susannah forced a cheerful reply, "Yes, they will, sweetie."

The time to lay past demons to rest had arrived. As she struggled to overcome the fear that had plagued her for years, she told herself that the darkened carriage was only a space, a space she shared with a child she adored.

Unable to see where they were going, Susannah attempted to gauge the direction Conroy took and the time it took to reach their destination. Concentrating on the time and keeping up a brave front for Grace helped her bear the confinement that would have otherwise resulted in heart palpitations and severe breathing problems. As it was, her breath came in shallow gasps.

The bumpy ride took less than half an hour, but she felt no relief when the carriage came to a stop. Within moments, Conroy unlocked the carriage. "Yer ride ends here, ladies."

He picked up Grace and swung her down to the ground before helping Susannah from the small conveyance.

Susannah surveyed their surroundings quickly. Thick woods hid the ramshackle cabin they'd come to. She could hear the trickle of a creek running close behind the dwelling. From the corner of her eye, near a thick cluster of underbrush, she caught the movement of a shaggy tail. Fred had followed them.

A terrible sinking feeling washed through her. She'd credited the dog with more intelligence than the poor sad-looking animal possessed. He'd learned with ease the few tricks she and the girl taught him. When she had released his leash, Susannah had hoped he would run home. She knew if Fred arrived home alone, Aunt Cellie or Adam and Jane would be alerted that something was amiss.

But she could not despair. With a jerk of her head, she gestured toward the narrow dirt road, hoping he would catch on that the silent command meant to go home. She did it twice until she was caught.

Elliot Conroy leered at her through narrowed eyes. "What's the matter with you?" he growled.

"I have a kink in my neck." She made the gesture again, this time rubbing her nape. "From the ride."

She didn't dare turn to see if Fred had responded to her desperate charge.

"Get going," Conroy ordered. "Get in the cabin."

Straightening her shoulders, she took Grace's hand and marched into the cabin like a queen on her way to her throne.

"We're gonna wait for Lieutenant Reardon to miss you."

"Are you holding us for ransom?" she whispered.

"You might say." He shoved her through the door.

Grace appeared alarmed for the first time as she stepped into the cold cabin. Her eyes grew big as she looked around. Obviously unused for years, the cabin had layers of dirt coating its floors and windows. A three-legged plank table listed to one side, and a bare cot sat next to a stone fireplace. Two rusted pots were overturned on the hearth.

"What is this place?" Grace asked in a halting voice.

"This is where we shall wait for your father to find us," Susannah replied, before Conroy could answer and possibly frighten the little girl.

Grace gazed up at her questioningly. "Are we playing hide-and-seek with Papa?"

"Yes, hide-and-seek."

Grace smiled, at ease once more.

Susannah heard a creak.

Grace tugged at her hand. "Look, Miss Partridge, a secret hiding place."

Susannah saw a dark hole. In the center of the cabin, a trapdoor had been carved in the uneven plank floor. A rope ladder fell to unknown depths. Elliot Conroy held open the door.

Goose bumps rose on her arms. Her throat constricted. "Wha . . . what is that?"

"It's where you and little Gracie will be stayin' for now."

She took two stumbling steps back. "No. No, I can't go down in there."

Conroy shot her a menacing scowl. "You will, Miss Partridge. Unless you want me to find Gracie another game to play."

"No, no."

*Be strong. Be strong. You can do this.*

The trembling began in Susannah's hands. Her knees shook and her heart pounded. Thankfully, her cloak hid the physical manifestations of her fright. She could think of no worse fate than being forced down into the dark hole.

"What other game?" Grace asked.

Taking a deep breath, Susannah said, "Let's do as the nice man says, Grace."

The hulking seaman seized Susannah's upper arm, gripping her painfully. "You first, Miss Partridge. Get down there."

Terror-stricken, she closed her eyes as soon as her feet made contact with the rope. She stopped, took a deep breath, and haltingly climbed down the rope ladder.

When she reached bottom, she opened her eyes. She was in a space about six feet deep and seven feet wide. The dirt walls were shored with slats of wood. The pit held a stool, one canteen, and a single candle. She had descended into the devil's grave.

Cold, hard shudders racked her body. When the trapdoor closed it would be darker than tar. She had nothing to light the candle. This was far worse than the punishment meted out by her mother when she was a child.

Her head spun in dizzying fear as she held up her arms to receive the child she had been charged to protect, and had failed. Inhaling deeply, Susannah silently vowed to be strong for this child she loved so dearly. "Come, Grace."

"This is scary."

"We won't be afraid of a silly old hole."

"No, I'm not afraid." But she sounded uncertain.

"That's a good girl." Susannah perched on the stool and drew Grace into her lap.

"Will Papa be able to find us here?" The five-year-old's shaky tone held a shade of doubt.

"Oh yes," Susannah assured Grace, though she did not believe it likely. "Mr. Conroy, there is nothing down here to light the candle."

"You aren't afraid of the dark, are you?"

She lifted her gaze. Conroy stood above them peering down, one hand on the door. "No. No, of course we aren't. I just thought it would be nice of you to allow us a bit of light."

Chuckling as if she'd made a joke, the dark, hairy instructor closed the trapdoor.

Susannah held her breath as the pit became dark, pitch-dark. She could not even try to get out until she heard Conway leave the cabin. All she could do was make their ordeal bearable for Grace.

"I think we should sing while we wait for your papa, Grace. What would you like to sing?"

" 'Beautiful Dreamer.' "

"My favorite song."

Trace looked forward to going home. Tonight he would grovel at the governess's feet, beg her forgiveness, and make wild, passionate love to her. A light flurry of snow fell as he strode from the gymnasium.

Susannah had shown enormous courage by coming to him and revealing the embarrassing details of her past. She hadn't had to confess her mistake to him. He would never have been the wiser if she had fabricated a less humiliating story.

Trace understood Susannah's mistake. He'd made a similar mistake of the heart. He'd believed Louise had loved him. He hadn't realized that as an accomplished actress, she was highly skilled in the art of deception. He, like Susannah, had been a trusting soul, wounded by an untrustworthy partner.

This afternoon, when Susannah had approached him from across the gymnasium, his heart had demanded he forgive her. If she'd had ten men masquerading as her husbands, he could do nothing but welcome her home. He should have taken her in his arms then and there, in front of the world, Grace, and their ugly dog.

Ugly dog? He had no sooner thought it when he saw Fred bounding toward him, dragging his leash. Trace hunkered down on his heels and patted the heavily panting dog. "Hey, there, boy. How did you get loose?"

He knew that his children and the animals obeyed Susannah. Fred would never run away from her. Something must have happened to Grace and Susannah. The first stab of alarm struck just as the dog leaped away when Trace reached for the leash. Fred barked and ran a few feet ahead, stopped, stared, and barked again.

"You're trying to tell me something, aren't you, boy?"

The god-awful fear that something had happened to Grace and Susannah gripped his belly like a burning vise. Fred had been with them earlier; the big dog knew whatever had happened.

Trace had no choice but to follow him and hope that he was not on a wild-goose chase.

Fred headed out of the academy grounds and up Main Street with Trace close behind. Midshipman Rand Noble, driving a horse-drawn sleigh with a young woman nestled by his side, waved and pulled up beside Trace. "Are you chasing that poor dumb animal, sir?"

"Yes. He wants me to follow him. I . . . I think something's happened to Susannah and Grace."

Noble didn't hesitate. "Get in—I'll drive you. Sir."

Fred barked incessantly, spurring Trace into action. He hopped in the back of the sleigh. "I won't forget this."

"But you were taking me home," the young woman cried in protest.

Trace recognized Mary Millbanks.

"Unfortunately, we seem pressed for time at the moment," Noble replied, giving a piercing whistle and a shake to the reins of the two handsome geldings drawing the sleigh.

Once again, lieutenant ahead, Fred led them out of town and onto the road leading to Baltimore.

"Mama will be angry with me if I am not home in time for supper," Mary objected.

"I shall explain to her," Trace promised. "But we can't stop now."

"Susannah is an intelligent young woman," Noble said. "I'm certain that all is right. Your dog may be leading us to a pack of wild rabbits."

But deep in his gut, Trace knew differently. Fred had never behaved this way. Something had happened to Grace and Susannah. He had to find them.

\* \* \*

To keep from frightening Grace, Susannah stifled any expression of her horror of being buried alive in this small, dark pit. Although she could not see the walls, she could feel them closing in on her. Until now, she would never have imagined that anything could be worse than being locked in the root cellar by her mother.

The walls were impossible to scale. Shouting for help was unlikely to bring anyone but Elliot Conroy. Neither she nor Grace had done anything to harm him. Susannah could come to only one conclusion: the bitter seaman meant to extract revenge on the lieutenant through them. But how, and for what crime? Trace had won a wrestling match with Conroy, and he'd worn a Confederate uniform. Neither warranted this treatment.

She silently berated herself for not having had the presence of mind to inform their intimidating kidnapper the moment he stepped out of the alley about Trace having been a Union spy. If he knew the agonies Trace had suffered as a result, perhaps Conroy would have felt gratitude instead of resentment toward the lieutenant. He might have released Grace and her. But fear had made her mind go as blank as her bird's.

She and Grace were consigned to this nightmarish hole for whatever time it took for Conroy to contact the lieutenant with his demands. And for Reardon to respond. It might be hours. Or never. A series of hard, cold shivers ripped through her body.

"Miss Partridge, what shall we sing now?"

"Well, what about 'Goober Peas'? We haven't sung that in the last five minutes," Susannah said, brushing her lips against Grace's temple.

"Papa will find us, won't he? He's smarter than almost anybody."

Susannah fervently hoped so. She was relying on the fact that when the lieutenant discovered them missing, he would move heaven and earth to find Grace. She wasn't certain that he would move a finger to find her.

"Yes, he is," Susannah assured Grace, opening her cloak to enclose the child within its folds. "Your father is so smart that he could find a needle in a haystack."

"That's what Twinkle said."

"Twinkle is very smart, too."

"I don't talk to her much anymore."

"Why is that, Grace?"

"Now I have you to talk to."

Susannah's heart flooded with warmth. The dirt walls fell away. She snuggled Grace closer to her. "Yes, and I have you! You've made me very happy, Grace."

"Let's sing 'Beautiful Dreamer' again."

"Wouldn't you rather sing 'Goober Peas'?"

"No."

Grace knew all the words to only two songs. They sang 'Beautiful Dreamer' for the tenth time.

Less than three miles out of town, Fred came to a sudden standstill. Whimpering, he turned his head from side to side as if he was lost. Rand Noble pulled the sleigh to a stop, and then Trace spotted the narrow dirt road leading into the woods.

"Look, carriage tracks," he shouted as he leapt from the sleigh.

Midshipman Noble followed suit. "Hurry, Mary."

"Are you mad?" she shrieked. "I refuse to run after a mongrel dog chasing hares through the woods."

Trace started after Fred, calling back over his shoulder, "I can't wait, Noble."

"I'm right behind you. Sir."

In fact, the midshipman caught up with him in a matter of seconds—just in time to come to an abrupt halt at the rumbling sound of a carriage approaching from the woods. Both men ducked behind the undergrowth.

"It's Conroy!" Trace jumped out of the brush and directly into the path of the oncoming vehicle.

Taken by surprise, Conroy pulled up on the reins, causing the frightened horse to rear up. Wildly struggling against his bit, the horse broke free on one side and the phaeton-like vehicle wobbled and fell to its side.

Trace pounced on a shaken Conroy as Noble ran from the bushes. Circling the seaman's throat with one hand, Trace pinned his shoulder to the snowy ground with the other. "Where is my daughter?"

Wincing in pain, Conroy closed his eyes.

"What have you done with Grace and Susannah?" Trace demanded, applying more pressure against his captive's throat.

Conroy rasped a defiant answer. "If you want to see them alive again, you'll resign your commission. A Confederate don't belong in this man's Union Navy."

Noble kicked the snow at the side of Conroy's head. "If you want to stay alive, you'll tell us now, you worthless—"

But Trace's attention had drifted. "Look, Fred is halfway down the road. He's heading in the direction that Conway came from. Tie Elliot up," he ordered the midshipman. "I'm going after Fred."

"With pleasure. Sir."

"You can't hogtie me and leave me here," Conroy objected loudly. "It's snowin'!"

But Trace didn't hear. Driven by a fear like he had never known, he ran down the road panting heavily. Icy pinpricks of snowflakes stung his face before melting against his skin. Each gasping breath he took became a smoky cloud in the frigid air. Pierced by stabbing pain, his lungs felt close to collapse. But he could not stop. If anything happened to Grace or Susannah, he would never forgive himself.

There were no words to describe how much he loved Grace, his own angel, pure and sweet and defenseless.

And Susannah. If he found so much as one hair on her head harmed, he would kill Conroy. He would? Yes, he would. The seaman had gone too far, taking Trace's loved ones. Loved ones. He could no longer deny his heart. He loved Susannah Partridge.

She was his woman. The one he wanted for all time.

The vixen had slyly worked her way through his defenses and into his heart. He loved her for breaking down the barriers he'd created to protect his heart. He loved her for challenging him, enchanting him, provoking, amusing, and seducing him. And he meant to take her in his arms and tell her so at the first opportunity.

At last Trace came to a clearing in the woods. Barking with new frenzy, Fred jumped at the door of a rotting wood shack set in the middle of the clearing. Trace had no doubt that Susannah and Grace were being held here. He'd found them.

His pulse raced with dread as he burst through the door. It appeared as if no one had inhabited the one-room cabin in a long time. It was cold and forbidding. No fire burned in the fireplace; no smoldering ashes hinted the place had been occupied recently.

Fred sniffed and whined his way around the cabin.

"Grace!" Trace's booming call shattered the silence. "Susannah!"

"Lieutenant?"

Susannah's voice, muffled but strong.

In less than two strides, he was at Fred's side. The whining dog scratched at a spot on the floor.

"Fred?"

Trace's pulse doubled its beat at the sound of his daughter's voice coming from beneath the cabin.

"I'm here, Grace," he called. "Papa's here."

"Yay!"

"You'll be free in a seconds, Susannah," Trace promised, knowing her fear of small spaces.

Frantic, he hunkered down in search of the opening just as Noble ran through the door. "Are they here?"

"Yes," Trace responded in a ragged rasp, his heart pounding with fear. "Conroy buried Susannah and Grace."

"You found us, Papa! You won the game."

What the hell was Grace talking about? Did she think this was some sort of game? "There it is, a notch in the planks. It's a trapdoor," he mumbled, fumbling with the notch. "A place below to hide from Indians." Gritting his teeth, he pulled the trapdoor back. The sight below tore at his heart. Susannah sat on a stool in the center of the earthen pit, engulfing Grace beneath her cloak. They both looked up, blinking at the dusky light.

"Papa! Papa! You found us! We knew you would, didn't we, Miss Partridge?"

"Yes, we did. I . . . we knew you would find us, Lieutenant."

So that was it. Susannah had made the kidnapping a game of hide-and-seek. She'd saved his daughter from being frightened out of her wits. The plucky little governess who feared small spaces had proved more courageous than any woman he'd ever known.

The warmth of a love greater than he'd dreamed possible filled Trace. Alive with the tingling, thumping, roaring sensations coursing through his body, he tore down the rope ladder. When he jumped the final rungs, he found Susannah standing, holding Grace in her arms.

Scooping the beautiful governess and Grace into his arms, he lowered his head and crushed them to his heart. He felt the warmth of Susannah's tears against his cheek.

"Papa, you're smothering me," Grace protested.

"Is everyone all right down there?"

Trace looked up to see Midshipman Noble and a drooling Fred observing them through the open trapdoor.

Susannah laughed. "I'm fine, Midshipman. Better than I have ever been."

"The lieutenant appears to have taken a shine to you, ma'am," Noble added with a mischievous twinkle in his eyes.

"More than a shine," Trace murmured in a voice husky with love and relief.

Susannah's eyes met his as she gave Grace up to Trace. "Once again you have come to my rescue."

"You need me."

She sighed and nodded her head in acknowledgment. "It would appear so."

"I wanna go home now, Papa. I'm hungry."

"As fast as we can, Monkey, we'll be on our way."

After giving her a noisy kiss on the forehead, he handed his daughter up to Rand and turned back to Susannah.

"And I need you, Susannah," he confessed, locking his gaze on her misty amber-gold eyes. "I need you just as much as you need me, maybe more."

She appeared genuinely surprised as her lips curved into a faint smile. She inclined her head. "You need me?"

"Yes, Susannah. I don't know how I can live without you . . . how I lived before you. You have filled my heart and my home with love," he said, whispering the words in her ear, pressing her to his heart. "I love you, Susannah, with all my heart. You are my heart."

He heard her sigh softly. Wary of the reason, he stepped back, took her small hands in his and gazed into her eyes.

Flecks of gold sparkled deep in amber pools. Her eyes, her smile shone with love. Luminous, her small sweet being lit the small dark hole like the summer sun. His heart slammed against his chest.

"I . . . I never thought to hear you say those words," she said.

"And if I ask you to marry me—"

"A marriage of convenience?"

Trace shook his head, grinning. "No. Never that. This will be a marriage of necessity. I have recently learned that I can't live without you, Miss Partridge. I can't live without your love."

"Sir? Do you need help getting out of that hole?"

Midshipman Noble never failed to be polite.

"Coming, Noble."

\* \* \*

Trace carried Grace and kept a loving arm wrapped around Susannah as they walked through the snowy woods back to the sleigh. The light flurries had become a heavy snowfall.

"Fred deserves to ride back with us, don't you think, Noble?" Trace asked.

"Yes, I do. He will also provide warmth with that coat of his. Sir."

It no longer bothered Trace that Rand nearly always addressed him as "sir," only as an afterthought. Of course, at the moment, nothing could bother him. He hadn't felt this happy in years.

Soon they came upon Conroy, tied up and lying by the side of the road. He'd begun to look like a snowman. Trace regarded the bitter seaman with pity rather than the fury he'd felt back in the cabin. "Conroy, if you agree to leave the academy—just disappear—we'll set you free."

"What?" Nobel objected. "The scoundrel should be punished for what he's done."

"Leaving the academy will be punishment enough. Living with his tormented soul will be even more punishment," Trace said.

Conroy's eyes narrowed in disbelief as he regarded Trace. "You're gonna let me go?"

"It's up to you. Do we take you back to the academy, or do you disappear?"

"I'll go."

"If you ever show your face in this town again, you'll be sorry," Trace warned. "We'll press charges, and your disgrace will be public. Do you understand?"

"Yeah, I understand."

As Noble untied Conroy, Susannah watched. "There's something else you should know. Lieutenant Reardon was a spy during the war. He worked to save Union lives, not destroy them."

Conroy frowned. "Yer not a Johnny Reb?"

Noble cocked his head. "I didn't know that."

"And it made no difference to you," Trace replied. "You accepted me as an officer and instructor. You accepted me as a man, and you will always be my friend for that. The war is over."

"Yes sir." Midshipman Noble's blue eyes twinkled as he saluted Trace.

Picking up Grace to carry her the rest of the way, Trace clasped Susannah's hand. As they walked to the sleigh, he knew he had found peace and contentment at last. "Let's go home."

# CHAPTER 20

On Christmas Eve, Susannah stood ready to receive the gift she'd been waiting for all of her life, a loving husband and children.

The love she'd given to Trace Reardon and his daughters from the time she entered their lives had been returned in abundance. In a matter of minutes she would become the lieutenant's wife, and mother to Emily, Amelia, Alice, and Grace.

Boughs of rich evergreen holly, festooned with red velvet ribbon, adorned the Reardon parlor. The refreshing fragrance of pine filled the room from the ten-foot Christmas tree and the handful of pine needles tossed into the fire. For days the lieutenant's daughters had worked on the strings of berries and popcorn that now looped around the tree along with a smattering of red bows and snowflake lace. Miniature white candles burned at the tips of the limbs. Even the flames that danced and crackled in the fireplace appeared festive as they warded off the cold, snowy night.

Aunt Cellie had wasted no time. The dressmaker had been called and Susannah pinned into a gown before Trace finished explaining his intentions. While there hadn't been time to create a true wedding gown, the holiday confection of evergreen velvet and lace that she wore made Susannah feel like a princess on holiday.

The snug off-the-shoulder bodice formed a plunging vee neckline displaying milky decolletage and delicate, shimmering shoulders. Wide bands of Cluny lace trimmed the daring neckline, voluminous skirt, and cap sleeves.

She peered into the looking glass, unable to believe the reflection was of the same woman who had fearfully arrived in Annapolis only a few months ago.

She added jewelry at the last, her mother's cameo and exquisite pearl earrings, a gift from Trace.

The entire household took part in the ceremony. Jane had fashioned Susannah's hair, pulling the flaxen mane into a smooth buttermilk chignon. Adam cut the small bouquet of holly, bound with flowing strands of white ribbon. Babette had toiled throughout the day preparing a Christmas goose fit for a wedding feast.

Even the animals gathered for the ceremony. Fred looked quite handsome bedecked with a red ribbon around his black and white neck. Bilge called the wedding party to attention from his cage beside the Christmas tree.

"All hands ahoy! All hands ahoy!"

Midshipman Rand Noble and Lulu from the Sugarplum Sweet Shop had been invited and joined the household staff in the parlor. Susannah and the girls waited at the top of the stairs for Aunt Cellie to play the wedding march.

The girls all wore dresses of white lace and carried bouquets similar to Susannah's, but smaller and fastened with red ribbons instead of white.

Emily, who prided herself on poise, fairly sizzled with excitement. "I am so glad Father decided upon you, Miss Partridge."

"Yes, we are accustomed to you," Alice, who feared change, declared. "We shan't have to learn to like someone new."

"Will you do all the things a mother should?" Ever-curious Amelia wanted to know.

Grace sidled up to Susannah and tugged on her skirt. She looked down into the youngest's pensive silver-blue gaze.

"What is it, Grace?"

"May I call you Mama?"

Susannah's eyes misted with tears. Despite the layers of crinolines and the heavy skirt of her gown, she sat on her heels to be eye-level with the dark-haired child. "I would be so happy if you would call me Mama."

Grace's smile shone brighter than the candles lighting the Christmas tree. "Mama," she whispered, testing the word.

Rising, Susannah regarded Emily, Alice, and Amelia one by one. "I promise to do my very best to be a good mother to all of you. I love each of you with all of my heart and . . . and you may call me anything you like." Her voice trailed off as she realized what she'd said. "Well . . . perhaps not anything."

"We shall call you Mother," Emily stated, her gaze flickering to her sisters as if she spoke for all of them and dared any to disagree.

Struggling to stave off tears of joy, Susannah gave each of her daughters a warm hug. "You have just made me the happiest and most blessed woman on this earth."

From the parlor, the piano sounded. Cellie struck several discordant notes as she played the wedding march, but what she lacked in ability she made up for in gusto. Determined to be a part of Trace's nuptials, she'd practiced daily. Susannah suspected it was because the day Aunt Cellie had prayed for had finally arrived. Her nephew was taking a wife.

Preceded by the girls, two by two, Susannah listened with joy. Each chord, off or not, was incomparably beautiful to her ears. And when her eyes met the lieutenant's, she knew it was not the love of the girls alone that made her blessed.

Resplendent in his dress uniform of navy and gold, with its stiff stand-up collar and sleeve trim of gold stripes and stars, Trace Reardon waited for her by the fireplace. Even the gleaming handle of the cutlass cradled in his scabbard and the bright white of his gloves conspired to dazzle her. The minister who would marry them stood next to the lieutenant, but Susannah's eyes fastened on her groom alone.

The courage and strength reflected in the set of his broad, squared shoulders caused her heart to flutter in appreciation. With every breath he took, Trace exuded a simmering male energy that warmed her in hidden female places. The gleam of intelligence in his eyes challenged Susannah; his compassion served to calm her. Never in her wildest fantasies had she thought to marry such a remarkable man, a devoted father, a courageous war hero, a thrilling lover. A warm, tingling sensation flooded Susannah's body. Her knees trembled, and she paused to regain her composure.

Towering above all the others in the parlor, the lieutenant presented a powerful force, rugged and compelling. His lips curved into a devastatingly attractive crooked smile, triggering a rapid rat-a-tat-tat of Susannah's heart.

Her eyes locked on Trace's, and she was entranced by the love shining there for her. Soon they would be man and wife. None too soon for Susannah.

"Ladies and gentlemen," a beaming Admiral Porter addressed the midshipmen, faculty, and distinguished guests at the first formal Naval Ball. He'd declared the ceremonial dance the start of a tradition to be honored every January and concluded his remarks with a passing tribute. "I would like to give thanks to those without whom this evening would not have been possible, Lieutenant and Mrs. Trace Reardon."

Susannah could barely contain her pride. With her arm tucked primly beneath her husband's, she shared the platform behind Superintendent Porter with Trace, the mayor of Annapolis, and invited political guests from Washington.

Her heart swelled with love as Trace briefly lowered his head in acknowledgment of the applause. One person did not applaud.

A flash of a fan caught Susannah's eye. It came from below the platform in the front row of the captive audience. Above the hand-painted cherub fan, Clara Devonshire's small dark eyes glared at her. Susannah smiled.

"And now, you may carry on," the admiral ordered with a flick of his wrist. "Enjoy yourselves, and dance."

The academy orchestra took its cue and launched into a rousing rendition of "Listen to the Mockingbird."

After hours of intensive labor, the gymnasium of Fort Severn had been transformed into an elegant ballroom. The star-spangled sky blue ceiling above was adorned with a scroll that read *Dieu et les dames,* "God and women," the midshipmen's creed, which could not be covered up, but, fortunately, not too many of the guests looked up.

"Mrs. Reardon, may I have this dance."

"I would be most happy, Lieutenant Reardon."

Her heart fluttered at his touch, at the warmth of his hand in the small of her back as he guided Susannah off the platform and onto the dance floor. She knew that Trace's touch would warm and thrill her for the rest of her life. It was just that way between some men and women.

His eyes were alight with desire as he drew her into his arms. She knew the look very well, knew what to expect. Her pulse raced with anticipation.

"You look beautiful tonight," he said. "You are the most beautiful woman in the gymnasium."

"Thank you, but I do believe you are biased. And if I make an acceptable appearance, I owe it to Aunt Cellie. She helped select my gown before she and Edgar returned to Lowell."

Tarlatan ruffles trimmed the low neckline and hem of her sky blue silk dress. Initially, she'd worried about the daring neckline and plentiful cleavage revealed.

Trace had not commented, but now he wore a troubled frown.

"What is it, Trace?"

He lowered his voice to the point where it was barely audible. "You know, because of this ball they are calling the Naval Academy, 'Porter's Dancing Academy.' "

"Let them. Admiral Porter has done more for the midshipmen's morale than any other superintendent."

"The old naval sea dogs don't consider morale important."

"Well, they should. Why, if it were not for the admiral and you, there would be no young men interested in enrolling in the academy next year. Everyone can see how happy it has made the midshipmen to have the gymnasium and ten-pin lanes."

Trace nodded, but still appeared disturbed. "The former superintendent, Goldsborough, was heard to say that in his time they educated the head of the midshipmen"—Trace leaned closer to Susannah's ear, and mimicked Goldsborough—"but now, by Neptune, they educate the heels."

"How silly and single-minded!" Susannah scoffed beneath her breath. "More quality young men will be drawn to the academy and become officers in the navy thanks to the superintendent's foresight."

"I hope that you are correct."

"Aren't I always?" she teased.

Trace chuckled. "Always, my beauty. Always."

"And, mark my words, someday people for miles around will be coveting invitations to this ball. Look around! We're dancing among first classmen and their partners, among the president's cabinet officers and members of Congress."

"I agree. It's an impressive party. But I have not been looking for senators; my eyes are only for you," he drawled, giving her a rakish wink.

Susannah's heart beat a bit faster as she laughed. "I am delighted that the southern charm you once locked away has returned in full force."

"Southern charm is inbred. Surgery is required to remove it."

"My sister was surprised to learn I'd married a southerner. Especially one who will now be instructing classes in torpedoes and submersibles."

"Is she upset?"

"I don't think so. Mabel is an understanding

woman. Surely she could not fault us for wishing to celebrate the holiday together. Besides, I described every detail of the ceremony to her." Susannah paused and sighed. "No wedding could ever have been more perfect."

"And our marriage is legal in every way. You *are* my wife," he added, with a grin.

"Who must remind you that tomorrow night is our night with the girls in the ten-pin lanes."

For the past two weeks, when the midshipmen were all in their dormitories studying, Trace had taken Susannah and his daughters to the lane and taught them how to bowl. With only a bit more practice, Susannah thought she might be able to win a game. She wondered how her husband would accept being bested at the sport by a woman.

"As if any of my women would let me forget ten-pin night," he said with a grin. But in the next moment his eyes drifted to her cleavage and lingered there. His dark brows dove into a frown. "I think we should go home now. I want to take you home."

She knew what her husband had in mind. Susannah's cheeks flushed as she met his gaze. His look of longing ignited her desire as suddenly as the strike of a match would ignite a burst of flame. But the dance had barely begun. It was still early in the evening.

"I . . . I think we should stay a bit longer," she hedged.

"But we have much to do yet," he insisted.

"We do?"

His sensuous lips parted in a seductive smile. His voice softened. "It's time to start making babies."

"Babies?" Susannah blurted. When last they'd talked, one more child had been agreed upon.

"Yes, I have decided that the four girls need four brothers." A slight twitch of his lips betrayed his amusement. "I cannot be expected to live my entire life outnumbered by women."

"But eight children?"

"Do you not think eight will be sufficient to share our happiness? Would you like more?"

"Heavens, no," she said and laughed. "Eight is quite enough. But given the number, I think we must steal away at once. The sooner we get started, the better."

But as they whirled closer to the edge of the dance floor, toward their escape, Midshipman Noble blocked their path. He forced Susannah and Trace to come to a halt.

Noble flashed a broad grin. "Good evening."

"Good evening," Trace responded somewhat tersely.

"I understand congratulations are in order to the new instructor of torpedoes and submersibles."

"Thank you, Midshipman."

Susannah watched with pleasure as Trace allowed a smile of triumph. The task he sought, he'd finally earned.

"And now, may I have this dance with your lovely wife, Lieutenant Reardon?"

"When are you going to get a woman of your own, Noble?" Trace replied. "One woman, I mean."

"Never."

"You shall fall in love one day," Susannah predicted. "Do not say 'never.' "

But still grinning, the academy's oldest midshipman shook his head. "This fickle heart of mine loves too many to settle on just one woman. I have roving eyes like my father before me." He raised his eyes to the ceiling. "I have taken the motto as my own: *Dieu et les dames.*"

Trace's frown deepened in mock annoyance. "I'm not certain that my wife is safe dancing with you."

"I shall return her in good stead."

"And soon, if you please. We have urgent . . . business."

Fred slept in the girls' chamber, but Bilge now shared Trace's chamber, along with Susannah. Trace preferred his wife to the bird but could not have one without the other. Her compassion extended to the bird abandoned by Harling the deserter. She refused to allow Bilge to be by himself.

"All hands ahoy! All hands ahoy!"

Trace did his best to ignore the cockatiel. He'd hurried Susannah from the ball and, once behind closed doors, he'd practically torn off his clothing. Only to have Susannah linger in the dressing room.

He lay in bed waiting. Beneath his nightshirt, his muscles coiled with tension. His pulse raced, and his manly regions ached for Susannah. Waiting. He could not get enough of her. Night and day, the longing for Susannah held him in a feverish grip. It seemed the more he had of her, the more he craved.

When at last she emerged from the dressing room, his breath caught in his throat. Her glorious mass of pale gold hair fell past her shoulders in a cascade of silken waves. He swallowed hard. His fingertips tingled in anticipation of weaving through the fine, soft strands. Trace's gaze fell to fix on Susannah's sweet body.

She wore a gossamer gown of rose silk and ivory

lace that molded to her body, moved with her as she moved. Soft mounds of creamy breasts rose above the deep neckline. And in a move meant to torment and tease him, his provocative wife slid the tip of a finger into the valley of her cleavage, and out again. Brushing her finger back and forth, Susannah repeated the motion, toying in absent-minded fashion as she slowly approached the bed. The tip of her tongue moistened her top lip. She flashed a hussy smile. He loved it.

His wife enchanted him. And Trace had reached the limit of his endurance. He wanted her. His heart hammered and his mouth felt as dry as a western desert. He wanted her now. Jumping from the bed, he pulled her into his arms, crushed her against him, and fell back with her into the big four-poster bed.

They rolled together playfully until he was over her. Susannah's breasts pressed against his night-shirt—damn the nightshirt—as he brought his mouth down on hers. With a soft moan of desire, she melted into him. Trace caressed her eyelids and cheeks, sprinkled a trail of love to the sensitive hollow of her throat. His lips lingered in that sweet recess while he listened for the soft sigh he knew would come, the sigh that warmed and excited him. It came. As provocative and sensual as the echo of a siren's song.

From the first, Trace had learned what Susannah enjoyed when they made love. Just as quickly, he'd discovered that giving her pleasure tripled his own. He'd never loved like this before, and he knew he would never love this way again. He was with the woman he was always meant to be with, to have, to hold, forever.

Unable to ignore the ache in his lions any longer, Trace gently pulled Susannah's gown over her head, and when she was free of it, he flung it aside.

"Bail! Bail!"

Bent on ignoring the bird and following his instincts, Trace skimmed the outline of Susannah's body with his fingertips, fingertips that trembled with eagerness and expectation. He traced her full hips, circled her flat, satiny belly, stroked her petal-soft thighs.

If it was possible, Trace would spend the remainder of his days and nights like this, listening to the faint sounds of her pleasure. Thrilling to her body as it arced and reached out for him. But tonight, as he parted her thighs, she resisted, and pushed up on his nightshirt.

He stayed her hand. "No, Susannah."

"Yes, Trace." She pushed again until her hand rested on his bare chest.

Stifling a groan born of lust, and love and desire, he attempted to explain. "Susannah, I cannot—"

"Yes," she whispered, in the darkness. "I have seen you and love you, love all of you."

"Seen me . . ." his voice trailed off as he tried to make sense of what she said. When and how might she have seen his scars? Could she have seen them and still married him?

"When you were ill with malaria," she said quietly. "Your scars mark you as a man of great courage, a man I adore. A man who would risk his life for another, a man with an indomitable heart. Let me help you to heal."

But she had already healed him. Her patience and love had renewed his spirit, given him life again.

"Let me love you, Trace," she coaxed.

Needles and pins, warm and prickly, slid down

his spine. Her soft, sultry voice hummed in the night. "All of you."

Surrender came swiftly. Without waiting for his answer, Susannah's lips brushed his shoulder with exquisite tenderness. He felt her touch, her full, sweet lips pressed against the ravaged tissue like a cooling miracle balm. But Trace felt no pain, no embarrassment. The will to deny her drained from him. He freed himself from his nightshirt and he gave himself up to her.

Her kisses, deep and delicious, wove a torrid path from his shoulder to his manhood. Flesh against searing flesh, Trace trembled from the passion that enveloped him. The preacher's daughter practiced loving abandon. She brought him to the edge of a dizzying precipice. His heart thundered; his body shuddered.

"It's time, my beauty," Trace murmured in a voice thick with passion. "It's time."

At last one with Susannah, with a groan of unbridled pleasure he buried himself deep within her warmth and joined in the ancient rhythm of lovers since the beginning of time, Trace soared.

There was nowhere he and Susannah could not go, nothing they could not do, as long as they were together. They would fly to the heavens and beyond. Their love would take them higher than ordinary mortals dared to go. They would spend eternity together.

Later, much later, Trace fell to her side. Stripped of his last ounce of energy, he levitated in the afterglow of her love.

"Susannah?"

Her face, flushed and dewy, appeared above him. "I think we have made an excellent start, Trace."

"You do."

She grinned. Her eyes sparkled with certainty. "We shall have a baby before the year is out."

He didn't doubt it. "Does the idea make you happy?"

"Oh yes!" she exclaimed. In her enthusiasm, she flopped back on the bed and rolled over. She rolled over too far.

Susannah rolled out of Trace's reach.

The thud startled him from the languid after-effect of loving.

Good God! She'd rolled off the bed.

Trace dove to the side of the bed. Her lily white figure lay sprawled on the floor. "Susannah! Are you all right?"

Instead of the halting reply he expected, his anxious question garnered gales of laughter. "You . . . floored me!"

Before he could reply, she dissolved into waves of laughter once again.

He fell to the floor beside her. Reenergized, he devoted himself to examining every inch of her beautiful body, with his lips, with his tongue, and with his tingling fingertips. After all, what kind of husband would he be not to take every precaution? Trace could not sleep unless he made sure his accident-prone wife hadn't been hurt.

His lips found her belly button, and when he raised his head, he asked, "Have you any pain there?"

She giggled.

"Love you. Love you. Love you."

For once, the bird had it right.